Oh My Blessed Father

Book 2

"Dum Dum"

Coming of Age in the '60s

By

Ted Burton

Oh My Blessed Father

Book 2

"Dum Dum"

Coming of Age in the '60s

By

Ted Burton

Schooner Publishing

Ottawa, Ontario, Canada

Published in Canada by Schooner Publishing

ISBN: 978-0-9938868-1-2

Dedication

Dedicated to the memory of Mary Veatress Burton who taught me the strength of love and the importance of the Golden Rule.

Table of Contents

Introduction – Book 1 Highlights

It's been a while since I last spoke to you about my life and the comings and goings of the Cooper family. So I thought I should summarize the previous book's highlights (if you can call them that) in order that this continuation of my story will make more sense to you.

When I last left you, it was the summer of 1962 and we were heading east down the 401 highway towards our new home in a small town called Newburgh located in the Kingston area of Eastern Ontario. Our car was being driven by a stranger. Our father, or The Old Man as we called him, had arranged for this guy to help get us to our destination. I have no idea who he was now or if we ever saw him again or not. In the car, besides myself, was my mother Mary, my youngest sister Lily, our dog Poncho, and in a cardboard box was our cat, Pepper. The Old Man was driving a rental truck containing all our belongings on the way to our new home. Travelling with him were my older brothers Billy and Gordie. Our second oldest brother Ernie was at army cadet camp in Ipperwash at the time and was to meet up with us in Newburgh after the move.

Our oldest sister Claudia was married to Tom Kilkenny who was an MP in the Royal Canadian Air Force and they were currently living in a suburb of Montreal with their four children Lizzie, April, 'Little Tom', and Matthew. The oldest Cooper son (and second oldest sibling) Brad, who was also in the RCAF, was married to Catherine and they also lived in a suburb of Montreal (not the same suburb) with their two children Cheryl and 'Small Catherine'.

We were leaving another small town called Hillsburgh which is located north of the GTA (Greater Toronto Area) in what you might call Central Ontario. We had lived there for four years, so we were not at all pleased to be leaving behind our friends with whom we had shared many experiences and adventures. For both Lily and me, our best friends were our neighbours who lived right across the street from us. My friend was Sammy Smale who many people (but never me) referred to as Sammy Snail. He was about a year younger than me. His younger sister, Jenny was about the same age as Lily. We had all promised to not let our friendship end due to distance. Mom said that I could come back to Hillsburgh to visit Tommy and stated that Tommy was welcome to come visit us in Newburgh anytime. The same was also true for Lily and Jenny. But we both wondered how often that would really happen in spite of all the best intentions. Yeah, I know that I said in the first book that my best friend was my brother Gordie, but Sammy was my best non-family friend. And of course, Ernie, Billy, and Gordie all had good friends that they were leaving behind both in Hillsburgh and from the town of Erin (five miles away) where they attended high school.

Lily and I were both students of the public school in Hillsburgh. However, I had just graduated from Grade 8 at the ripe old age of 13 and I was now ready to head to high school. But it wasn't going to be in Erin. While mentioning the Hillsburgh school, I would be amiss to not mention how reluctant I was to be saying goodbye to a certain girl who was in the same classroom as me the previous school year although she was in Grade 7. Her name was Wendy Monahan. You may recall my clumsy attempt at saying goodbye to her during our school year ending hayride. Would I ever see her again?

Anyway, that's where I left off, but I just realized that it would probably make more sense to start at the beginning and provide you with a bit more background.

My story began on Christmas Eve in 1952 when I was 2 years old and had uttered my first complete sentence, "Is Daddy going to tear down the Christmas tree this year?" And then I related many stories that helped explain why a two-year-old would ask such an odd question to his mother and older sister. As I recounted the many instances of verbal, mental, and sometimes physical abuse, I hope you were able to realize why 'Daddy' so quickly became The Old Man.

I explained that I was born in Halifax, Nova Scotia and had moved to Ontario when I was one year old. My parents, Garfield Cooper and Mary Simpson were both Newfoundlanders although Mom was born in Saskatchewan. My oldest sister Claudia and my older brother Brad were born in Newfoundland as well. After the family moved to Halifax, along came, in quick succession, Ernie, then Billy, Gordie, and finally me in 1949. Did I tell you my name? Sorry, I'm Benny. Lily came 4 years later in Orangeville when we lived on a farm near there. For many years, we all called her Sissy. And Brad was known as Buddy. And you may recollect that I said that I was the seventh son. That's because I failed to mention 'Dear Little Brother' who was born between Claudia and Brad and had passed away at a very young age. The other son was a stillborn baby that tried to enter our world after Gordie and before me.

I told you about all our moves from various houses in Toronto, to even more numerous farms and small towns all situated north of the GTA near the town of Orangeville. And eventually, we ended up in Hillsburgh where we were all amazed to be able to stay for the extraordinarily long time of four years.

I was nine years old when we first moved to Hillsburgh and had adopted the motto "Don't ask me, I'm only nine." It used to drive Gordie crazy so I uttered it often. You also heard The Old Man's favourite expressions, "What am I an eight-day clock or a sewing machine? I've been around the world, I know the score. I'm drunk again. Where the hell's the Old Bag? Where the hell's my supper? What's this shit? It looks like my hass'ole. Who are you fucking now, you old bag? I wasn't born yesterday. You're dirt under my feet! Dirt! Dirt! Dirt! I could take the whole bunch of you with one hand tied behind my back. Why are you turning the kids against me, Mary? I installed Conn Smythe's phone for Christ's sake." And so on and so on. However, I was also able to tell you about the good times that a large family could

3

experience while growing up in the '50s. There were some humorous times (at least they were humorous to us) and some of those fun times even involved The Old Man.

I introduced you to a few members of our extended family. There was Mom's older sister Rebecca who we always referred to as Aunt Becky. She lived in Grand Bank, Newfoundland but visited us many times staying for weeks at a time. Her favourite expression was 'Oh My Blessed Father' and we would often repeat it. An incident with Billy and me, while Aunt Becky was coming down the stairs, produced the phrase 'Aunt Becky's coming!' which would always drive us into hysterics. Anyway, we were glad that our move would no way affect how often we would get to see Aunt Becky. But we weren't so sure about Mom's cousins 'Fred and Them' who lived in Toronto. Fred was Mom's first cousin Fred Foot. 'Them' included Fred's wife Violet (Vi), their grownup children Ron and Lucy, Lucy's husband Tom Locke, and their children Lizzie and April. No, I am not confused. Yes, Lucy who was about the same age as Claudia was also married to a Tom and coincidentally they both had children called Lizzie and April. I don't think they were even aware of it. And I should mention, The Old Man's many sisters, whom we sometimes visited, were at the time living in Toronto and Detroit.

If you recall my talking about Flat and Them, that was different from Fred and Them. Flat and Them were our collection of figurines that came free in our cereal boxes. They were gone now. Most were lost in the Great Cereal Wars while Flat is still somewhere in outer space. Our other toy collection was our Dinky Toys. Billy had his army vehicles, Gordie was a lover of trucks, and I amassed a fleet of farm equipment. We still had most of them.

I was thinking that I should give you a quick summary of some of the so-called highlights of my story up to this point. Then I realized that I was in essence just rehashing the chapter headings from the first book. So in second thought, I suggest that you now reread the Contents section of Book 1 and that should accomplish the same goal. Hopefully, that may bring back some of the memories for you.

I paused my story when we left for Newburgh because this was to be our new beginning. It was now 1962 and the new decade was just starting to make its presence felt. Also, The Old Man said that he was a changed man. He had a good job as a telephone lineman, so we would be able to live a good life. And best of all, he had quit drinking. That was now all behind him. Or so he said. Did I believe it? Well, I didn't believe in the Easter Bunny or Santa Claus and had stopped believing in the existence of some superior being that watched over us. I did believe in ghosts though. So, no, I didn't really think that The Old man had turned over a new leaf; however, I was willing to wait and see. And now finally, you will be able to see for yourself.

1 – Another Dam Place

Mom always said, "If you don't have anything good to say about someone, don't say anything at all." But she never said anything about writing. So after a short break, I've decided to keep on with my narration. To begin with, I will describe my first impressions of my new hometown. Newburgh had more in common with Hillsburgh than just the name. The population of both towns was around 500 to 600 people at that time, and Newburgh too had a large hill at one end of town. The hill in Newburgh was even steeper than the one in our former village. But we didn't live at the top of the hill this time. No, we lived at the other end of the town on the street farthest from the hill. And we no longer owned our home; instead, we were renting once again. But we were still living in a town; our farm days were over. We were renting the house from a family called Chance. So of course, we only referred to this abode as Chance's Place. At first inspection, I was quite impressed with the house. It had lovely hardwood floors and French glass doors dividing the living room from the hallway and the stairs leading up to the bedrooms. There was a large kitchen and a separate dining room. When you went up the stairs, you came to the top of a small hallway with four doors opening onto it. The first door on the right was Lily's bedroom. She now had her own bedroom with real walls, no more blanket partition. This fact helped to appease Lily somewhat about the move. The other door on the right became Mom and The Old Man's room. On the left, the one door led into a large bedroom which was assigned to Ernie and Billy. It had a door off of it which led into a smaller bedroom (but still a fair size) that was left for Gordie and me. So Gordie and I had to walk through Ernie and Billy's room to get to ours. The last door directly straight ahead at the top of the stairs – where you would expect a bathroom to be – was actually just a large walk-in closet. The bathroom? It was in the backyard – an outhouse. That was a first for us, at least that I could remember. A lot of people in Newburgh still had outhouses. I couldn't believe it. I felt like we had moved away from civilization. And the phone? We still had one but once more it was a large wooden box hanging on the wall with a crank handle on the side. Nobody in Newburgh had a dial phone yet. Hence, that accounts for The Old Man's transfer to this town. To introduce them to the modern era of communication. But the bathroom was another matter.

On the first night in our new home, we were awakened by the sound of a large explosion followed by what sounded like an air-raid siren that continued wailing for a long time. I thought the town was being bombed. I was close. In actuality, a U.S. Air Force plane crashed in a field just south of town killing the crew (Was it two or four? I can't recall). That was the explosion. The fire alarm, to alert the Newburgh Volunteer Fire Department into action, was what sounded like the air-raid siren. That was our welcome to Newburgh. The next day some of the other kids told us about their experiences during the night accompanied by all the gruesome details. I was sort of glad that I remained in bed and missed all of the 'excitement'.

In short order, we became aware of the two most distinctive features of Newburgh. Other than the hill, that is. The first was the dam. It is situated on the Napanee River which runs from town towards the town of Napanee seven miles away. The dam towered about 10 to 15 feet above the water depending on the time of the year and which end of the dam you were standing on. In the summer when the water was fairly low, the dam actually worked like one. In the spring, water rushed through it because of the large tunnel in the middle. I was amazed to see kids dive off the dam into the water below. I already told you the height of the dam, as for the water it was at most five feet deep in the deepest spots. You definitely had to know how to dive shallow. Not that you had much choice. If you dove straight down, you would hit your head on a large rock protruding from the aforementioned tunnel. But everyone seemed to know what they were doing and I never saw anyone get hurt. I'll have much more to say about 'the dam' as this story unfolds.

The other main feature of Newburgh was the nicknames. Practically everybody had one, well at least the boys anyway. And they weren't necessarily complimentary. But nobody seemed to mind that much. I'll give you some examples now. At the top of the hill lived the two brothers Top Cat and Big Boy. Partway down the hill, there were three brothers – Schroeder, Linus, and Pigpen. At the bottom of the hill, Sneezy and Maynard (I thought that was his real name for the first year) took up residence. On the road towards the dam lived Flip (Flip the Sausage) who I was told was aptly named. Further into town, there were another two brothers – Pooh and Birdbrain – who lived with their father Great Elk. Just to confuse things, a father of one of the boys was also called Sneezy. However, we were still just Billy, Gordie, and Benny. Whoops, no we weren't. I almost forgot. Billy now insisted that he be called Bill and Gordie followed that up with his own demands to be referred to as Gord. 'Bill' I could manage most of the time, but 'Gord' just never seemed to roll off the tongue easily. Ernie was still Ernie (call him Ern at your own peril) and Lily was of course still Lily (not Sissy, remember). Me, I was still Benny or as Mom often would call me – 'Dear Little Benny'. I think that was started by Lily when she was two or three. "Oh look Mom, here comes Dear Little Benny home from school," she blurted out one day. The handle stuck.

There were three other facets of Newburgh that I should tell you about. One being the hockey arena – there wasn't one. Right in the middle of town, at the bottom of the hill, sat a large, low building on a fair-sized lot. On first glance, I thought it was an arena. What gave it away though, was the large sign on the front of the building which said 'Newburgh Sales Barn'. I didn't know what that meant at first. At least not until I attended my first cattle auction there. Not exactly the place to take your first date. Another significant building in Newburgh was right beside the sales barn. There sat an old tar-papered structure that looked ready to burn down at a moment's notice. Which would have been scary because Dorchester's Service Station was situated right on the other side of it. This ominous edifice was a factory. The Kitchen Brush Factory. For the first year, I always wondered what a 'Kitchen Brush' was until someone explained to me that it was just a brush factory and Kitchen was the name of the owner. And the third highlight of Newburgh that I want to tell you about is another industry – the cheese factory. It was at the end of town near where we lived. You couldn't miss it, even with your eyes closed. Because you could smell it. This disgusting looking stuff would dump out of the factory, right into the little stream beside it. In keeping with Newburgh traditions, this stream will hereto always be referred to as 'Shit Creek'.

A few days after we arrived in our new residence, a boy came to the door to introduce himself and to see if I wanted to play baseball. He was a little younger than me but not by much. His name was Brendan Casey. I agreed and off I went to meet his friends. Also playing the game were Schroeder, Linus, Sneezy, and Flip. As well there was another boy that I haven't mentioned yet – Very Dorky. That's what everyone called him, I swear. I eventually determined that his real name was Barry Dorchester. Very Dorky originated from the way that Barry's older brother Brian used to pronounce Barry's name when he was a baby. Brendan Casey and I were just about the only kids there that went by our real names. All of the participants in the game except for me attended the Newburgh Academy, the local public school. At first, they didn't believe that I was going into Grade 9 and would be going to the high school in Napanee on the bus. I was the smallest one there – no surprise. When the game started, I was positioned at second base which scared the wits out of me. I was no Ty Cobb when it came to baseball. I was used to languishing in the obscurity of the outfield. Sometimes I had been inserted at shortstop. Why? Because I was short. I never understood the connection. Anyways, when the first ball was hammered my way, I made a brilliant catch and tagged out the guy on second.

"Boy, not only is this kid smart, he's an athlete too!" commented Sneezy. I just blushed.

Not long after, Sneezy and the rest of the competitors soon realized the error in their judgement. I never stopped another ball that came my way.

"Maybe he's not so smart either," somebody suggested.

But it was all good-natured jesting. And I soon became good friends with many of those players.

That night Gordie (see I told you I couldn't get used to Gord) and I met a couple of local girls. We were just at the end of our street in front of a church when they introduced themselves to us. I don't remember who they were anymore. I only remember what one of them asked us.

"What religion are you?"

"None," replied Gordie.

"What do you mean, none? You have to be some religion," she replied.

"Well we used to be United, but we don't go to church anymore," explained Gordie.

"Thank God!" the girl exclaimed, "You're not Catholic. I hate Catholics."

Both Gordie and I didn't know what to say to that. I was shocked. That was my first real experience with religious bigotry like that. I wondered what she would have said if we

11

had told her that we were atheists. I assume that would have been OK compared to Catholicism. When I say that was my first experience with prejudice based upon religion, I am not being entirely truthful. When The Old Man was drunk he used to sometimes rant against Roman Catholics. But that was different. The Old Man said many things when he was drunk. Both my oldest sister Claudia's husband Tom and my oldest brother Brad's wife Catherine were Catholic. And when The Old Man was sober, I never heard him make a big point of it. Besides this was coming from someone my own age. I couldn't understand the reaction at all. I thought to myself, "What the devil difference does what building people sleep in on Sunday mornings have to do with anything?" That's absolutely true. That's how naïve I was about those things. I remembered Brendan Casey was Catholic. I only knew that because he told me that he was going to be going to school in Brockville to become a priest. I finally got up enough nerve to answer.

"I like Catholics. They are just the same as us."

That was the extent of the theological discussion. I never talked to that girl about religion (or anything else, for that matter) again.

I already told you that I was starting Grade 9 at the high school in Napanee (Napanee Regional High School). What I didn't tell you was that Gordie would also be attending Grade 9 along with me. I hadn't mentioned earlier that Gordie had failed his first year of high school in Erin. I guess there were a few things about his first year in Erin that I failed to mention. Like the amount of time that Gordie spent in the Erin pool hall when he should have been in class. But this is my story, isn't it? So forgive me for omitting a few details that I was not directly involved in.

Billy (I mean Bill) passed his year and was therefore commencing Grade 10 at N.R.H.S. that September of 1962. I know that Ernie was in Grade 12 that year, hence either he failed his last year at Erin, or I lost count somewhere along the line, or Ernie decided to repeat a year for reasons that are beyond me. I don't recall. Regardless, the four of us boys now got to travel together on the same bus each school day. Lily would stay in Newburgh to continue her education (Grade 4) at the previously mentioned Newburgh Academy. We would wait for the bus in front of The Newburgh Lunch – the local restaurant (or snack bar really) at the bottom of the hill by the river. This also was the location where we would gather for any activity, or more often than not, just hang around. I enjoyed the camaraderie of the bus ride. We would usually discuss the previous night's hockey games and scores in elaborate detail. Almost everyone had a favourite team and if that person's team had suffered a defeat the night before, then he would be subjected to endless harangues. The New York Rangers were dreadful that year so I told everybody that I was a Leaf fan. Gordie got kidded about every Boston Bruin loss (they were worse than the Rangers) even though he also tried to claim loyalty to the Maple Leafs. Bill still cheered for the Canadiens. Birdbrain (Jim Stonehouse) was also a Habs' supporter while his younger brother Pooh (Phil) favoured the Detroit Red Wings. I also met some more Newburgh residents once we started going on the seven-mile bus ride to Napanee.

I was introduced to one boy who wasn't much taller than me. He was called Sean Becker and didn't seem to have a nickname. He lived in a house by the river very close to where we boarded the bus, so naturally he was always the last to arrive. Another good part about busing was being late for school when the weather was bad. I remember one particular day that we got buried in a large snowdrift. Many of the boys had to get out and help push the bus free. By the time we got to school, we were told to go home. It was great.

High school itself was a big change from Public school. I now actually had to study, especially History which I found challenging. I hated trying to remember dates. The only thing that I remember from History that year was Miss Crusher – the young woman teacher with the large chest size. It was said that you could see her start to enter the classroom a minute before she actually arrived. For Geography, our teacher was Chalky Chapman. His lesson consisted of Chalky circling the room writing copious notes on every square inch of every blackboard in the smallest writing possible. We were expected to copy every word into our notebooks for posterity. At the end of the period, Chalky Chapman would be covered from head to toe in chalk. More memory work. I still don't know how many sheep they have in New Zealand.

However, my and Gordie's least favourite subject was Agriculture. A new subject for both of us. Neither of us saw a need for taking this course but it was mandatory in Napanee. I was no longer interested in learning about farming. I wanted to be an architect now. The only interesting part that I can recall was when we got to hatch chickens in this big incubator. Gordie and the Agriculture teacher never did see eye to eye. His name was Mr. Major but everyone called him Major Major, but not to his face mind you. Except for Gordie, who did just that one day. Major Major was so infuriated that he walked down the aisle and knocked Gordie right off his stool. In second thought, maybe it was an interesting class.

I haven't mentioned about The Old Man in Newburgh yet, have I? Well, there was nothing new on that front. He was still drinking as much as usual – at least each payday which was still every two weeks.

By the late fall, we had also already built up a fair-sized credit at the local general store for things such as a new stove and a minor necessity called food.

Before I relate the story that I meant to tell you, I just realized that I never mentioned that there was a door at the back of the house off the kitchen. This made it easier to go to the 'bathroom' without having to go out the front door and then having to circle around to the back of the house. You need to know that fact. One early Saturday evening, The Old Man arrived home well on his way to inebriation and not alone. He had a teenage boy with him that I would guess was sixteen or possibly seventeen at the maximum (the drinking

14

age was twenty-one in 1962). I had never met him before but Gordie thought that he lived at the top of the hill. His name was Kenny Turner. They walked through the living room without saying a word. At the time, Mom, Ernie, Bill, Gordie, Lily, and I were situated in the living room watching something on the TV. The Old Man and Kenny headed into the kitchen (where else?) with a case of 24 Red Cap. At the same moment, Poncho crawled into his favourite hiding spot – under the china cabinet. In a matter of a few seconds, the expected outburst occurred.

"Where the hell are you, old bag? Come and meet my friend, Kenny. He's a great guy. Give you the shirt right off his back. Wouldn't you, Kenny? Hey, old bag, we're hungry. Get us some food, will you!"

Mom hesitantly started to rise in order to go into the kitchen and warm-up the supper, when Ernie spoke. "Why don't you let him starve, Mom? He won't thank you for it anyway. He'll probably just say it looks like his asshole. And if you're lucky, he won't throw it on the floor."

"No, Ernie," Mom argued. "I know your father. I better go in there or he'll be a lot worse." So that's what Mom did.

"Hello dear," The Old Man said with a sickeningly sweet voice. "This is my good friend, Kenny."

"Hello," was all Mom replied. Kenny grunted a hello in return. "I put the dinner in the oven," Mom continued after a brief pause. "It will be ready shortly."

"Thank you dear. Get us a beer out of the fridge, will you dear? And one for Kenny."

"That's a first," I said, "beer in the fridge. It must be something he learned from Kenny Turner."

We heard Mom next. "I'm not getting your beer. And I'm not serving beer to a boy the same age as Billy. You can get it yourself. If you want to get in trouble with the police for serving a minor, go ahead. But I'm not going to be part of it."

"You goddamned gray-haired, old bag! How dare you tell me what to do! Get us the fucking beer, now!"

Mom walked back into the living room without bothering to respond to that tirade. "Good for you, Mom," Ernie encouraged. "You don't have to listen to every word that bastard says."

"That fucking old bag thinks she's queen of the fucking world. She's getting too goddamned smart for her own britches. I fought in the war; I installed Connie Smythe's phone for Christ's sake. This is the thanks that I get for it. Goddamn that gray-haired, old son of a bitch." We then heard The Old Man's fist slam down on the kitchen table. "I'm sorry Kenny that you had to put up with that gray-haired old bag. I'll get you another beer."

"You don't have to apologize for the old bag," Kenny slurred. "That's OK."

Before what Kenny had said had even sunk into my brain, Bill whizzed by me and rushed into the kitchen and began shouting.

"How dare you come into our house and call my mother an old bag, you drunken piece of shit! Get the hell out of our house right now! And don't ever come back!"

"I'm sorry, I didn't mean..." Before Kenny could complete his apology, Bill had the front door open and was pushing Kenny out through it. He then slammed the door shut. I looked over my shoulder and out the front window to see Kenny stumble and fall on our front-walk.

"What the hell do you think you are doing, Billy?" The Old Man demanded to know. You let my friend back in here, right now! The old bag put you up to this. She's turning the family against me again."

"You shut up too or you'll be out the door next. Don't you call my mom an old bag anymore!"

"What? She's a gray-haired old bag and always will be. What's wrong with speaking the truth?"

That was enough for Bill. Either the anger gave Bill extra strength or else The Old Man was too stunned or too drunk to respond, but before I knew what was even happening, Bill heaved The Old Man out the front door and locked it.

"And stay out you son of a bitch!" Bill yelled at the closed door.

"You think you're fucking smart, don't you? Wait 'till I get my hands on you!" That was The Old Man screaming from the kitchen. He must have run around the back of the house and into the back door. We couldn't believe how fast he did it. Maybe, he wasn't quite as drunk as I first guessed. But Bill wasn't to be out-foxed that day. He quickly threw The Old Man right back out the front door while the cursing and hollering continued. By this time, Ernie had locked the back door as well. A few seconds later, we heard The Old Man banging on the kitchen door. Bill then grabbed the case of beer and deposited it out the front door as well. We didn't know what to expect next. I know that I was watching out for a large rock to come smashing through one of the windows. However, the next sound that we heard was the engine of the car. The Old Man, Kenny Turner, and the Red Cap left and went somewhere else to drink.

"Yeah, way to go, Billy!" Lily exclaimed. We all seconded the motion including Poncho who then came out of hiding and barked at the closed front door as if to say 'Good riddance!"

"Thanks Billy," Mom added, "I just hope that we don't pay for it later. That's all."

The funny part was that when The Old Man finally did come home sometime in the early hours of the morning, he went straight to bed without saying a word.

2 – Doctor Claus

In the fall of 1962, there was a total eclipse of the sun. Everyone said it went totally dark for a few minutes in the middle of a sunny afternoon. But I had to take the others word for it because I missed it completely. Where was I? Sitting in the outhouse. I didn't know anything special had occurred until a few hours later when Lily told me. What could I do about it? You know what they say, "When you gotta go, you gotta go." I didn't think I cared much. So how come I still remember missing not seeing the sun?

One evening in November of that same year, Gordie, Lily, and I were looking at the Christmas catalogue and trying to decide what we were looking forward to seeing under the tree that year. Gordie and I both had our eyes on this new table hockey game. It was far more advanced than our old model. The players could actually move up and down the ice, there was a large score-clock above the ice, and it used what looked like a real puck. It also came with players for all six N.H.L. teams.

"Look Mom," I exclaimed, "here's what Gordie and I want for Christmas. Can we get this hockey game here? It looks real neat."

"I don't know, Benny," Mom snapped in return. "I don't

even know if we'll be having Christmas this year."

Mom had caught me totally by surprise, not only by what she said but more importantly by the short tone of her voice. I hadn't known her to speak to one of us like that before – unless we had asked for it. I must have worn a shocked and hurt expression on my face because Mom immediately changed.

"I'm sorry, Benny. I didn't mean to bark at you like that. I was just thinking about Christmas and worrying where the money will come from."

"The hockey game would be for the both of us," rationalized Gordie. "And probably Bill too. He said he would like a new one."

"I don't want a hockey game," said Lily. "Can I look at the book again, Benny? I think I want the stove and fridge that I saw. Maybe Santa can get that for me."

"I'm not sure that we have enough money to get any presents this year, whether you share or not," Mom continued to explain. "Other than what Santa brings, I mean," she added for Lily's benefit. "With us moving and other bills, we hardly have enough money for food and clothes. In fact, if Mr. Hooper at the general store stopped the credit, we wouldn't even have enough for food. I'm sorry to be bothering you three about this but I don't know what to do. I'm at my wits' end."

"Can't Brad or Aunt Becky give us some money?" I inquired.

"They would, Benny, but I don't want to ask them. Brad, Claudia, and Aunt Becky already do enough. Brad and Claudia have families to look after too. Aunt Becky can't really afford anymore either. No, I won't ask them." Mom hesitated for a moment. "I have another thought though."

"What's that?" asked Gordie.

"I don't really want to do it, but I don't know what other choices I have. I'm ashamed to do it."

"What, Mom?" It was my turn to ask.

"I was thinking about writing Dr. McGuire. He knows

all of you. He said to me before we moved that if there was ever anything that he could do for us, he would be glad to help. But that's a lot to ask from someone else. Maybe, I can ask him to send us a hundred dollars or so. That would be enough to get the presents that you want plus some other extras for Christmas. I don't know. What do you think?"

"He said he would help us, didn't he, Mom?" Gordie replied first. I then uttered a few more reasons why Mom shouldn't feel shame in asking this favour.

"I guess you're right. I'll do it. It's going to be a hard letter to write though."

"I'll help," I volunteered helpfully.

So that's what happened. A few days later, Mom wrote the letter and I Okayed the contents. Mom asked Dr. McGuire if he could lend us one-hundred dollars until we got back onto our feet. Not long after, we got a letter from Dr. McGuire in return. Enclosed was a cheque for two-hundred dollars and a note. Dr. McGuire said that he was pleased to help us anyway that he could and he didn't want us to pay him back. That kind of charity is hard to believe today but that's the way it really happened. I'm sure it was nothing for Dr. McGuire; however, I've never forgotten the sacrifice that Mom made to her own pride in order to write that letter. And I've often wished that we could have repaid the doctor for his kindness in some manner or another. Thus on Christmas morning, we opened our present of the new table hockey game. I should also mention that Lily was a recipient of new kitchen appliances as well.

Consequently, right after Christmas 1962, our hockey league was revived. We even expanded. A new team – the Montreal Canopeners – was added to the league as competition against the Boston Beans and the New York Riders. Bill, of course, was the Montreal franchise. We gave the league an official name. We called it the W.H.L. or the World Hockey League; we never did understand why the N.H.L. was called 'National' even though it spanned two countries. We started to keep track of standings, scoring leaders, penalties (yeah, and we even had fights!), and other such statistics. The standings would hang on Ernie and Bill's bedroom wall. We sent away for extra players for the game so that each of us could dress 16 players – 9 forwards, 6 defencemen, and 1 goalie. We would carve the players' numbers on their sweaters. We also used black tape to put a mask on Jock Planter (Jacques Plante) and a helmet on Barley Beans (Charlie Burns). Nothing but reality for us. The W.H.L. was cruising along with the three-member teams until we noticed that we had played five games in a row between the New York Riders and the Montreal Canopeners. Where were the Boston Beans? Had they folded? No, it was just that they were getting harder to fit into the schedule. For reasons which I will explain.

As 1963 progressed Gordie became less visible around the house. He had met a girl. Paula Cutler was her name. He had become more interested in seeing Paula than spending time with his brother Benny. Was I jealous? Yes. Did I miss playing with Gordie? Yes. Did I sit at home and sulk? No. Well not all the time, anyways. I too started to develop other interests besides playing games. There was a girl in Newburgh that I had started to notice. She lived near the top of the hill. She was still in Public School, so she wasn't on our bus. However, whenever I passed her on the street she would have a big smile for me. So I would return the smile. So far the most we had said to each other was 'Hello'. That was the extent of it until one cold, February, Saturday afternoon, I was sitting in the Newburgh Lunch with a group of guys when Carol English (that was her name) and another girl walked in and sat at the far end of the counter. Today, we smiled at each other but didn't even say 'Hello'.

"Why don't you go sit with your girlfriend, Benny?" Birdbrain said suddenly.

"What are you talking about, Jim? I don't have a girlfriend," I refuted.

"You can't fool us, Benny," argued Birdbrain. "You're in love with Carol English. How can you let her sit down there by herself? You should join her."

"I don't love her and besides she's not by herself."

"You like her a lot then and she sure likes you. Don't you know that?"

"I don't think so. We've never even spoken to each other."

"You don't have to. Didn't you see that smile and the sparkle in her eyes? And yours too. It's love alright. Aren't I right, Pooh?"

"Sure thing, Birdbrain," his brother agreed.

"You're crazy, Birdbrain," I continued to dispute.

"That may be, but I'm right about this. Just watch."

At that point, before I could raise any objection, Birdbrain had slipped the engraved bracelet off my wrist and was walking down to the far end of the counter. I didn't mention the bracelet before, did I? Once again, more details that I forget to mention until they become central to the story. Excuse me. Anyways, the bracelet was a gift from Claudia and Tom that Christmas. It was silver (not real) and had 'Benny' engraved on it. It opened up so that you could insert something (a very slim photograph, for example) inside. At any rate, what I started to say was that Birdbrain went up to Carol and placed the bracelet with my name written on it upon her wrist.

"Thank you, Benny," Carol said excitedly.

I decided not to admit that it wasn't my idea. "You're welcome, Carol," I mumbled in return.

Birdbrain came back to our end of the restaurant and spoke, "See I told you. She's your girlfriend."

I had no rebuttal. I guess he was right. I was just the last one in Newburgh to realize the truth, that's all. Carol was my girlfriend. Over the next few months, Carol and I would spend more and more time together. Most of it consisted of standing together, holding hands, and saying a few words. In front of the post office was one of our favourite standing locales. We would stand there for hours and converse only a few words. I am exaggerating a bit; in truth I did manage some sentences. And sometimes we would walk. As I said, this progressed slowly. Accordingly there was still time for other adventures.

I described earlier the circumstances around my cessation of the smoking habit. What I didn't explain was that that made me the only Cooper male still living at home who didn't partake in that particular sin. Ernie and Bill would often smoke up in their bedroom with the window wide open blowing smoke out into the great outdoors. They assumed that this fooled Mom and that she would never have noticed the smoke-filled room or the butt-filled ashtray on the windowsill discreetly hidden by the curtains. Although they were both of legal smoking age – Ernie was eighteen and Bill was seventeen – they thought it best to hide this custom from their mother. They didn't want to unduly upset her or cause extra worries. Since Gordie had only just turned sixteen, he took the safer route and would only do his smoking in a natural setting – out on the street. Bill was smoking enough that he had developed the brown stain of nicotine on two fingers of his right hand. One day Mom questioned Bill about it.

"What's that on your fingers, Billy?" she asked.

"What? There's nothing on my fingers," he answered.

"That brown spot there on those two fingers. What is that?" Mom followed up.

"Oh that," said Bill. "I didn't notice that. I guess that's where I had to go outside to the toilet a while ago and we were short of toilet paper. I better go wash it off."

With that response, Bill disappeared into the kitchen and we all heard the water begin to flow from the tap. Mom just looked at me, smiled, and shook her head. Mom knew what was going on; she was no fool.

One Saturday night, we were all watching the Leaf game. All except for The Old Man that is. We hadn't seen him since he left to get his car filled with gas that morning around ten o'clock. We were all dreading the moment when his drunken face would appear at the front door. By the time that the hockey game was over (another Toronto win) and Juliette had graced our television screen, there was still no sight of a car in the driveway or the sound of The Old Man on the front step. At that point, Mom decided to call it a night and went off to bed with Lily in tow. In point of fact, Lily had fallen asleep on the living room floor before the third period had started. The rest of us decided to stay up and watch Lon Chaney in 'The Wolfman' on Channel 7 (Watertown). We had all seen it before but that didn't matter. It was a classic and well worth another viewing. We just hoped that we would be able to watch the whole thing in peace and not be interrupted by comments such as, "What the hell's this shit that you're watching?" Well, we made it. Just! At the moment that the credits were beginning to roll by, a car pulled in the driveway. We quickly turned off the television and headed up to our respective bedrooms. Poncho and Pepper followed us up the stairs. Before the four of us had donned our matching yellow-brown and blue-blue pyjamas, we heard the distinctive, staggering steps of The Old Man on the stairs.

"Hey, fucking old bag. I'm drunk again. Where the hell's my supper? You gray-haired old cunt! I'm so hungry that I could eat a horse. Could you please get me something to eat, dear?"

"It's one-thirty in the morning, Garf," Mom sighed. "I left you a plate in the fridge. Just stick it in the oven on two-hundred for a half-hour or so."

"In the oven! In the oven! What the fuck do I know about ovens? I mean, I cooked on the ships during the war. I'm not doing it now. I fought in the war for this?"

"Take your arms off me, Garf. I'm trying to sleep. Leave me alone."

"You lazy son of a bitch. All you want to do is stay in bed all day fucking everything that moves. You think I don't know what's going on. I wasn't born yesterday. I've been around the world. I know the score. What…"

"Four to two for Toronto," Bill shouted. "That's the score!"

"What! Who said that? You think you're so fucking smart." I heard Ernie and Bill's bedroom door open and The Old Man's voice getting much louder. "Is that you Billy, Bill? Whatever the fuck you call yourself these days. You think you're so fucking smart, don't you? The whole goddamned family! You're all dirt under my feet! You think I forget you throwing me out of my own house. I should teach you a goddamned lesson. I could take all of you with one hand tied behind my back. Oh, why bother with you? It's that old bag I want to teach a lesson. Get up you gray-haired son of a bitch and get my supper! Right now!"

I then heard loud steps across the hall followed by my Mom's cry in pain. "Garf, you're hurting me! Please, let go. I'll get up."

"Ahhh!" That was Bill. Gordie and I opened our bedroom door to catch the sight of Bill jumping The Old Man from behind, grabbing him, and pushing him back into the hall. "You leave my Mom alone," Bill demanded. "I'm not taking your shit anymore."

The Old Man quickly eluded Bill's grasp and clenched his fist on Bill's crotch. Even when he was drunk, The Old man demonstrated great agility and surprising strength. I saw a look of pain cross Bill's face. Ernie quickly headed for the hall to help Bill but before he arrived to the rescue, Bill raised one leg and pushed it against his aggressor. The Old Man tumbled backwards down the stairs. He crash-landed awkwardly at the bottom. All of us ran to the top of the stairs to peer down below. Lily ran out of her room crying and ran to Mom. To our surprise, The Old Man swiftly jumped to his feet and glanced upwards.

"Goddamn you! Goddamn you all! The whole fucking family has gone nuts. I'm going to watch TV. May you all rot in hell!"

We then heard the TV blaring on some late-night movie. After we all had inquired on Mom's condition, she took Lily back to bed. We discovered Poncho crouched under Ernie and Bill's bed and Pepper curled up under my and Gordie's covers. After waiting a few minutes to ensure that The Old Man wasn't returning with a butcher knife or some other weapon in his hand, we all returned to our own rooms to attempt sleep. I heard Bill exclaim, "God, my nuts hurt. That bastard's a strong son of a bitch." I can't answer for the rest, but I know that I lay there awake for a few hours until I could hear the buzz of the test pattern coming from the television below. That was one of those nights that I prayed. And it worked.

The next day, you know what wouldn't melt in The Old Man's mouth and he was for sure giving up drinking for good. He apologized to Mom, Bill, and the rest of us for his behaviour the night before. He had suffered no permanent damage from his trip down the stairs. Mom said The Old Man was like a cat – he had nine lives. From his exploits in the war, falling off telephone poles, being ejected from rolling cars, and now falling down the stairs, we figured that he must have just about used up all nine of them. Or was that just wishful thinking?

We started to think seriously about a suggestion that Brad had made to Mom and the rest of us a while back. He wanted all of us to pick up stakes and move with him and his family to either the Barbados or Florida. Without The Old Man of course. None of us kids were keen on the idea. I'm not sure why now. I think my main argument against the scheme involved not wanting to leave Canada. I particularly remember not wanting to go to Florida. First it wasn't in Canada, second it was in the United States, and third it had no snow, hockey, or other such things that we loved. During one discussion I became so adamant about my opposition to the proposal, that I picked up a nearby penknife and threw it towards the atlas lying on the floor. It landed with the blade embedded in the middle of the state of Florida. I couldn't have done it better if I had tried. In conclusion, Mom just wasn't up to forcing us to make that big of a move, so no action was taken on the relocation plan. Brad however still decided to leave the Air Force and soon headed down south by himself to scout out the territory. He would write us letters telling us how beautiful it was down there, but as time went on we became even more reluctant to make the shift. We had all developed new friends in Newburgh and, as I had detailed earlier, that included the opposite sex.

3 – Firsts and Farewells

Gordie and I had a radio up in our room that we would listen to at night as we attempted to study or complete other homework. It was especially effective when studying History. The music could help me concentrate on Miss Crusher's History as opposed to her anatomy. We couldn't get CHUM anymore but for some reason we could pick up WBZ from Boston. They, like CHUM, would also have a Top 30 countdown. I recollect the number one song at the time. It was 'In Dreams' by Roy Orbison. Both Gordie and I loved it. We couldn't wait until they got to number one so that we could hear it once more. Although, I have to admit that I couldn't focus on my lessons when it was being played.

As the year progressed and we continued our bus ride to school in Napanee, we met more and more people. Before the bus arrived in Newburgh, it had already made stops in the towns of Moscow, Yarker, and Camden East. Eventually I learned the names of many of these passengers. The students from Moscow were always kidded about being Russians. Along the way to Napanee we would stop at another little town two miles down the road from Newburgh to pick up more riders. This little town which was even smaller than Newburgh was called Strathcona. It was noted for its paper mill and its smell. Some days it could have put Shit Creek to shame.

At N.R.H.S. there was something new for 1963. We now took shop. There were three types of shop during that first year – Metal, Wood-working, and Drafting. A few students helped get the shops ready for the new semester. Among those 'volunteers' was Ernie. A reporter from the local newspaper – The Napanee Beaver – interviewed them and Ernie even got his picture in the paper. The reporter asked them if they were having fun and Ernie sarcastically replied, "Oh yeah, for sure." So the article in the paper described how the boys not only were doing work and making extra money but that they enjoyed it as well. Ernie got a good laugh over that one.

I wasn't a big fan of metal shop right from the start. We were introduced to these giant lathes (at least they seemed huge compared to me) and we were expected to know how to run them with little or no training. I guess you could say that I was intimidated by them. We were required to produce some kind of tool for our first project. I chose to manufacture an ice pick; however, I never even finished the handle. Wood shop was much the same. Although the machines weren't quite as threatening in size, they were just as much or more dangerous. Still, I managed to complete my project this time. I made what probably every male student in Ontario has made – a cutting board shaped like a fish. Real exciting! Drafting was much more to my liking. We sat at these large easels using neat looking rulers and right angles to compose various drawings. I thought it was great fun. I was in the minority opinion there, so that only solidified my desire to become an architect.

Another subject that I failed to point out earlier was Physical Education. This also was not one of my favourites. Soccer, the one sport in which I felt that I had a chance to compete in, in spite of my size, was not part of the agenda. We spent a lot of time on sports in which I was utterly useless such as football. We were graded on how far we could throw or kick a football. Or, on how well we could tackle a two-hundred and fifty pound opponent. I had no chance. I didn't shine in Track and Field either. Finally, we did take one sport that put me on a level playing field and that I enjoyed for a change. That was gymnastics. At last an activity where size didn't matter. I was one of the few kids in the class that could climb to the top of the gymnasium on the rope. I must have inherited this skill from The Old Man.

The boys usually took Phys. Ed. on one side of the gym while the girls were on the other side with a moveable wall between us. Once in a while they would open the wall and we would take our classes together. This would be for things like dance. The best part of that was seeing how the various-shaped, female classmates looked in their baggy, blue, one-piece gym suits. Once a week our lesson was given in a classroom by the same instructor and it was called Health. They still segregated the sexes for this session. That was so they could talk about things such as sex education. One time we had to take a written quiz which determined your health rating. I remember this because my score indicated that I should be dead. I'm still not sure what part of my lifestyle was the main contributor to that result.

Anyway, I was still alive a couple weekends later when The Old Man inevitably got drunk again. It was dinnertime and Mom, The Old Man, Gordie, Lily, and I were sitting around the dining room table having homemade fish and chips. This was one meal that you could usually depend on The Old Man not complaining about as it was one of his favourites. Neither Bill nor Ernie were home at the time. Things were going smoothly until Gordie spoke.

"Is it OK if I go out after supper, Mom? I promised Paula that I would see her later."

Mom never got a chance to respond. The Old Man commented first.

"What do you want to see her for? She's a whore just like the old bag, your mother. You just want to fuck all night."

"Garf! Don't..." Mom started before Gordie interrupted.

"You shut your fucking, disgusting mouth! You worthless piece of shit," Gordie shouted towards The Old Man.

"I'm not taking this crap from my own kids!" yelled The Old Man as he picked up his plate of fish and chips and threw it towards Gordie. It soared between Gordie and Lily and hit the wall smashing into a thousand pieces.

"Don't Dad," Lily pleaded. "Please!"

"You shut your fucking yap too! Don't you start on me now. You're just another whore like that gray-haired, son of a bitch of a mother of yours. I'll throw any dish I want."

And true to his word, The Old Man grabbed his coffee cup and heaved it towards Lily. It just grazed my shocked sister and disintegrated against the wall and joined the remains of the plate of fish and chips on the floor below. Lily burst into tears while Mom jumped to her feet to protect her youngest daughter. I stayed motionless. My only movements were my shaking and sobbing. But not so for Gordie. He jumped into action. He ran around to the other side of the table and brushed up against The Old Man who was attempting to stand up at the same time. This action caused The Old Man's chair to tip over backwards while he was still in it. The next thing that I knew The Old Man had recovered his feet and had the chair poised over his head ready to strike Gordie with all his might. I finally was able to force a few words out of my trembling body.

"Gordie! Look out!"

Gordie had only enough time to duck down so that the legs of the chair slammed down against his back rather than over his head. I too now jumped to my feet and ran towards the combatants. To do what, I wasn't sure. I heard Mom's pleadings before I discovered what my actions would have been.

"Garf, what are you doing? You're going to kill your own son. Gordie! Are you all right?"

"I think so," replied Gordie as he slowly stood back up. The Old Man froze looking at the chair like he couldn't understand how it got into his hands.

"Benny, go phone the police," Mom continued.

"No, I'm OK now," said The Old Man. "I don't know what got into me. You don't need the police. There's no need for them. I'm sorry. Gordie, you're OK, aren't you? Don't cry Lily. Everything is OK now. I just lost my head for a minute. What am I doing?"

"Call the police, Benny," Mom repeated.

And so I did. I was in tears as I told the man on the line what the problem was. "My father hit Gordie." While we were waiting for the police to arrive Gordie kept The Old Man's attention sidetracked by talking to him about the war. How Gordie was able to do this, I couldn't understand. I couldn't even look at the bastard. I hated his guts. How could he say those awful things about Lily? She had a few weeks yet to go before she turned ten years old. To talk to Mom like that was bad enough but I guess I had developed hardened skin against it. I had heard it over and over. However, the accusations against Lily made my blood boil. I wondered what Bill would have done had he been home. I recalled his inspiration for chopping wood. Using the axe even crossed my mind. We'd all be better off if The Old Man was dead, I thought. But that contemplation only lasted for a second until I realized the effect it would have on Mom if her 'Dear Little Benny' was languishing in a prison cell for committing patricide. And that would be the best result that I could hope for. I could envisage a lot worse possible outcomes if I attacked The Old Man with an axe. Who was I fooling anyway? I could hardly get up enough nerve to speak let alone take some kind of physical retaliation. That was the frame of mind I was in, as first Ernie arrived home and shortly thereafter the police appeared. At first, it sounded like the same old story. The police said that they couldn't do anything. It was a family matter and nobody had been hurt (other than a sore back for Gordie). Eventually, they stated that the only way that they could be involved would be if Mom charged The Old Man with assault against Gordie. Mom wasn't too sure she wanted to do that because of the reaction it would cause from The Old Man. Eventually, with persuasion from Ernie, Mom decided that was the best course of action and she told the officer that she wished to file a charge against The Old Man. Nevertheless, they still didn't take The Old Man with them when they left. He was just told that he would have to appear in court later. That didn't seem to make The Old Man any better or worse that night. He performed his usual late night in the kitchen routine accompanied by various outbursts of profanity, rage, sorrow, and drunken utterances.

Not long after, The Old Man stood in front of a judge and pleaded guilty as charged. He had been very apologetic since the incident and had refrained from further drunk and disorderly conduct. In other words, payday hadn't arrived yet. He was sentenced to two months in jail. I remember thinking that justice was funny. Smash up a car and they put you away for three months; attack your own family and the punishment is two months. It didn't seem right to me.

That was in April 1963. While The Old Man was in jail, the Leafs won the Stanley Cup for the second year in a row by defeating Detroit with a score of 3 to 1 on April 18th. It was a fun time to be riding the bus to school. I was able to get back at Pooh for all the times that he harangued me after a Leaf loss. Things couldn't have been any better. I even gathered up enough courage to kiss a girl for the first time in my life. The 'who' I kissed, was Carol. If you were wondering where I kissed her, it was at the dam. Our relationship had progressed from holding hands in front of the post office to hugging and kissing at the dam.

At the end of April, The Old Man was released from jail. He had spent a little over three weeks of his two-month term. We were informed that Garfield Cooper had been a model prisoner. He was well-liked by everyone including the guards. He had once more joined the AA and had sworn never to touch another drop of alcohol again. And once more a member of the AA came to our house to tell us how Garf had changed his life around. Charging him with assault was the best thing that ever happened to him. He now realized the error of his ways and had found the straight path to salvation. It was now up to us to support him and put our trust and faith into his convictions. That was the most important thing in the world. If his own family couldn't back him up in a time of sickness then who could he turn to? What option would he have other than returning to a life of drink? We were so lucky because many alcoholics never realize their affliction, but Garf had not only recognized this problem but had also taken it upon himself to reverse his life and show total commitment and love to his family. I wasn't sure if we were supposed to rejoice at our good fortune or show a little more restraint and humility. Mom just nodded and said 'yes' in all the right places. As for me, I suppressed the urge to throw up.

But maybe I was being too cynical and hasty in my judgements. It was now the end of the school year and the beginning of summer and The Old Man had still not picked up a bottle of beer. It had been two months and three paydays and counting since he had become a changed man. He had stopped attending the AA meetings a couple of weeks before; nevertheless he had so far continued to resist the urge for a drink. Sammy Smale came to Newburgh to visit for a couple of weeks as soon as school ended. It was great to see him again. When I told Sammy that The Old Man had stopped drinking, he told me that he would bet a hundred dollars that The Old Man would be drunk again when the next payroll was distributed. Neither of us had a hundred dollars so I didn't take him up on his wager. I felt a little awkward while Sammy was there because I still wanted to spend some of the time with Carol. I was now fourteen years old and getting a little old for our usual games. I remember that we attempted to play Dinky Toys again but our hearts weren't quite into it. We couldn't recall what we found so entertaining about toy cars. And any thoughts about Flat and Them never even crossed our minds. Sammy was very understanding and encouraged me to go out with Carol whenever she called. He also indicated that he had no desire to join us on our 'walks'. He would just say, "Go on and have some fun. Don't do anything that I wouldn't do." Still, I felt guilty and tried to stay with Sammy for most of the time during his two-week visit.

I just realized that I neglected to tell you that at the beginning of June, Poncho gave birth to five pups. Two had died shortly after birth and miraculously The Old Man hadn't drowned the remaining three. That also reminds me that I didn't tell you about the first time that I had noticed that Poncho had left blood spots on the kitchen floor. At first, I thought that she was injured and I wanted to take her to the vet. Gordie straightened me out. What did I know? We had always had male dogs before. About four weeks after the puppies were born, Sammy and I came home after an exciting day of hanging around the streets of Newburgh. As soon as we walked in the front door, Sammy commented, "You owe me a hundred bucks." I peered into the kitchen to see a case of 24 Red Cap sitting on the floor by one of the kitchen chairs. The chair was occupied by The Old Man.

"Is that you Benny, dear? Come here. I need to talk to you about those damn pups."

I hesitantly entered the kitchen. I was afraid of what I might see. I expected to view the sight of three puppies floating in a laundry tub. I breathed a sigh of relief when I saw them alive and well with Poncho in the corner.

"Yes, Dad?"

"We got to get rid of those pups right now."

"I'll find homes for them," I promised.

"No. They have to go today. Right now."

"But they're not old enough yet."

"I don't give a damn. Come with me and we'll drive out to some farms and give them away."

"Now?" I questioned since I wasn't sure yet how much

of the case of beer had been consumed.

"It's either that or else I put them in a sack and throw them into the river. It's your choice."

Shortly after, Mom, Lily, Sammy and I went with The Old Man to visit some of the farms west of Newburgh. At first, I didn't think that The Old Man was that drunk. After all, he wasn't cursing and ranting yet. However, I soon came to realize the error of that judgement. He was swerving all over the road. I wondered why we had been so stupid to agree to go with him. After what seemed like hours of terror followed by tears, we had found new owners for the three dogs and were returning home. I was beginning to think that we had made the right choice when we took a corner on the wrong side of the road. Coming straight towards us was another car. Lily screamed and Mom yelled, "Look out!" The other car swerved one way and The Old Man spun the other way and kept on going after bouncing in and out of the ditch. I turned around and looked out the back window to see the other car in the ditch. Then the driver – Mr. Hooper – and four cub scouts scrambled out to inspect the damage. The Old Man didn't even slow down. I was so glad when we pulled in the driveway.

"Remind me to stay home next time, will you Benny?" Sammy commented after we had returned safely into the house.

"Ditto for me," I replied while watching Poncho search everywhere for her pups.

When Mrs. Smale arrived to drive Sammy home, she offered to take me back with them. I was invited to stay at their house for two weeks. At the same time, Jenny would stay at our place to spend some time with Lily. Mrs. Smale even volunteered to bring me back home when she was coming to pick up Jenny. Even though I was reluctant to leave Carol for two weeks, I jumped at the chance to return to Hillsburgh. Not only to see my old hometown once again but best of all, to get away from The Old Man for a couple of weeks. I longed for some peace and quiet. So I took the

Smales up on their kind offer and was soon on my way to Hillsburgh with Sammy.

Surprisingly, I felt a little awkward in Hillsburgh. Maybe it was because I spent all my time with Sammy and his friends. I was used to hanging out with the older kids. The ones who were friends of Gordie. You know who I mean – all the ex-NOBS. For some reason, I never saw any of them. I never crossed paths with Wendy Monahan during the visit either. I wasn't sure how I would have reacted to seeing her. I was going steady with another girl now. I must have been 'going steady', after all, Carol was wearing my bracelet, wasn't she? And Wendy had a boyfriend now – a classmate of Sammy's. Sharon, with whom I had skated along with Wendy, gave me that news when I ran into her one day. I don't know but I still think I would have loved to have seen Wendy. The biggest change in Hillsburgh was at the twisting hill at the south end of town. It was under construction and being straightened out. I guess The Old Man wasn't the only one to roll a car there. Another new feature was the 'beach' at the south end of town. This new attraction was located on the same road that went towards Erin except that you went in the opposite direction. The facilities included a manmade beach on a manmade lake with an adjacent restaurant (also manmade). Sammy and I went swimming there a few times. Well, not swimming really. The only water that I could manoeuvre at that time was the frozen kind. But I waded a lot and looked at the girls in their bikinis. Hey, even guys going steady are allowed to look now and then, aren't they? Again, I didn't see many people that I had met before. For some reason or another, Sammy seemed to know all the good-looking girls though. That's about all that I remember from that two-week stint in Hillsburgh. It was completely uneventful, which was exactly what I was looking forward to. I had lived enough events at home that I wished to forget. After being returned home and being exchanged for Jenny, I had a couple of surprises in store for me. I remember thinking to myself, "how come if I go away for a few weeks everything changes?"

The first thing that I heard was that we were moving again. The second was that Ernie wasn't going with us. This time the relocation wouldn't cause a big change. At least not to us three boys. We were just moving to Napanee – seven miles away. Therefore we would still be attending N.R.H.S. and would keep in touch with the same friends. Lily was the one that was most affected. She would have to change schools once more. I think the main reason for moving was so that The Old Man could go to a bigger town where not everyone knew his business. In a small town like Newburgh when you go to the washroom (or should I say outhouse), all the locals know how long you were there and what you did. The Old Man certainly didn't enjoy the fact that it was well known that he had assaulted one of his kids. No one said anything or treated him any differently. It just made him uncomfortable. As for Ernie. He just wanted out. The Old Man told him it was time to get out and earn a living. So Ernie took him up on his suggestion and got out. He had finished his Grade 12 and was now ready for the working world. And he wanted to start out somewhere with familiar surroundings and friends (and less turmoil). You guessed it – he was moving back to Hillsburgh. It was almost the end of July. Ernie was leaving in two weeks and two weeks after that the rest of us were picking up our roots and replanting once more. I was shocked about Ernie leaving. I again repeated my long-ago promise to Mom that I was never going to leave. We were all getting old too fast. I longed for the days when I was only nine.

Aunt Becky came to visit us during the month of August. Her presence was enough of a distraction from our everyday routine that it made Ernie's departure easier for all of us to handle. He had called and told us that he had got a job working in a plastic factory in one of the other towns in the Hillsburgh area. The Old Man behaved like a normal human being while Aunt Becky was there; consequently, I can't think of much more to inform you about her visit. I do know though, that this time Pepper refrained from jumping on Aunt Becky's back.

I assumed that I would find it really difficult to say goodbye to Carol even though we would only be seven miles apart and could see each other on a regular basis. However, the more that I thought about it, the more I started to realize that I wasn't as upset as I expected to be. I can recall one incident that contributed to that realization. One Sunday we were sitting in front of the Newburgh Lunch holding hands. I was being my usual quiet self and was struggling for a source of discussion when I looked up and saw a '55 Ford with its grill removed parked near us. I then decided on a great conversation icebreaker.

"I like the grill in that car," I said boldly.

The response wasn't quite what I had in mind. Carol let go of my hand, dropped her chin, and turned her face away from me without uttering a word. I didn't know what I had done wrong and I was afraid to ask, lest I dug myself into a deeper hole. We sat silent for the next five to ten minutes without exchanging as much as a grunt or a nod. Not knowing what to do or say, I glanced toward the grill-less car once more. I eventually raised my line of sight above the hood towards the top half of the car. I then noticed that there was a good-looking blonde girl looking back at me through the windshield. Embarrassed, I lowered my eyes and stared back towards my dangling feet. After a few seconds, I looked up again and the blonde smiled. Again I lowered my head. And then it hit me. I had a reason why Carol was mad at me. Maybe she thought that I had said, "I like the girl in that car." Could that have been it? That was the only logical explanation for her behaviour. I was about to correct the situation but I couldn't figure out how to broach the subject. If I tried to explain it, then Carol would know that I did notice the blonde. I could say something about the grill again. Then I thought, "Why bother?" If an innocent remark would cause that kind of reaction maybe I should just let Carol speak first. I told you that I can be stubborn and stubborn I was. I came to the conclusion that I wasn't going to speak until Carol spoke first. Three days later, Carol finally spoke to me. She just said that she was sorry for being angry and I accepted her apology and life returned back to normal. She never explained why I had received the silent treatment and I never offered a justification for my lusting after a complete stranger. The blonde was kind of cute though. I wonder who she was.

4 – Fire and Water

A week later we moved from Chance's Place to our new home in Napanee. We were no longer house renters. No, we didn't buy a house. We rented, but it was an apartment, not a house. We lived in a two-floor apartment located over one of the Napanee businesses situated in the centre of the town. We weren't on the main street (Dundas – the name of the main street for a lot of Ontario towns stretched along Highway 2), but we were very close to it. Even though this was an apartment it was very roomy – probably larger than our house in Hillsburgh. From the street, you climbed a long set of stairs into a large entrance room which was adjoined by another room which became our dining room. Further along, there was a large kitchen and the living room. These rooms were separated from the entrance-dining room combination by the stairs up to the bedrooms. Located at the top of these stairs and to the right was the best feature of the house – a bathroom. No more freezing your rear off in the winter. And no more odours from the chamber pot under the bed. That was something to celebrate. And there were four bedrooms. One for Mom and The Old Man, one for Bill, one for Gordie and me, and one for Lily. All in all, I was quite pleased with our new setting. Lily too seemed to settle in fairly quickly.

The animals weren't as pleased however. Poncho wasn't that fussy about the location; she didn't like managing all the stairs. And Pepper was forced to stay inside. We thought the streets were too busy for him to wander unattended.

Napanee wasn't so bad either. The population was somewhere around 5,000 or so which was a large town to me. It had a large downtown business section with numerous banks, stores, restaurants, and offices. And it was a long walk from one end of town to the other. At one end of town, the Newburgh Road, Highway 2, and the Napanee River all converged at a high railroad trestle. This is where you would stand if you were hitchhiking to Newburgh. If not, then you would walk for twenty-five minutes or so to the far end of Napanee. Here was the local arena. Another definite plus over Newburgh. But I still missed the old burgh. Mainly the people. I would see them at the school but I would miss just hanging around the dam or the Newburgh Lunch with my friends. And most of all, I missed the nicknames.

Just to keep boring you with meaningless details, I will once more inform you about what grades everyone was entering. Anyway, it helps me visualize the time period better. In September '63, I began Grade 10 along with Gordie and Bill. Yes, that's right, Bill. He had failed his year and was repeating this grade once more. Again, I don't recall the particulars that caused this repetition. However, we wouldn't be sharing any classes. Bill and Gordie were now enrolled in the four-year Business and Commerce curriculum whereas I remained in the five-year Arts and Science program. But I wasn't too lonely. There were some familiar faces in my classes though; among them was Sean Becker from Newburgh. He was to provide some interesting times that year. There were some recognizable faces at the front of the classes as well. Among them were Major Major instructing us in the fine points of Agriculture once more, and Chalky Chapman covered in just as much chalk dust with blackboards full of an endless supply of useless and boring Geography notes. But alas, Miss Crusher had departed to provide education and fantasy to some other part of the province. But the boys weren't too disappointed when we saw her replacement. Our History lessons were now being taught to us courtesy of Miss Legg, the most aptly named teacher there ever was. She was a long-legged beauty that wore short skirts and often sat at the front of the classroom on top of her desk facing the students. It drove all of the boys to distraction. Our Mathematics teacher had also been replaced. I guess the last one had hit one kid too many (don't feel too bad if you don't remember this part, I didn't tell you about it). Our new teacher seemed to be in a competition with Chalky Chapman. He also would be covered from head-to-toe in chalk, literally. He was bald as an eagle and would often be sporting a white top. His name was Mr. Eagleson or more specifically – Bald-Headed Eagleson. Then there was the Science teacher – Mr. Humphrey. I think he was about eighty years old. He made even the late Mr. McKenzie seem young and alert. That's about all the teachers that you need to know about for now. Before I tell you some of the stories involving this group of instructors, I should inform you that Lily was beginning Grade 5. She was starting a new school for her, of course. The public school was situated right beside N.R.H.S., so that meant that the four of us could walk together to school. We didn't all finish at the same time, though. So depending on the day, any combination of us four would make the return trip to our downtown apartment.

And now back to the first incident involving one of the above teachers. As I explained earlier, at that time Sean Becker wasn't much taller than I was. So one day, some of the bigger boys thought it might be amusing to hang Sean on the coat hook inside the closet at the front of Miss Legg's classroom. They chose Sean over me because he was much more willing to go along with whatever scheme was dreamt up. He relished these moments so he could provide a much more entertaining outcome. So there was Sean hanging from his collar, hidden inside the closet when Miss Legg made her appearance. After a few minutes, she abruptly stopped the day's lesson and inquired the whereabouts of Sean.

"Has anybody seen Sean. I'm sure I saw him in the hall earlier."

Nobody replied. Nobody except for Sean.

"I'm in here, Miss Legg."

"What? Where? Where are you?"

"In the closet."

Miss Legg extended her long legs off of the desk and headed towards the closet. And then she hesitantly opened the door and peered in to view Sean dangling from the coat hook.

"Mr. Becker. What are you doing in there?"

"Oh, just hanging around, Miss Legg."

"Well, get out of there this minute and take your seat."

"I can't. I'm hooked on this place."

"Come on out, now!"

"I really can't get down myself. I need help."

"How did you get up there, then?"

"With some help."

"You and you, help Mr. Becker back down," Miss Legg demanded as she pointed to the two biggest boys in the class. Two of the main conspirators as well, I might add. As this whole scene evolved, the room full of students was erupting into a bigger and bigger state of laughter.

"In the future, Sean, please try to stay in your seat," commented Miss Legg.

"But it wasn't my fault, I..." Sean started to refute until the icy stare made him just add, "Yes, Miss Legg. I will."

That autumn the count of Cooper brothers at home once more returned to four. But it wasn't Ernie that rejoined the fold if that's what you're thinking. No, it was Brad and his family that came to Napanee to live with us. Brad had completed his scouting expedition to the Barbados and Florida and had settled on a house in Fort Lauderdale, Florida. However, their house in Canada had sold before the closing date of their new American home. So they joined the rest of us Coopers to take up residence in Napanee until the end of February in 1964. I told Brad that he had it all backwards. Most people live in Florida during the winter and return to Canada for the spring. Brad's family had grown since we had last seen them. Along with Brad and Catherine and their two daughters Cheryl and Catherine (now referred to as Cathy partly in the Cooper tradition of shortening names and partly to differentiate her from her mother), there was now a new son – Brent. Cheryl was four years old, Cathy was three, and Brent had only been in the world for six months. The Cooper household was filled with kids again. The rest of us were pretty old now. I mean Lily was already ten and I was fourteen. This must have been an adjustment for Mom but I'm sure she loved it. To me, it was great except for the fact that Gordie and I lost our bedroom. As did Bill. Brad and Catherine occupied our room along with Brent while Bill's room was given to Cheryl and Cathy. We three boys got the living room. We had a pullout chesterfield and a cot to share. We took turns rotating on the cot. The cot was not that comfortable but at least it afforded a private bed. We didn't mind that much because now we had a TV in our 'bedroom'. What a luxury! The one thing that I had trouble getting used to was the fact that six-month-old babies don't want to sleep near as much as I did. I thought that babies liked to sleep. Either Lily did or I just didn't remember those times as clear as I thought that I did. I do know that Pepper wasn't excited about having a toddler around.

I remember Catherine telling us about this new group that was popular in Great Britain. She said they were really popular 'back home'. "They're great," she told us. But I had my doubts when she told us that all four of them had long hair with bangs that came down to their eyes completely covering their foreheads. And their name was weird too – The Beatles. I spoke to Gordie later to determine his opinion.

"They may be good but what's with the strange haircuts?" I stated.

"Yeah," Gordie replied, "if they need a gimmick like that they mustn't have much talent."

"You're right, Gordie. Roy Orbison doesn't need funny hair to sell records. He just has a great voice. I'm sure The Beatles can't touch Roy."

"Or Gene Pitney or Del Shannon either for that matter," Gordie summated.

"And don't forget Bobby Vinton," I added.

"I'm trying to. I'm trying to," said Gordie as he looked at me with pity and walked away shaking his head.

Shortly after, Gordie purchased the new Roy Orbison album 'In Dreams" and played it for Brad and Catherine. I was surprised when Brad said that he thought it was really good. I wondered if maybe there was some hope for Brad's musical taste after all. Until he said that Roy Orbison had a voice that sounded like an opera singer. Then I began to doubt my own choice in music. "I've got to give The Beatles a listen," I thought.

That winter I took up a new sport – hockey. Not the tabletop version this time but actual hockey at the Napanee arena. They had leagues there for various ages of boys sponsored by the Ontario Minor Hockey Association (O.M.H.A.). I registered at the arena and then went to the Canadian Tire store with The Old Man and Mom to acquire all the necessary equipment. This included a duffel bag to put my gear in and to top it all off, a brand new Toronto Maple Leaf sweater with number 14 on it. That wasn't for my age but for Dave Keon, of course – my favourite Leaf and second favourite player. My favourite player was Andy Bathgate but he played for the New York Rangers. And I didn't want a Rangers sweater. I think moving further away from Toronto and being surrounded by many Montreal Canadiens fans had finally made me more committed to the Leafs. The Rangers were only my second favourite team now. And they stunk. The Leafs were the Stanley Cup champs.

I had never played a minute of hockey before in my life not counting a few games of scrimmage on frozen ponds and rivers. So I wasn't very good. Well, I was a pretty good skater but when it came to trying to shoot the puck I couldn't lift it off the ice. I could manage a slap shot with a rubber ball when playing road hockey; however, a puck on ice was a different matter altogether. When I warmed up for my first game (there were no practices), the coach asked me what position I played. Thinking of the number 14 on my back, I answered, "Centre." So that's what I became – a centre and occasional left winger. I was too small to play defence. Our team was called the Beavers. And I soon learned that I was one of the better players on the team. We were utterly hopeless. We got demolished in every game. We made Charlie Brown's baseball team look like winners. One game, the other team had no goalie for the first period and we still never scored. Scores like 13 – 1 were common. After about a half-dozen games, there was an outcry to do the humane thing and put the Beavers to rest. Accordingly, we were disbanded and the players were split among other teams. I was transferred to the Wolves which quickly moved me up to the second place team battling for the championship. I also quickly became the second worst player on my team. The worst player would have been much better if he had been smart enough to learn what offside was. He could bring every rush to a standstill. As for me, I was still waiting for my first goal.

The other thing that I remember about hockey was the long walk to the arena. Sometimes The Old Man drove me but more often I would go by foot. Like any Canadian boy, my stick would be over my shoulder with the duffel bag hanging on it stuffed with all my equipment. The one part that I hated the most about the hike was the fact that I had to saunter right past a Jehovah Witness Kingdom Hall. I kept expecting someone waylaying me and trying to convert me to the religious ways of life. I always walked faster when I passed that place. The one time that I couldn't walk fast was the night that I had four hamburgers and two hot dogs for dinner. However, I did manage to score my first goal that night. At least that's what the scoresheet (and the newspaper) reported. I still haven't touched the puck. Oh, by the way, Bill played hockey too.

Let's backtrack a bit. I got ahead of myself in this narrative thinking about my exciting hockey career. On Friday, November 22, Gordie and I were just leaving the school to head for home when one of the boys told us that President Kennedy had been shot. This boy wasn't the most reliable source of information so we didn't believe him for a minute and we expressed this opinion to him.

"No, I am not kidding. I just heard it on the radio. Kennedy has been shot," he insisted.

"Well maybe Fred or Larry or some other Kennedy that we've never heard of got shot," Gordie argued. "But not President Kennedy. Who would shoot the President?"

"I don't know but it's true. President Kennedy has been shot. You'll see."

"Yeah, yeah, yeah," responded Gordie as we headed on our way. "Did you believe him, Benny?"

"No, are you kidding? I'm not that gullible."

When we arrived home, you know what we discovered. Brad, Catherine, Mom, and even The Old Man were riveted to the TV set, transfixed by what they were witnessing. Even with it all in front of them, they couldn't believe it either. Like the rest of North America, the entire family spent the entire weekend in front of the television watching it all unfold. We sat in shock as Kennedy's death was announced, Lyndon Johnson was sworn in, Lee Harvey Oswald was arrested, and Jack Ruby stepped out of the crowd to kill Oswald. It seemed like there was a new development every second. We all stayed glued to the TV afraid to even get up to go to the bathroom. It was a very strange and unforgettable experience. I thought back to the night that we all stayed up late to watch the election results. How we had to wait until the next morning to know that Kennedy had won. Ernie had been elated. I imagined that he was doing the same thing as us at that moment. And I wished that Ernie could have been with us now.

Back at school the next week, things abruptly returned to

normal. After one particular gym class, we were in the locker room changing when we were suddenly pulled from our routine by the sound of the fire alarm. Each of the boys looked at each other wondering what to do. Everyone was in different stages of undress. Some were already in the shower. I was being my usual slow self and still had my gym shirt and shorts on. All of a sudden we heard the frantic cries of "Fire! Fire! Fire!" as our gym teacher (Mr. Peabody) ran through the locker room.

"Get out! Get out!" Mr. Peabody continued.

"But we're not…" someone began to say.

"I don't care. Do you want to burn to death? Let's go now! Hurry! Fire! Fire" our teacher continued to bellow as he ran on towards the girls' locker room.

So everyone jumped up and ran outside on the double. We were the first kids outside. And it was freezing out. Some boys were only in their underwear, others had only a towel wrapped around them, and a few wore only clenching teeth. A few seconds later more of our schoolmates appeared outside sporting winter coats, hats, and gloves. Even all the girls who had been taking gym next to us were properly attired for a Canadian winter. I kept moving to keep my bare legs and arms somewhat warm. A minute later, another one of the teachers ordered the three or four naturalist boys to get some clothes on. So they had to run back into the fray and each grab an article of clothing to cover their exposed parts. I watched the reaction of the other students as all of this was going on. The girls seemed particularly amused and interested in the entire proceedings. It was probably about a half an hour later, before I had frozen completely, that we were directed to reenter the school. Everything was safe we were told, as it had only been a false alarm. After we had all made our way back into the school, finished dressing, and slowly made our way to our scheduled next class, there were only about ten minutes remaining in that period timeslot. The subject for my shortened lesson was History.

"I guess we won't have time for that test now," declared

Miss Legg.

In the excitement, I had forgot all about the test. I looked at Sean Becker and he was wearing a grin from ear to ear. And then the voice of the principal began blaring from the intercom.

"I am very disappointed in the actions that just occurred. It appears that some hooligan purposely pulled the fire alarm in order to get all of the students out of the school. I am not sure what he was trying to prove. That was a very dangerous and illegal thing to do. The fire department does not take it lightly. We will discover the perpetrator of this despicable act and he will be severely punished. Also the police will be interested in talking to the young man that caused this inexcusable disruption of our education process. Further, I am extremely disheartened by the way that a few people reacted to the situation. Some fool ran through the school yelling 'Fire!' and unnecessarily alarmed the school populace. Others took the opportunity to display acts of exhibitionism. What kind of people do we have at this school? These entire proceedings are a disgrace that reflects badly on the entire Napanee Regional High School. Believe me, when I say that this crime will not go unpunished. Now, let's get back to the job of education. Thank you."

"OK," Miss Legg began with a smile before we could react to the announcement, "as I was saying, I will reschedule our test next week. Now, it's almost time to head off to your next lesson. I'll see you tomorrow."

As we were exiting the classroom, Sean leaned towards me and whispered, "I wasn't ready for that test. I was wondering how I would get out of it."

"It wasn't you that pulled the alarm, was it?" I asked.

Sean just smiled and walked on down the hallway. No culprit was ever identified and no suspects were ever questioned.

Another incident that springs to mind involves Mr. Humphrey's Science class. I'm not sure exactly when this happened but this is as good a point as any to place this in the narrative, I guess. Remember Mr. Humphrey was the teacher who I described as eighty years old. One day, he was delivering a chemistry lesson which required the use of a Bunsen burner. He hooked a hose up between the burner and the gas nozzle before he began the lecture. As he began the instruction, he held the lighter above the Bunsen burner and turned on the gas. A stream of water shot up out of the Bunsen burner and nearly hit the ceiling. The look on Mr. Humphrey's face was priceless. I thought that he was going to have a heart attack. But he didn't say a word. He merely turned off the gas and checked his connection to make sure that the hose was attached to the gas and not the water faucet. He seemed satisfied that everything was setup correctly and then turned the gas back on. Again a rush of water burst from the Bunsen burner and this time soaked Mr. Humphrey from head to toe.

"What the hell?" he squawked. He looked completely bewildered and was at a complete loss for words. "Can someone help me, here?"

"I will, Mr. Humphrey. I'll have a look," answered Sean Becker.

Sean went to the front and spent ten minutes inspecting all of Mr. Humphrey's connections. Finally, he opened the doors below the sink and had a look below. After a couple of minutes, Sean surfaced back to the counter. "Try it now," he stated.

Mr. Humphrey turned on the gas and ignited a beautiful flame out of the burner.

"Well, thank you Mr. Becker. You are quite helpful. That did the trick. What was the matter?"

"No problem, Mr. Humphrey. I am glad to help. Somehow the lines just got mixed up. It'll be OK now."

"Thanks again, young man."

"You're welcome."

After the class, I was not totally surprised when Sean said to me, "What an old fool. Who does he think switched the lines to begin with?"

"You?"

"Of course."

"I thought I recognized your handy work," I admitted. "And you pulled the fire alarm, right?"

Again the only answer that I received was a smile.

5 – It's a Rabbit

Christmas, for most households, is a time for the entire family to get together to share each other's company, presents, great food, and love. Since Ernie was returning home for Christmas and all the Cooper kin except for Claudia, Tom and their children would be there, I was expecting a great Christmas. But alas, I was forgetting that this was the Cooper clan where things never work out that way. How could they with The Old Man around? The two cases of 24 Red Cap sitting on the kitchen floor on Christmas Eve was the first sign of trouble. Although Brad and Catherine attempted to assist with the consumption of all the beer, The Old Man still got his fair share and more. He stayed up all night in the kitchen mumbling and cursing while Bill, Gordie, and I tried fruitlessly to get some sleep in the next room. Poncho and Pepper were lucky; they went up to Lily's room. We all fully expected The Old Man to wear himself out and to be in one of his sombre 'butter wouldn't melt in his mouth' moods on Christmas Day. Wrong again. The Old Man was still going strong. He dozed off for an hour or two here and there but his drunken stupor put a damper on gift openings on Christmas morning and didn't allow us to get any enjoyment throughout the remaining festive day. About five o'clock, just before supper, he was flying high. He was as drunk as I'd ever seen him and that's saying something. And his language and demeanour were getting nastier by the minute. All of us just tried to stay clear of him and hoped that he would soon pass out before any major confrontation erupted. Soon though, in final preparations for the Yuletide feast, Mom and Catherine needed more room in the kitchen; that is, they needed The Old Man to move someplace else. Hence Mom politely made a request to The Old Man.

"Garf, could you please move for a minute? Catherine and I need to get the turkey out of the oven."

"What? Goddamn you fucking old bag! Can't a man just have some peace in his own fucking house? I do all the work around here. I work my ass off to bring home the money for the whole goddamn family and this is the thanks I get. You fucking gray-haired old bag! With your lazy fucking sons and sluts for daughters. Look at Brad laying around the house all day long doing fuck all. And that whore of a wife of his. They're a good fucking pair. And look at Lily sitting on the couch on her ass watching television. She's nothing but a whore just like her gray-haired old bag of a mother. Don't try to tell me what to do and where to go. This is my fucking house and I'll do whatever fuck I please. Goddamn it!"

At that point, he swung his arm with all his force and knocked the pot of potatoes off the stove. It went crashing across the floor spewing boiling water in every direction. Luckily, none of it hit Mom or Catherine. Catherine was backing out of the kitchen at the same time that Brad, Ernie and Bill were entering. I could see that they were all steaming mad. Gordie was right behind them. Lily was sitting on the couch crying. I had at least stood up but my feet wouldn't move away from the edge of the chesterfield. I wished that I could have joined Poncho behind it. I was shaking. I wanted to kill the son of a bitch. I wanted to smash his skull to smithereens. I had never felt such anger. And it frightened me. I could see that The Old Man had swung back his arm again; this time the pan of turnips was his target. Before I or anyone else could react, Bill went into action. In a fraction of a second, he stepped forward, grabbed an open beer bottle off the kitchen table and slammed the bottle on the back of The Old Man's head. "Take that, you son of bitch!" Bill yelled at the same time. The bottle didn't even break. We just heard a dull thud and watched as The Old Man collapsed on the kitchen floor. Soon Bill was on top of him swinging his fists frantically at The Old Man. And the next thing I knew, Brad and Ernie were standing over the combatants.

"Let me hit the bastard," exclaimed Ernie.

"After me," said Brad. "That bastard deserves it!"

Somehow I had managed to move away from the couch and was now standing beside Gordie. I watched as Bill hit The Old Man a few more times. There was blood flowing from his face covering the linoleum floor.

"Stop it!" pleaded Mom. "You'll kill him. He's not worth it. I don't want any of my sons going to jail on Christmas Day. Please Billy, don't hit him anymore. Ernie, Brad get him to stop. Billy!"

After a few more strikes, Bill finally ceased the beating but remained straddled on The Old Man. Everyone remained silent and inspected the damage to The Old Man's face. He didn't appear to be as badly injured as we all first thought. Other than a nosebleed and also most likely a very sore head, he seemed to have come out of the battle relatively unscathed. Bill at last broke the silence.

"Are you going to behave yourself if I let you up?"

"You fucking bastard, what are trying to do kill me?" shot back The Old Man. Billy pulled back his arm to strike The Old Man once more. "I'm sorry, Billy. Please, don't hit me again. I'll be OK. I don't know what got into me. I'm sorry. I'm drunk and I don't know what I'm saying. I love your mother and all you kids. The beer makes me crazy. Please, let me up. I'll be fine now. You smartened me up. OK, let me up, now. OK?"

Slowly Bill stood up and moved away from The Old Man towards Ernie and Brad. Everyone was watching what

The Old Man would do next. He eventually got to his feet and stumbled towards the kitchen sink. "I need to wash off this blood. I bleed like a bull sometimes. But I think I'm OK." The Old Man started to run water and to rinse his face. Billy turned to leave the kitchen. At the same instance The Old Man suddenly pulled a pocket knife from his pants pocket. He quickly engaged the knife and with surprising speed and agility lunged for Bill's back.

"Look out, Billy!" we all screamed in unison.

Ernie and Brad managed to push Bill away from the attacking weapon just in time. Then Brad wrestled The Old Man to the floor as Ernie knocked the knife out of his hands. After Brad struck a few more blows to The Old Man's head and body, The Old Man again begged for clemency. I won't bother going into all the details; essentially the previous scenario that I described before (when Bill was on top of The Old Man) repeated itself. Ultimately, The Old Man was once more on his feet but this time he was crying.

"I'm sorry, I'm sorry. I love you. I love you. Please don't call the police again. I can't take any more time in jail. Please! I'm going to bed now. Mary, will you help me clean myself up. I'm going up to bed. Billy, please forgive me. I wouldn't hurt you. I have to go to bed. Help me upstairs, will you Brad? Jesus, my nose hurts. God, what a lot of blood. My head hurts too. I don't blame any of you. I got what's coming to me. I got to go lie down. Oh shit, I'm sore all over."

And so The Old Man went to bed and not a sound stirred from him until late the next day. The rest of us somehow sat down to our Christmas dinner and pretended that life was normal. All in all, another typical Christmas for the Cooper family, wouldn't you say?

Ernie returned to Hillsburgh a few days after Christmas. He probably had enough and had recalled only too well why he had left home in the first place. At the same time, The Old Man again swore off any form of alcohol. He said it was driving his family away from him. He was definitely finished drinking forever. A few weeks later, a payday had arrived and

The Old Man had passed off his entire payroll to Mom without spending a cent on beer.

"Take this," he said to Mom, "before I get any bad ideas. If I don't have the money, I won't crave any beer. See, I'm not an alcoholic. I don't need to drink. It's just a bad habit. If I don't have money, I won't miss it. If I ask for money later, don't give it to me. Then I'll be fine. You'll see, Mary. I'm a changed man. I've finally seen the light. Everything's going to be different from now on."

As for me, things hadn't changed much. I saw Carol English a few times over the Christmas holidays and we had exchanged gifts. When I went to Newburgh, we would walk the streets and sit by the dam and cuddle to keep warm. When she came to Napanee, we would stroll around the town and go to the local Chinese restaurant for a coke and fries. We both thought that this relationship would continue as far in the future as we dared to glance. Then one Saturday morning in January 1964, I was awoken from my sleep on the chesterfield bed in the living room by the sound of Carol speaking to Mom. I listened to their conversation.

"Benny's still in bed sleeping, dear. Do you want me to wake him up?"

"No that's OK, Mrs. Cooper. Let him sleep. I was just in town with my mother shopping and I thought I'd say hello. Just tell Benny that I was here."

"Are you sure you don't want me to call him, Carol? Benny should be getting up soon anyway."

"No, that's OK. I don't want to disturb him. See you later, Mrs. Cooper."

"OK, dear. Bye for now."

I was wide-awake, listening to the entire dialogue. And I didn't move or say a word. The more I thought about it; the more confused I became. Why didn't I say something? Why didn't I get up? Didn't I want to see Carol? I love her company, don't I? It at first made no sense to me. Until I finally came to the conclusion that my subconscious was right. I didn't want to see Carol as much as I thought I did. I wanted to spend more time with my friends. I wasn't ready to go steady. In other words, I wanted out of the relationship. I had to tell her. "How?" I thought. I'll never get up enough nerve to inform her about my feelings – or lack of them. I'll just have to wait and see what happens.

As it turned out, I didn't have to wait as long as I thought. Gordie's girlfriend Paula Cutler was babysitting for her sister in Strathcona and she had asked Carol to join her. It was all planned that the four of us would spend the evening together. The night's entertainment turned out to be Gordie and Paula making out in one living room chair while Carol and I sat in another. We were hugging and kissing but my mind was elsewhere. I looked at Gordie and Paula and they seemed lost in a haze of love. Did I want that? No, the whole situation didn't seem right to me. I was uncomfortable. I had too much fun to experience yet. This was getting far too serious for me. Look at Gordie and Paula. How sickening. Help, I want out. Then, I got my wish. There was a knock at the back door.

"Maybe that's Malcolm," Carol explained. She then jumped up and went to the back door. I heard Carol say, "Hello Malcolm, how are you?"

"That's Malcolm Stagg," explained Paula. "He said that he might drop by."

"Oh," I said. A few minutes passed and Carol was still in the back kitchen.

"Malcolm's still talking to your girlfriend, Benny. Why don't you go punch him out?"

"Why?" I asked. "I like Malcolm. He can talk to Carol. I don't care."

"Don't you love Carol? You've got to fight for her. You've got to stand up for her. Go punch Malcolm's lights out."

"No, I don't think so. I'll just sit here and wait."

"You're not much of a man. You've got to fight for what's yours."

"Carol's not mine. She can talk to Malcolm. I don't

mind."

"Please yourself then."

Paula and Gordie went back to making out and I sat and waited. About fifteen minutes later, Carol returned to the chair. We hugged and kissed some more but I didn't say a word.

"What's the matter, Benny? Are you jealous?" asked Carol.

"No. Why should I be jealous? You were just talking that's all."

"But I left you to talk to Malcolm. Aren't you mad?"

"No. I don't mind. Malcolm's a nice guy."

Anyway, you get the drift. We bantered like that for the rest of the evening. We still kissed and held each other but it didn't seem right to me. When Gordie and I left, I said a sweet goodbye to Carol, but that was the end. I now knew it was all over. I never went out with Carol again. Maybe she thought that I was so mad about Malcolm that I couldn't forgive her. Or maybe the whole thing was planned to awaken some fire of passion in me. I don't know. I just saw it as an opportunity and I took it. I was free to spend as much time with my friends and brothers as I wanted once again. And maybe the odd girl, if I got lucky.

On his next payday, The Old Man gave all his earnings to Mom again. However, on the following day he asked for some of it back. Remembering what The Old Man had told her, Mom refused and got the following reaction.

"What? What do you mean no, you old bag? Give me some fucking money now. Jesus Christ, what do you think you are – queen of the goddamn place?"

And The Old Man hadn't had a drop to drink yet. Mom had said that The Old Man could get drunk just thinking about drinking. To avoid an argument, Mom relented and handed some money back to The Old Man. Of course, he bought beer, got drunk, and performed his usual 'I've been around the world; I know the score' monologue. The next day, The Old Man criticized Mom for giving him money.

"How can I ever quit drinking if you don't help me, Mary?"

Mom knew that when it came to The Old Man, you could never win.

On February 9th of 1964, we all watched the debut of The Beatles on The Ed Sullivan Show. With it being a Sunday, The Old Man was sober – there was no place to buy beer on a Sunday. As we all watched and listened, The Old Man advised that he couldn't understand what all the fuss was about.

"Oh my God, look at that. You can't even see their ears. What are all those girls screaming about? I can understand them crying; the music makes me cry too."

"You're right Dad. They are pretty awful," agreed Brad.

"I can't hear the music for all that stupid screaming," informed Gordie.

"They're not that bad," suggested Bill.

"I kind of like them," stated Mom.

"Me too," said Catherine.

"Paul is so cute," added Lily.

"Cute?" disagreed The Old Man. "I've seen better looking things in the barnyard."

I didn't say a word. I just sat and observed. By the time that they had started the first few bars of 'All My Loving', I was hooked. They performed four more songs and in spite of the negative comments from Brad and The Old Man about their appearance, I knew that this was the music for me. Bobby Vinton was putrid garbage. I had caught the Beatlemania bug.

There was no medicine to cure that bug. But the thought of medication reminds me of the time that Cheryl and Cathy got into the medicine cabinet in the bathroom. They discovered what they thought was chocolate which in reality was a bar of Ex-Lax. Cheryl, the older of my two nieces, did not share fairly and ate most of the bar. Cathy only got a small amount. And boy did Cheryl ever pay for that avarice. She went to the bathroom for days. Cathy escaped with hardly any side effects. This was another example that Mom could use for the outcome of greed. It rivaled the story of Billy seeking out the biggest apple on the tree. It was Gordie that informed me about Cheryl and Cathy's mistaken identity crisis.

"Did they get into shit because of it," I asked.

"I guess you could say that," giggled Gordie.

"That's crappy," I replied.

"Yeah, they're a couple little shit disturbers – those two."

And we both laughed uncontrollably as the bad puns continued. A few days later, we were in hysterics again. This time it was The Old Man that was the brunt of our joking. We were watching the game show 'Concentration', which was hosted by Hugh Downs, on television, when The Old Man walked into the living room. I don't know how many of you remember that show but it went something like this. When it was your turn, you chose two squares on a board to uncover different prizes. When your prizes matched or you had a wildcard, you got that prize added to your list. Then the prizes were removed to reveal two squares of the puzzle hidden beneath. The puzzle would be a combination of pictures and letters to spell out some famous saying. For example, the board could have eventually been uncovered to reveal the number '2', a picture of a bee, the word 'ore' on a bar of gold, a rope tied in a knot, another '2', and then a bee. You figure it out. Well, this time there was about four squares of the puzzle revealed when The Old Man came into the room. There wasn't much to see to identify any picture or letters. But The Old Man had the answer.

"I know it right now. It's a rabbit," he surmised.

Gordie and I started to laugh.

"What are you laughing at? It's a rabbit. Any fool can see that."

We laughed some more.

"You just wait and see. It's a rabbit, that's for sure. Why can't they see that?"

We fell on the floor. My sides were aching.

"What's wrong with you two," Dad said as he started to laugh as well. "Isn't it a rabbit?"

That was too much for me. I couldn't control the laughter. Gordie was just as bad as me.

"I'll leave you two. You're being silly. You'll see that I'm right. It's a rabbit."

The Old Man left the room and we lost it all together.

"It's a rabbit," Gordie said.

"Aunt Becky's coming!" I answered. And we rolled in hysterics for hours.

Speaking of The Old Man and television, we were finally getting smarter. We were tired of trying to watch one show only to have The Old Man enter the room after a few beers and force us to change the channel to something that he said he wanted to watch. One night we were watching the Leaf game when The Old Man came home after being out drinking. We quickly changed the channel to some John Wayne movie that was on the Watertown station just before The Old Man made his entrance.

"What's this shit you're watching?" he asked. "Why don't you have the hockey game on? Let's have the Leafs on. What's the matter with you tonight?"

"Alright Dad, if you insist," said Bill.

And we all watched and enjoyed another Leaf win. That was the same month that I returned home from playing hockey with the Wolves, and experienced quite a surprise when the Leaf game came on the air. There was a player on the Leafs called Bathgate. Yes, it was my favourite player – Andy Bathgate. He had been traded to the Leafs that day from the Rangers. The Leafs had given up Bob Nevin, Dick Duff, Bill Collins, Arnie Brown, and Rod Seiling in order to receive Bathgate and Don McKenney. Mom was upset that the Leafs had traded Duff and Nevin. They were two of her favourite players. I liked them too and I also thought that Rod Seiling was a good young defence prospect. But I was ecstatic just the same. My favourite player was now a Toronto

Maple Leaf. I didn't have to be a closet Ranger fan anymore. I now could be a 100 percent true blue Leaf fan without reservation. Go Leafs Go! Go Leafs Go!

I guess it was around early March, that Brad and his family left for their new homeland in Florida. The house purchase was now legally completed and all the paperwork to allow them to move to the United States was now in place. The apartment seemed incredibly quiet after they left. We all got our own bedrooms back but the apartment felt huge and empty. We now had to count on Poncho and Pepper to make our home bustle. It was weird to just have the four siblings at home once more. After all, we had only experienced that situation for a month or two before.

The spring of 1964 was uneventful except for two memories that stand out. The first was hearing about the death of Uncle Ben – The Old Man's younger brother. He had died of cancer in spite of only being in his early fifties. Although I didn't know Uncle Ben, I found his death quite unsettling. After all, I was his namesake. The Old Man didn't make the trip back to Newfoundland to attend the funeral. It was too far and too late to drive and the cost of a plane trip was prohibitive. I'm not sure they were ever that close anyway. The other thing that I recall was that the Leafs won the Stanley Cup for the third year in a row. They beat the Detroit Red Wings 4 – 0 in game seven to attain the right to hoist the Cup over their heads. But what I'll always remember was game six. That's the game where Bobby Baun was carried off on a stretcher but resurfaced in sudden-death overtime to score the winning goal to prolong the series. And he did it on a broken leg! I couldn't wait until I saw Pooh (Phil Stonehouse) again. The Leafs had beaten his beloved Gordie Howe led Red Wings. That would be worth a lot of ribbing. At least until the next season.

I soon heard that I was going to get a chance to spend more time teasing Pooh than I thought. We were moving back to Newburgh again. Before the school year was even over, it would be time to pack once more. Again it was Lily that would be affected the most. Bill, Gordie, and I would maintain the same school and the same friends. However, Lily would have to switch back to the Newburgh Academy. She put up such a fuss that it was finally arranged that she would finish the year at the school in Napanee. She would just share the bus ride from Newburgh to Napanee with her brothers. I should mention that there was one aspect of the move that disappointed me. I had started roller-skating at the Napanee arena that spring. You could skate around in circles to all the great songs of 'The British Invasion' that year. Songs by groups like Gerry and the Pacemakers, the Dave Clark Five, the Rolling Stones, the Animals, and many more – not to mention The Beatles. And more importantly, there was one particular dark-haired girl that was always there and had a big smile for me. The last time, she even said hello. I still had to find out her name.

6 – Wedding Bells

Our new house in Newburgh was positioned at the bottom of the hill on the street just past the Newburgh Lunch. We were situated on a small tributary of the Napanee River on a street supposedly called Water Street although there were no signs to corroborate that piece of information. The main branch of the river was on the other side of the Newburgh Lunch right before the hill started its steep incline. Between the town's eating establishment and the river proper was the road leading down to the dam. Further down Water Street, was another small dirt road with access to the dam. So as you can see, we were well located in very close proximity to all the major hot spots of Newburgh, right in the centre of all the action. That was the good news. The bad news was that we had no inside bathroom again. The worse news was that we had no running water either – at least none fit to drink. When you went in the front (and only) door, you were standing in a large kitchen. It reminded me somewhat of our kitchen in Hillsburgh except there was no wood stove. The heat was supplied by an oil furnace in the living room and we had an electric range for cooking. The other difference was the kitchen sink. It had a large metal pump and handle overlooking it. This pump supplied rain water right out of a large cistern in the basement; so it was not fit for human consumption. For our drinking water, we had to walk down Water Street a few houses and use the pump attached to the well belonging to one of our neighbours. Lily and I could now act like Jack and Jill and go 'fetch a pail of water' hopefully without the same tragic outcome.

To continue the tour of the house, turn right into the living room and dining room area. The separator for the two rooms was the oil furnace. This again reminded me of Hillsburgh. At the far end of the living room, you would find the stairs up to the sleeping quarters. After ascending the stairs, you would discover yourself located in a large open room which would become the boys' bedroom. Bill would be in a single bed positioned beside the double bed belonging to Gordie and me. Under our bed you would find the chamber pot. Near the top of the stairs was a door leading into a small bedroom which was assigned to Lily and finally to the left of it was another door into the room designated for Mom and The Old Man. The bathroom – or should I say toilet as there was no bath involved – was as I mentioned earlier, outside. You had to go out the front door and around the back by the river. No, not to the river itself. It wasn't as bad as that! There was an outhouse attached to the back of the house. It was no ordinary latrine either. It was a two-seater so that you could share with others. Doesn't that sound cozy? What I didn't mention yet was who lived right next door to us – Sean Becker. You could wave to him whenever you took a trip to the privy. You could also see Sean's hound Snoopy, who like his namesake could be found sleeping on top of his doghouse. We were never sure if he dreamed about the Red Baron.

That summer was a chance to become reacquainted with some old friends. Besides Sean Becker, there were the Stonehouse brothers – Birdbrain (Jim) and Pooh (Phil). The move also allowed me to get to know some others a lot better. I began to spend a lot of time with Brendan Casey, with whom I discovered, I shared many interests. One of which was definitely music. Another was the Leafs. He advised me that he was no longer going to school to be a priest and that he would be joining me at N.R.H.S. Brendan had recently concluded that maybe the priesthood and he were not exactly a good fit. I could have told him that. There were three other boys (which I only mentioned in passing before) that would often hang around with us. They were Sneezy (Kenny Shaker), Flip the Sausage (Roy Henderson), and Very Dorky (Barry Dorchester). Alongside Sneezy, Flip, and Dork, Brendan and I were conspicuously lacking in colourful monikers. But that oversight would soon be partially rectified.

One warm, sunny day in late June, Brendan, Sneezy, and I were sitting on the stoop in front of the Newburgh Lunch when we were soon joined by Birdbrain, Pooh, and my brother Bill. Pooh and Bill were grilling Birdbrain about the details of his date the night before. Apparently Birdbrain had gone to the Napanee Drive-in Theatre with Judy Winchester, a girl who lived half way up the hill. It was a double date actually. The driver of the car was Malcolm King, not to be confused with Malcolm Stagg, the one who rescued me from the predicament that I described earlier. And Malcolm was with his girlfriend Peggy Day, whose father was the other Sneezy. Is this all getting too confusing for you?

"So how did you make out?" asked Pooh.

"With his hands," I volunteered.

"Well, the movie was pretty good," answered Birdbrain seemingly ignoring my comments.

"No Birdbrain, how did it go with Judy?" persisted Pooh. "That's what I meant."

"Not great, she was cold as ice to tell the truth."

"Why?" I inquired. "Wasn't Malcolm's car heater working?"

This time Birdbrain couldn't disregard me any longer. He gave me a dirty look and shook his head before responding.

"Benny! For someone who's supposedly so smart in

school, you sure can be a dumdum sometimes."

Everyone laughed while I tried to explain that it was only my futile attempt at humour and I understood the whole conversation. But it all went for naught.

"In fact," continued Birdbrain, "from now on that will be your name. I now officially christen you Dum Dum."

"All right," agreed Sneezy. "Dum Dum it is. It's perfect."

"I second that," said Pooh.

And that's how I, Benny Cooper, became Dum Dum. The name didn't upset me the least. I now felt like a regular Newburgher. I had a nickname! Wasn't that great!

A few days after becoming Dum Dum, I became dumbfounded. Gordie told me that he was getting married. And soon. He advised me that he would be marrying Paula Cutler in late July and then he would be moving out of the house to an apartment in Napanee. I couldn't believe it. Gordie (I guess I should finally break down and call him Gord) was only seventeen. Paula was sixteen. What were they thinking? I thought if that's what love does to your brain, I'm glad I got out of my relationship when I did. I knew they were serious about each other, but marriage – whew! I never saw it coming. Maybe I was aptly named by Birdbrain. But I wasn't alone in shock. Mom was not only stunned but extremely upset as well. She feared that Gord was making a terrible mistake. She told me so. However she refrained from arguing with Gord. She knew that her attempts of persuasion would only drive Gord closer to Paula and further away from us. So Mom stayed quiet and pretended agreement. Gord wasn't fooled for a minute. Mom's silence was far worse than her bark. I too never said much to Gord. Not for any reason other than I didn't know what to say. Gord's mind was made up and I wasn't about to change it. Bill told Gord that he was making a mistake but that was about the extent of his arguments. Lily couldn't understand it all. She just thought Gord was being foolish. The Old Man thought it was great news.

"Way to go, you old devil," The Old Man told Gord. "Paula's a hot one, eh?"

The one person that did try to entice Gord to rethink his marriage plans was Sean Becker. He spent hours in our kitchen reasoning with Gord. He contended that Gord was far too young. He had an entire teenage life to enjoy yet. Why cut it short to enter the working world already? He should be having the time of his life now. But it was all to no avail. Gord could not be convinced. He was looking forward to quitting school, getting a job, and beginning a new life with Paula. And that was that.

Sean soon spent so much time at our house that he began to address Mom as 'Ma'. And then whenever Birdbrain or Pooh would drop by, they would say "Hello Ma." Before long, Brendan and Sneezy were also saying, "How are you doing, Ma?" Mom was really popular with all of our friends. She was always pleasant to every one of them and made them feel comfortable. Mom was quite happy for us to have friends over for several reasons; the main one being that it usually meant that The Old Man would be more reluctant to enter into one of his drunken tirades. Soon 'Ma' began to sound so familiar around the house that we all started to use that appellation. Except for The Old Man of course. We were all changing names. I was Dum Dum instead of Benny and Ma was no longer Mom. I should correct that and add that I was still Benny to Ma and Lily.

In early July, Very Dorky taught Dum Dum how to swim. Barry spent the time with me at the dam until I could master this new skill. I started by putting my head under the water and then by lifting my feet and floating. Before long I could jump in the river headfirst and swim underwater to the rock ledge in the middle. And then all that was required to swim was to eventually float closer and closer to the surface. And move my arms and legs. In a week, Barry had taught me the art of swimming. Next up, diving. I would start just going off the ledge and soon hoped to progress to spectacular dives off the top of the dam. That was the extent of my goals for the summer of 1964.

Brendan, Dork, Sneezy, Flip, and I kept busy in other ways. We went to a few movies with some of the older boys that had means of transportation. Boys such as Malcolm King, Gordon Day (Peggy's brother), or anyone else that had their licence and access to a car. I was introduced to James Bond when I saw 'Goldfinger' at a cinema in Kingston with Brendan and one of his older friends. Then all five of us saw Psycho at the Napanee Drive-in when we went with another older Newburgh boy. Flip and Sneezy snuck in the theatre by hiding in the trunk of the car. We scared them before the movie even started by not letting them out of their hiding place right away. And then there was Psycho itself. I'll never forget Flip being frightened to death and Sneezy pleading, "Don't go down the stairs! Don't go down the stairs!" Another film highlight that summer was 'A Hard Day's Night' which Brendan and I viewed with Malcolm King and Bill. All in all it was a great cultural summer respite.

Thinking about Gordon and Peggy Day reminds me of the time that I was at their place with Sean when their father Sneezy handed me a magazine.

"Look at this story. This kid's going to be a star in the N.H.L one day. You just wait and see."

I glanced at the magazine to peruse a story about a sixteen-year-old kid that was wowing the hockey world. He had already been drafted by the Boston Bruins and was expected to be playing for them in a couple of years. It said that he would be a surefire hit. His name was Bobby Orr.

"How can they say that he'll be a star? He's only sixteen. That's crazy. And he only plays defence," I said.

"You just wait and see," Sneezy repeated.

"He won't beat Dave Keon that's for sure," I retorted.

July screamed by and before I knew it, it was time for Gord's wedding. I was excited because Ernie had returned home to be the best man. For a few days at least, it was like old times with the four of us boys and Lily together under one roof once more.

"I never thought that you would be getting married before me," Ernie commented to Gord.

"Neither did I," Gord replied.

To me, the day of the wedding had a surrealistic atmosphere. I couldn't really believe that it was happening. Consequently, I can hardly remember any of it. Some of my earlier experiences like the 'Pit of Hell' are more vivid memories. The service itself was in the United Church near where we used to live at Chance's Place. The only part of it that I recall was the moment when the minister said, "We are gathered here today in the presence of God," and I looked around and then at Sean and said "Is he here?" Sean responded with an elbow to the ribs. I think the reception was at our place; I can't remember. There were thin, dainty sandwiches. I know that. And the next thing I knew Gord and Paula were gone. They had moved into their Napanee apartment and Gord had started working at the well-known furniture factory just up the street from them. Ernie had returned home to Hillsburgh and then there were three – Bill, Lily, and me. The place seemed empty.

In August, for entertainment, I started attending many of the softball games between Newburgh and other small towns in the area. Towns such as Camden East and Centreville. Birdbrain, Pooh, and Sean all played for Newburgh. I should mention that Sean was no longer my size. That summer he grew a foot taller. He seemed to sprout up over night. I was still waiting for my growth spurt. The Newburgh team was managed by Great Elk alias Ron Stonehouse, the father of Birdbrain and Pooh. The Newburgh baseball diamond was situated in a field which also served as a cow pasture. That made people think and look twice before sliding into a base. Flying from the backstop were three Pearson flags. That's the flag with the three green leaves in the middle on a white background surrounded by two blue stripes. At that time the Flag Debate was going strong and Great Elk supported Lester B. Pearson's choice for replacing the old Canadian Ensign. As did I. I also recall that after one particular game (a

Newburgh win), I was offered a beer which I declined. In my mind, I found it difficult to not associate beer with The Old Man. Therefore, I decided to remain abstinent. Another day, many of the boys were drinking by the dam and I again refused an invitation to join in the festivities. In this case, that was literally way too close to home.

There was a rumour in Newburgh that a secret cave existed which would allow you to travel from the top of the hill to some unknown location in the centre of the village. Sneezy and Dorky were discussing the story when Flip suggested that we spend the day searching for the hidden route. The whole thing seemed far-fetched and I voiced that opinion.

"I think you guys are nuts."

"What the hell?" said Brendan. "Why not? Let's go. It's as good a thing to do in this town as anything else. Are you coming, Dum Dum?"

"Sure. Why not? I'm getting kind of tired of sitting on this stoop anyway."

So the five of us went right to the top of the hill up past the road to Napanee. Here the main street turned into a gravel road. We passed the house where Top Cat and Big Boy lived and then kept going until we were beyond the home of Teddy Lennon (another Newburgh boy I haven't told you about yet). We went on into the surrounding fields and wandered all day without success. We did see lots of crevices in the ground which we crawled into but none of them led anywhere. If we had been the size of a mouse, we might have been able to go a little further. But even that was doubtful. We never found the cave. And we never saw Tom Sawyer or Becky Thatcher either.

7 – Run Like a Deer

In September both Bill and I started Grade 11 at N.R.H.S. while Lily was back at the Newburgh Academy now attending Grade 6. Hey, not near as many grades to remember now; I didn't even have to look at my notes. I had many of the same teachers as the previous year such as Mr. Humphrey (now eighty-one years old, I figured), Bald-Headed Eagleson, Mr. Peabody (the one who cried 'Fire'), and most noticeably, the very fittingly named Miss Legg. I no longer had to put up with the dusty scribblings of Chalky Chapman as I had decided to forego my geographical education. And it was so long Major Major, as thankfully we were no longer forced to enroll in Agriculture. My new class was Latin, taught by a young, geeky looking teacher who I would have described as a Woody Allen clone (if I had only known who Woody Allen was and what in the world a clone was). His name was Mr. Homey – the second most suitably dubbed teacher in history. Many of the kids used to pick on Mr. Homey because of his apparent timid manner but I thought he was great. You could talk to him like a regular human being. That was unusual for a Napanee teacher. And for some strange reason that I still can't understand, I discovered that I was a whiz at Latin. Maybe it reminded me of my early childhood when I had invented my own language. I thought, now if I could only meet a girl that spoke Latin perhaps I could carry on a civil conversation with her. My favourite expression was "Veni. Vidi. Vici." That's what I liked about Latin; it was short and to the point. There was a kid in our class called Otis. I laughed when we learnt that 'Otis' was Latin for 'long-eared'. I never found out what 'Dum Dum' meant. On the first test, I got ninety-nine percent. I think I misspelled one word. Latin was far more useful than Geography or Agriculture. You could never know when it might come in handy. I remember we were given this questionnaire in Guidance to determine what vocation we were best suited for. It was some kind of multiple choice. Surprisingly, upon completion of the quiz, it indicated that I should become a priest or minister. I guess it asked if I liked Latin but forgot the most important trait for a priest – belief in God. I never had much faith in those type of aptitude tests after that outcome. Well, at least I could take solace in the fact that it didn't indicate that I was already dead like that quiz in Grade 9 had concluded.

That fall, one of the other women in Newburgh told Ma about a job canning tomatoes and other vegetables in a nearby cannery. She even offered to drive Ma to and from work each day. Since Ma was tired of being short of cash and counting on The Old Man to supply money for staples, she decided to go for it. What if The Old Man was upset? He couldn't be any worse, could he? So Ma applied and soon joined the work force. The pay was no hell, but it got Ma out of the house and gave her a life outside the home. She was glad for the little bit of independence this afforded her. And surprisingly, The Old Man didn't protest that much. He probably thought that now he could have more money for beer. And as it turned out, he was right.

Poncho and Pepper now had the house to themselves during the day. They didn't seem to mind too much. Although Poncho would be pretty excited by the time one of us got home. One day, Bill and I couldn't find Pepper when we got home. Finally, Bill noticed with assistance from

Poncho that the basement door was not fully closed. We decided to ignore Sneezy's warnings (remember Psycho) and headed down the cellar stairs. We still couldn't see Pepper anywhere. And then Bill hesitantly peered over the edge of the large cistern and surveyed inside.

"Pepper!" he exclaimed.

I slowly glanced into the cistern full of rainwater, to view Pepper floating on top. My heart sunk before I noticed that he wasn't floating. He was moving his legs as fast as he could. He made his way to the closest side and then Bill reached in and pulled him out.

"How is he, Bill?" I asked.

"Right as rain, Benny. Right as rain."

Other than being wet and scared, he was fine. It turned out that I wasn't the only Cooper to learn how to swim that year.

That Halloween a bunch of us boys were just hanging around in front of the Newburgh Lunch. What else was there to do? Lily and her friends had finished their 'trick or treating' and had headed home. We were too old for that, so we just sat around discussing possibilities for action. Birdbrain told us about the Halloween a few years ago when someone (who remained unnamed) pushed over Mr. Tompkins' outhouse. Mr. Tompkins was an elderly man who lived near the top of the hill. What that unnamed person didn't realize was that Mr. Tompkins was inside the outhouse at the time. That garnered a few laughs. Not so funny for Mr. Tompkins, I thought. But still a funny story. Besides Birdbrain and myself, there was the usual gang including Bill, Sean, Pooh, Brendan, Sneezy, Maynard, Very Dorky, Flip the Sausage, Top Cat, Big Boy, Schroeder, Linus, and Pigpen. Eventually we all got tired of the view and moved to the other end of town by the General store. Along the way, most of us picked up some broken tree branches to use as walking sticks. Or maybe, we could use them to knock apples out of a tree. Who knew? So there we all were – about fifteen boys standing around in front of a general store holding sticks and not exactly looking innocent – when a police cruiser came down the hill towards us. I thought we would just sit there, after all we hadn't done anything. But before I knew it, Birdbrain had made an executive decision.

"Let's get the hell out of here!" he yelled.

"Run, you bastards! Run!" added Pooh.

And everyone took off in every which direction. I didn't even see where Bill went. The police car slammed on its breaks and stopped a few hundred feet down the road. I then decided it was time to get my little, short legs moving. I rushed across the street in front of the cruiser and scooted between the two houses on that side of the road. I glanced over my shoulder to observe an extremely large police officer jump out the passenger side of the police vehicle and head towards my direction. "Oh shit!" I thought to myself. "I gotta get out of here. I can't explain what we're doing. And why we ran. I don't even know myself." It was pitch dark and I couldn't see two feet in front of me but that didn't slow me down. I ran straight into a wire fence and then somehow managed to clamber over it. I then bumped face-first into what I guessed to be an apple tree. My whole face was throbbing but I just kept moving as fast as I could. I saw the next fence through a distant street lamp just before I reached it and seemingly flew over it. "I knew the gymnastics lessons would come in handy someday," I contemplated. In truth, I have no idea how I traversed that last fence. I just found myself back into the open and crossing the next street parallel to the main one. I had no idea where my pursuer was but I couldn't imagine how he could have followed me through two fences and an apple orchard. I then heard someone screaming above the sound of my exhaustive breathing and thumping heartbeat.

"Run, Dum Dum, Run! Run like your mother was a deer! Go, Dum Dum, Go! There's a big fucking copper right behind you!"

It was Pooh. I could see him under the lights by the sales barn. He was heading for the thicket behind the barn. That was the inspiration I needed. I found another gear and ran down the sidewalk of the next street. I had had enough of fences and trees. I could hear the heavy footsteps of my tracker hitting the concrete behind me.

"Stop!" he shouted. "Stop this minute, you little devil!"

"Don't shoot," I thought. "I'm only a kid."

For a moment I thought he was gaining on me and I was going to be history. And then all of a sudden, I could only hear myself again. I didn't bother to look behind me; I just kept on going. Until I noticed the hut behind Stonehouse's place on my left. I was relieved to find it unlocked and I soon scurried inside to rest on one of the beds. I waited and listened. I expected the cop to break down the door and arrest me at any minute. But all was quiet. Except for my breathing. I thought I was going to have a heart attack. After about fifteen minutes, I got up enough nerve to peek outside. I could see no one in the darkness. I looked towards the back of the house and saw a light on. I hurried and went in the back door. Nobody knocked when they went into Stonehouse's. Luckily, the door was always open. Great Elk was sitting on the couch watching TV.

"Hello Ron," I said sheepishly. No one called him Great Elk to his face. At least, not more than once.

"What the hell happened to you, Dum Dum?" Great Elk questioned.

"Why? Is it that obvious that I've been up to something?"

"Look in the mirror. Your face is a mess. There's blood all over your shirt. No wonder they call you Dum Dum. Don't you even know that you're bleeding? Go wash up."

"OK, Ron. Thanks."

I went in the washroom and inspected the damage. Great Elk was right. I was a mess. I was too busy worrying about my escape to even take notice of my injuries. I removed my bloody shirt and then spent five minutes washing away the blood from my face. I wasn't that bad. Just a bloody nose and a fat lip. I put the soiled shirt back on and rejoined Great Elk in the living room. I described the evening's goings-on before suggesting that it was almost time for me to head on home.

"I think that's enough fun for me for one night, Ron. I'm gonna go home soon. I'll wait here just a bit longer if it's OK with you."

"Here," he said, "let me get you one of Pooh's shirts to wear home. And leave that bloody one here. You don't want Garf to see you like that. You don't need shit from your old man as well."

"Thanks, Ron. That's great."

After another ten minutes, I was back on the road to home. I was still nervous and kept to the shadows. When I got home, I was relieved to see the house in darkness. I entered the front door and made my way up the stairs to the comfort and safety of my bed. I didn't bother to put on any lights. Other than tripping over Poncho and inadvertently pushing Pepper off the bed, I made it without calling any notice to myself. I lay wide-awake still breathing heavy for quite a while. However, I was off in dreamland before Bill sauntered home.

The next day, I was brought up-to-date on the rest of the Halloween proceedings. Brendan and Flip had headed in the opposite direction than I did. They had the other cop chasing them for a few blocks. They ended up down by the cheese factory before they lost him.

"We ended up in Shit Creek," informed Brendan.

"Without a paddle," added Flip. "The stench drove the copper off though. See, and you guys thought that Shit Creek was a bad thing."

"I thought I was going to throw up," Brendan said. "I can't believe Flip. The idiot sat right in it."

"It wasn't so bad."

"I think I'd rather keep the fat lip. Thank you very much," I opinioned.

I found out from Bill and Birdbrain that an old wrecked car that was behind Dorchester's garage ended up in the middle of the street – upside down and on fire. No one knew (or should I say admitted) who had accomplished that ignoble feat. Also a manure spreader found itself on the road halfway up the hill. All in all, it was a typical Halloween Eve in small town Ontario of the sixties.

The move back to Newburgh did not stop Bill and me from pursuing the Great Canadian Dream and playing hockey. We still played in Napanee so we had to get there however we could. Sometimes The Old Man would drive us, other times Gordon Day or Malcolm King would give us a ride, and yet often we still had to rely on our thumb. We would stand at the top of the hill and attempt to hitch a ride to the games. It wasn't so bad really. Usually someone would venture by that recognized us and would take pity on us in our predicament. The sticks, skates, and duffel bags were a dead giveaway on where we were going. Hitchhiking between Newburgh and Napanee was a pretty common practice. There would be someone standing there with his thumb out more often than not. When we wished for someone to come by that we knew, we always hoped it wasn't Stan Howard. Stan was about the same age as Ernie and knew every face in Newburgh. And yet whenever he saw someone hitchhiking, he would wave hello to them and keep right on driving. I never did figure out what his problem was. A few times, I remember standing by the railroad trestle in Napanee in the freezing cold looking for a ride home when Stan went right on by. He did wave though. Real nice of him.

My hockey team that year was again the Wolves. Bill played for the Elks. I was still the diminutive centre modeled after Dave Keon or so I thought. Bill would have told you that he was a defenceman in the mold of J. C. Tremblay. In actuality, with Bill's temper he was really more like Howie Young. One night after arriving late for the game, I skated out just before the horn sounded to signal the start of action. The Old Man had driven me to the arena and Ma and Lily had come as well. By the time that I had arrived there were no team sweaters left, so I was wearing my blue and white

Dave Keon sweater with number 14 on the back. The regular coach wasn't there and when I skated to the bench, the replacement coach addressed me.

"Hey you, number 14. Get out there. You're playing defence tonight."

"But I play...."

"No buts. Just get out there."

And so I started the game on defence. I looked up to size out the other team. They were the All Stars and they were all much bigger than me. Then I noticed that one of the opposing centres was Barry Dorchester – Very Dorky. I don't know what it was about that night. But it was the best game I ever played. I never scored but I must have had three or four shots on net. I hit the post from just outside the slot. And I set up two perfect goals. And best of all, I chased down Dork on a clear-cut breakaway and stole the puck from him. The expression on Dork's face was priceless. He couldn't believe that I had stripped him of the puck.

"Way to go, Dum Dum!" someone bellowed from the crowd. It was Great Elk.

We won the game 4 – 2. After the game, Great Elk told me that I was the best player on the ice. Dork complemented me on my tenacity. Ma and Lily told me that I played great. Even The Old Man patted me on the back and said "Great game, Benny." I remember this well because that was the pinnacle of my hockey career. I should have hung up my skates that night and retired a winner. I never learned if defence was my better position. The next game I was back at centre. Another game I was asked to play goal but I declined. I've always wondered how that would have turned out since I was often the goaltender during street hockey games. Speaking of goalies, there was the time that I scored on Malcolm King who was the starting goalie for the Napanee senior team. It wasn't a real game though. It was a pickup game at the Tamworth Arena between us Newburgh players. I was setup perfectly by Birdbrain in the slot. Even Eddie Shack couldn't have missed.

In December, Ernie announced that another Cooper was getting married. He was going to be joining the married crowd next July. He and the bride-to-be came to Newburgh for Christmas. Her name was Ruth Arden. If the name sounds familiar that's because she was the sister of Ernie's old Hillsburgh friends Ken and Larry. I had never met Ruth before though. Ruth seemed very pleasant but a bit unsure of being introduced to the Cooper clan. Ernie had warned Ruth beforehand what a bastard The Old Man was. However, that Christmas The Old Man was on his best behaviour. I think Ruth wondered why Ernie didn't like his father. That wonder didn't last for long however. A couple days after Christmas and the day before Ernie and Ruth were set to return to Hillsburgh, The Old Man was his good old drunken, obnoxious self. In one way, I guess Ernie was relieved. He had been vindicated.

That was the Christmas that Canada received a new flag. The red and white flag with the large red maple leaf in the middle was designated as Canada's flag by the House of Commons on December 15. It wasn't my first choice but I thought it was a big improvement over the Ensign. Two months later on February 15, 1965 it officially became our new flag after passing the Senate and receiving royal ascent from the Queen. Now, I thought, if we could do something about 'God Save the Queen' and get our own national anthem.

Early in 1965, an ice storm hit our area. The streets were coated like a skating rink. You couldn't even walk up the hill. Some kids literally skated down it. So that meant no bus transportation and no school for two whole days. I failed to mention earlier that that was one of the good things about moving back to Newburgh. Bill and I could enjoy the camaraderie of our friends to and from school once more.

There were even more friends this time because Brendan, Sneezy, Flip, Dork, and others were now part of the busing population. The other thing that made the trip more interesting was all the construction – both for the expansion of the 401 highway and then the straightening of the Newburgh Road. The bus would often have to make extensive detours resulting in a prolonged trip. And shorter school day.

Before I continue on, I should inform you about something. It has to do with Gord and his married life with Paula. I don't want to go into details. Whoever knows the details about another's private life anyway? And I don't want to attach any blame. So I won't. Let's just say it wasn't exactly marital bliss. Or in other words, it was far from a marriage made in heaven. Whenever I visited them in their apartment in Napanee this realization was abundantly clear. The petty bickering and sniping would continue to pop up throughout the stay. I could see that Gord was not his old fun-loving self. But I never said a word. After all, he was only my brother and best friend. What right did I have to interfere? I just missed 'Gordie' and kept my mouth shut. And hoped and wished that everything would turn out for the best.

In late March, only a week or two after I had turned sixteen, we went to Toronto for the weekend to visit family. By 'we', I mean Ma, The Old Man, Lily, and me. Bill stayed home to spend time with his friends. The Old Man drove us up in his car of the time – a '56 Ford. We spent Saturday with Aunt June and her family and then went to visit Fred and Them on Sunday. It was great to once again see Fred, Vi, Ron, Lucy and Tom and their kids Lizzie and April. It had been quite a while since we had last seen them all. I couldn't believe how much the kids had grown. Lily would have been almost twelve then, so that would have made Lizzie around eleven and April about nine. I'm guessing here. I think April had a crush on me. She told her mom that she was going to marry me some day. April was kind of cute, but not only was she my cousin she was too young for me. But I was flattered nonetheless. Wait a minute, I just remembered that Lucy and Tom had a new son. He would have been about a year or two old then. His name was Matthew. If you are paying attention, you will have caught on that the tradition continued. That was the same name as Claudia and Tom's youngest. That was three for three. And once more Lucy denied any prior knowledge of my sister's choice of names. Weird, eh! All in all it was a good day of playing Auction (they let me play now even though I didn't know what I was doing) and sharing stories and Newfie jokes. Just like the old days. Ron even told me that I should be a jockey. I had pretty well forgot about that ambition. I was still the size for it, that's for sure. There was only one problem. I had yet to ride a horse. Who would have known that I used to worship Gene Autrey? That weekend The Old Man was not only well-behaved, he was actually fun to be with. I was kind of sad when it was time to head home after Sunday dinner. The one thing that I remember about the journey home was all the neon lights and flashy signs along the expressway in Toronto by the lake. I hadn't seen those before, not that I recalled anyway.

We arrived home close to eleven o'clock on the Sunday night. I was in an upbeat mood because it had been a good weekend. I could almost begin to visualize what normal family life was all about. Ma, The Old Man, and Lily went straight to bed while I decided to watch some TV. Bill, we assumed, was still out with friends somewhere. A few minutes after I had settled in front of the tube, there was a knock at the door. It was Sean Becker.

"Hi, Sean. What brings you here?"

"I was just passing by and I saw the light on. So, I thought I'd drop by and shoot the shit. How's your weekend?"

"Great. How's yours? What's new in the Burgh?"

"Interesting, interesting. I went fishing."

"Fishing? In March?"

"Yeah." Sean hesitated for a second before continuing. "I fished your brother from the river."

"What? Bill?"

"No. Not Bill. Gord."

"What? What are you talking about? Gord's in Napanee. And he doesn't swim."

"Yeah, he doesn't. But he decided to go for a swim just the same."

"Oh, Sean. You're just shitting me, as usual. You're full of it."

"No, I wish I was. I was walking home when I saw Gord standing on the bridge. I thought to myself, 'What's Gord doing here? It looks like he's planning to jump.' And before I knew it, the crazy fucker did just that. He jumped right into the river."

"You're not kidding," I realized. "How is Gordie? Is he OK?" I was close to tears.

"He's OK. As good as can be expected. Fine, he's fine. He's been released from the hospital. He's gone home. Bill is with him."

"What was he doing? Why would Gord try to swim now? The river's icy cold and running faster than hell. I don't understand."

"He wasn't trying to swim, Benny. He was trying to kill himself."

"Kill himself? Why? What? Why would he do that?"

"I don't know. He's not happy, I guess. I told him he shouldn't have gotten married. Now he's fucked up. I'm sorry, I mean he's confused. I don't know."

"How did he get out of the river? What happened?"

"I ran as fast as I could down to the dam. And when I got there, there he was. Gord was hanging onto the dam. He's a lucky son of a bitch. The water is flowing over the dam this time of the year. But he somehow floated to a part where the wall was higher. I grabbed down and pulled him out. He was scared shitless. And freezing. I took him home to my place. And called an ambulance. They took him to the hospital in Napanee."

"When did this happen? Tonight?"

"No, last night. Gord is home now. The police spoke to him."

"The police. What for?"

"Attempted suicide. That's a crime."

"A crime? What's the punishment if you're successful? Do they hang you?"

"It doesn't look like he's going to be charged. He just has to agree to get some help. You know, see a psychiatrist."

"I can't believe it. You're not shitting me, are you? I know you, Sean. You've made the whole story up."

"No, Benny. I swear. Where's Ma and your old man? They have to be told."

"Oh, yeah. They've gone to bed. Fuck, you're not kidding. I guess I better tell them. Oh, shit! This'll kill Ma. What do I say?"

"Go get them now. I'll tell them. Gord's fine, remember. He's fine. Calm down and call your parents."

"OK, Sean. I will. OK."

And I did. And Sean recapped his story all over again. Soon Bill arrived home and he did his best to comfort us. There was nothing to worry about. Gord was fine. He just got a little cold. He was no worse for the wear. And he seemed in good spirits now. He had just had an argument with Paula while they were visiting her family in town. He now saw it all as a big mistake. Gord said to tell us not to worry. He was fine now. He won't do anything so silly again. But no matter what Bill told us, I was worried. And shocked. And scared.

"Why, Gordie, why?" I thought. And I assumed Ma did too.

8 – Death in the Cellar

The next time that I saw Gord, I pretended that nothing had happened. I never mentioned his river incident and neither did he. It was constantly on my mind but it never came up. It was just like the night that the ghost appeared at my bedroom door. I figuratively pulled the sheets over my head and hoped it was all a bad dream. That was my way of dealing with adversity. Either that or look for a big chair to hide behind. After a while, I was finally able to enjoy Gord's company without thinking about bridges. And he seemed like his old self as well. At least like his old married self.

I haven't recounted many stories about The Old Man and his drunken ways since the story moved back to Newburgh, have I? Well, don't assume that he had suddenly changed. No, far from it. He was drinking, cursing, and ranting just as much as ever. I just can't recollect any particular incident that stands out more than any other. That's all. I mean, I could have written some tales about cases of beer on the kitchen floor, shouts of 'gray-haired old bag', threats, and other kinds of abusive behaviour. But it would have sounded too much like other parts of this book. So, use your imagination and insert such commotion in the last chapter or two. You'll get it right; you know what I mean.

"I'm drunk again you gray-haired old bag! Who 'ave you been whoring around with today? What do you think I am an eight-day clock or a sewing machine? I've been around the world; I know the score. I wasn't born yesterday. You old bag!" That kind of stuff.

The Old Man would often go out drinking with one of his co-workers, Bob. I have no idea what his last name was. He was only known as Bob. The two of them were inseparable. They worked together and drank together. They went to bars; they came to our place; they went to Bob's. The whole town would talk about that pair – Garf and Bob. Except, everyone would transpose the beginning consonants of their names transitioning them into something else. Thus it was common to hear the following.

"Where's Barf and Gob?"

"There goes Barf and Gob."

Or "Here comes Barf and Gob."

I am now going to jump this chronicle forward to the summer of 1965. I won't mention the fact that the Leafs didn't win the Stanley Cup that year (the dreaded Montreal Canadiens did). And I'll skip telling you that my hockey team – the Wolves – ended up in second place and lost in the finals. As did Bill's team – the Elks. I won't bother informing you about our Science class trip to the Sandbanks Provincial Park near Picton. I didn't go because my arranged ride forgot to pick me up after I had hitchhiked to Napanee to arrive at the designated rendezvous point. I was pissed off because there was a girl in the class who I had begun to develop a crush for. And I think she liked me. Her name was Lois Branch. So much for my visions of frolicking through sand dunes with Lois. I also won't bore you with the fact that I, Bill, and Lily all passed our grades. I went downhill in Latin and ended up with only ninety-seven percent. My Math result was similar. Just don't look at my English mark. That wasn't so pretty.

Anyway, back to the summer of '65, like I promised. I was offered a beer by the dam and I took it. That's right, I decided that it might be possible that I could drink and not turn out like The Old Man. Maybe I could drink beer and not turn nasty. After all, I had seen others get silly or sick but not many that became vicious or violent after imbibing. So I tried a beer. The first taste didn't do much for me but it was a hot day and it went down well. I declined the second beer. I was going to take this slowly. A week or two later, I went to a Newburgh softball game at 'Cow Dung Park'. The Pearson flags were once again flying from the posts of the backstop. Great Elk was not a big fan of the new red and white flag. He said it looked like a beer label. Besides, the Pearson flags were free and still in good condition. After the game, I was offered a beer from a cooler in someone's trunk. Then I had a second one and before long a third. I drank three beers in under an hour and I felt good – my first alcoholic buzz.

Not long after transforming into a drinker, I became a cold-blooded killer. Let me explain. I was walking in the woods by the dam carrying an old B.B. gun of Bill's that until that day hadn't been used for anything except shooting tin cans. I saw a robin sitting on the branch of a tree and without thinking I raised the gun towards the bird and shot. I had no idea that I would actually hit the poor, defenceless thing. I saw it topple off the branch and drop to the ground. I ran to the point of impact and looked below the tree. The robin was lying on its side, staring at me, and crying in pain. "What have I done?" I thought to myself. I was sickened by my cowardly actions. I wanted the bird to get up and fly away; however, I soon realized that the bird was beyond recovery and I put it out of its misery with the aid of a large rock. There was no way that I was going to fire that weapon again. I was in tears as I put the robin to rest. I then covered it with leaves and twigs. I went home, dismantled the gun, and threw it into the bottom of a clothes drawer. I never wanted to see it again. I'll never forget that day or the look the robin gave me as it lay dying. As you can tell, the feelings I experienced over that ordeal remain with me still.

In mid-July, we all went to Hillsburgh for Ernie's

wedding. By all, I mean The Old Man, Ma, Lily, Bill, and Gord. That's right, Gord came along with us as well but Paula stayed home. We stayed at Arden's farm which was on a concession road outside of town. That was great because the Arden's were very friendly and treated us like part of the family. The wedding itself was held at a church in downtown Hillsburgh. I can't remember the reception. I wonder where that was. I guess it was such a quick drive up and then back again that I don't recall many of the details. I know that a woman sang a song during the service. I also know that I really enjoyed the wedding but the best part for sure, was seeing Ernie and Ruth again. And spending time with Gord.

Later that July, I met a fifteen-year-old girl at the dam that I had never seen before. Her name was Pamela Curtin. She was from Guelph and was only in Newburgh for a few weeks visiting a family in town. She was quite friendly and we struck up a few conversations while swimming at the dam. Did I mention that I thought she looked pretty good in a two-piece bathing suit? Thus, I would go to the dam and swim as much as possible, as did a lot of others such as Brendan and Dorky. I noticed that Pamela seemed just as friendly with everyone and came to the conclusion that was just her nature.

On a late July weekend, Sammy Smale came to visit. It was a long time since I had seen Sammy. It was great to see him again. He also came to the dam to enjoy the swimming. I was diving off the lower part of the dam by now. Into the shallow part of the water just like the town regulars. I guess I was a town regular too, after all I did have a nickname. Sammy asked me to go back to Hillsburgh with him for a week and that sounded like fun to me. Although I had just been there for Ernie's wedding, I didn't get a chance to see any old friends then. It was just a quick jaunt. So I agreed to go. I assume it was fun but to be totally honest, I don't remember a thing about that trip. I can't distinguish that visit to Sammy's place from the previous one in 1963 two years previously. It's possible, we did the same things or we could have done something else altogether. What I do recall quite vividly was the reception when I arrived home. Mr. Smale had just pulled up in front our house and parked when Lily and Ma came out to greet me. But something was wrong. This was no normal greeting. Lily had been crying, that was obvious. Lily rushed to me and put her arms around me.

"Poncho's dead," she cried.

"What? How?" I replied.

"The Old Man did it. He kicked her down the stairs. He killed her. It was awful, Benny."

"Why? Why did he do that?"

"You know your father," answered Ma. "Who knows why? He had been drinking and I guess Poncho just got in his way. He kicked her right down the basement stairs. The poor thing died right there at the bottom of the stairs."

"Why didn't you call me and tell me?"

"It just happened this afternoon, Benny. We went out for a while. You know, to get away and when we got back…"

"She was dead?"

"Yes, Billy found her. We don't think Poncho suffered much. I think she died right away."

"How…how do you know what happened?"

"The Old Man told us. He said he was sorry. A lot of good that does. I'm sorry, Benny. We should have taken Poncho with us. We didn't…"

"Don't blame yourself, Ma. It's that asshole excuse for a father. Where's Poncho now?"

"Still inside, in the cellar. Bill's out back digging a hole. We're going to bury her soon. We waited for you."

"How come," I sobbed, "every time I go away something awful happens? I'm not leaving anymore."

I ran into the house and went past The Old Man without acknowledging him in any way. I went down the stairs to the basement to visit Poncho. I sat there in tears stroking the inert body of our dog until Bill told me it was time to take her outside.

"Why did The Old Man have to kill her?" I cried.

"Poncho never hurt him. Poncho never hurt anyone. She was the most gentle dog ever. I hate that bastard. No wonder Poncho always hid when The Old Man got drunk. She knew what she was doing. She was smart. How come she didn't go behind the china cabinet this time?"

"I don't know," said Bill. "I don't know."

The Old Man attempted to apologize to me as we went out the front door. Bill was just ahead of me, holding Poncho in his arms. Lily and Ma were outside waiting for us after saying goodbye and thanks to the Smales.

"I'm so sorry," The Old Man wept. "I did not mean to hurt Poncho, Benny. Please forgive me. I loved Poncho too. I'm sorry. I was drunk, Benny. Poncho was a good dog."

I just kept on walking and never even looked in his direction. I was afraid that I might start to take pity on him.

The next day, I went to the dam swimming. Brendan, Flip, Sneezy, and Dork were there. But no Pamela.

"She's gone back to Guelph," Brendan informed. "You were crazy to go away, Dum Dum. Pamela really liked you. She was asking for you. You didn't even tell her that you were leaving. You are a Dum Dum. Here's a good-looking girl who's crazy about you and you go to Hillsburgh right by Guelph while she's here. And then you come back home as soon as she heads back to Guelph. You..."

"Don't tell me any more," I interrupted Brendan. "I know. I'm a Dum Dum. Don't worry, I'm not going away again. I'll be right here from now on."

"Too late for that now, isn't it?"

"Yeah. Too late for sure," I replied before telling my friends about the circumstances surrounding Poncho's untimely demise.

August was a very busy month for me that summer. First of all, Aunt Becky came to visit. As was her custom, Aunt Becky was staying for a month at least. She slept in Lily's room which meant that Lily moved out into the single bed in the big open room. Bill and I were in the double bed beside it. To give Lily some privacy (or Bill and me privacy as well now that I think about it), The Old Man used the age-old trick of hanging a blanket between the two beds. Aunt Becky was pleased that she had a door that she could shut at night and didn't have to worry about Pepper attacking her in the dark. Instead he would sleep on the bed with Lily.

It didn't take me long to change my mind about never going away to anywhere again. Dork asked Brendan and me to spend some time with him at his family's cottage. Their cottage was on Beaver Lake which was not too long a drive directly north of Napanee. There were several benefits to this proposal which swayed my decision making process. One - this would give Bill the opportunity to have a bed to himself again. Two – I would be away from The Old Man. Three – Dork said he would teach me how to water-ski. Four – there were girls on the lake. Five – Dork's parents weren't going to be at the cottage so, we could party! Dork was now sixteen and had his driver's licence, so he drove us up to the cottage. Along the way we stopped at the Brewers' Retail Store in Tamworth and picked up two cases of 24 beer. I'm not telling how we managed that feat. I can't remember what brand we bought, perhaps Molson Export. Certainly not Red Cap. I couldn't understand what we were going to do with all that beer.

When we arrived at Beaver Lake, we stopped at the end of a lake road just before it seemingly went right into the lake. We then scampered into a small rowboat – the three of us, our clothes, provisions, and beer supply. After a short row, we arrived on a small island with two cottages on it. The one cottage belonged to the Dorchester's and the other was locked up and unused. It had belonged to Dork's aunt but had been sitting idle for years. Thus the setup was perfect. We were alone on an island in a lake to do whatever we liked. And so we did.

When we awoke around noon the next day, all our beer was gone. The bottles were still there but they were all empty. I couldn't figure that one out. We had to go get some more. There were other sources of entertainment though. The

Dorchester's had a motorboat with a 40 horsepower engine. After Dork took us on a tour of the lake, he showed us how to water-ski. Dork went first while Brendan drove the boat. Dork was a great water skier. He usually went on only one ski. He said it was too boring with two. Then it was my turn. Dork showed me how to float in the water with the skis on and then he accelerated the boat and up I went. It was a blast! I jumped the waves from the wake of the boat and I never fell once. I loved it. I didn't think two skis were boring. Brendan was pulled headfirst into the water twice before he got going. And then he just stayed centred in the middle of the wake. I was quite proud of myself. Maybe I had finally found a sport that I had a natural knack for.

We spent two weeks at the cottage having a great old time. Sneezy came up for a few days as well. We spent the days water skiing and the nights playing cards and listening to music. We would usually cook our own meals but would sometimes take the boat to the restaurant on the other side of the lake. One day we were asked to leave the restaurant because we didn't have any shirts on. We hadn't thought about it. We hadn't worn shirts for days. The expulsion also might have had something to do with the fact that we were also acting kind of silly. The restaurant was empty at the time but we didn't put up any kind of argument. We accepted the reasons for our banishment; besides, the waitress that kicked us out was kind of cute. We just got our shirts and went back.

Also we spent time swimming, rowing around the lake, and just relaxing. One day we wanted to listen to records, but our record player was broken. There was this very attractive blonde who was staying just across from us on the mainland. We hadn't met her. We had no idea who she was. I think she was staying with her mother. Dork and I told Brendan to go ask the blonde if we could borrow her record player. We couldn't believe it when he jumped in the boat and went over to her cottage. Dork and I were rolling in stitches. After a few minutes Brendan came back empty-handed. The blonde said she didn't have a record player with her. Whenever we ran out of anything from then on, we asked Brendan to go ask the blonde. He usually told us where to go. We loved the fact that we were completely on our own. We could eat or sleep whenever we wanted. If we felt like eating at four o'clock in the morning, who could stop us? That was a perfect time for a fried egg sandwich. If we slept in until two in the afternoon, so be it. We became so self-reliant that after a while, we decided to declare the island an independent republic.

"What should we call our new country?" asked Brendan. "How about 'The Peoples' Republic of Beaver Lake'?"

"No," said Dork. "How about Dorchestershire? What do you think, Dum Dum?"

"I love it. Dorchestershire it is. Long live Dorchestershire. Long live the Dork."

"Long live Dorchestershire," echoed Brendan. "I'll drink to that."

The two weeks went by amazingly fast. I thought it was the most fun that I could remember. We had the sun, the water, exercise, a lot of laughs, and the occasional beer. I didn't even mention that we also helped Dork build a new outhouse. On the way home, Dork suggested that we go to the Lake again next year. Brendan and I heartily agreed.

9 – The White Man

When I returned to our house on Water Street after my lake adventures, Aunt Becky took one look at me and spoke out quickly.

"Oh my Blessed Father, look at your son, Mary!"

"What?" I asked. I wondered if my drinking ways were that obvious.

"You're black," exclaimed Ma.

"What, I just showered this morning."

"No, not dirt. It's your tan," explained Ma as she laughed. "I've never seen you so dark. You're darker than your father."

"Oh," I said. "I hadn't even noticed. I haven't had my shirt on much the last two weeks. It was great, Ma. I can water-ski now. You should see me."

I chattered on, relieved that my indiscretions had not been discovered. So I was darker than The Old Man now. He always had a fairly dark complexion. Or was it red from all the alcohol? Bill and Gord both used to explain to me that Claudia, Ernie, Gord, and Lily resembled each other, while Brad and Bill were very similar, and I looked like the milkman. They also tried to convince me once that I was adopted. Funny guys, eh? In truth, I guess I do have more of the Cooper features than the rest of the family. They all definitely followed the Simpson line.

After this pleasant exchange, it was time for the customary bad news which followed a getaway. Here's what I was told by The Old Man. He was pursuing a job opportunity in Toronto and we might be moving. He may be offered a job as the superintendent of a small apartment building. Then we would get free rent. As well he could work at another job. So we would have lots of money. And Ma could stop working. And life would be perfect and sweet.

I was not impressed. We all spoke about it later when The Old Man was out. Bill stated that he wasn't going anywhere no matter what. And Lily advised that she wouldn't go either. I agreed with my siblings. Aunt Becky backed us up too.

"Maybe it's time to put your foot down, Mary. Tell Garf that you're tired of being dragged across the country every few years, disrupting the children's education, severing their friendships. What would happen if you just told him no? The worst outcome would be that he would stay here with you. The best would be that he stayed in Toronto, by himself. Let him."

"Maybe you're right, Becky. I'll refuse to go and see what happens."

"Of course I'm right. It's time to stand up for yourself and the children. You don't need the old geezer – pardon my French – anymore. You've got a job."

So that was our plan. A few days later, The Old Man left for Toronto alone to finalize his future career schemes. As of yet Ma hadn't told The Old Man about our reluctance. We were all hoping that the whole thing would fall through. Who would hire a drunk to manage a building? I waited a few days before telling my friends. Sneezy and I were sitting in Brendan's kitchen watching him make his breakfast consisting of a toasted peanut butter and sugar sandwich, when I eventually broached the subject. I was feeling a bit uneasy. Partly because of breaking the news of my possible departure and partly due to observing Brendan eat that disgusting meal. And then I finally revealed my secret.

"The Old Man wants us to move to Toronto," I blurted out.

"What?" said Sneezy. "You can't go, Dum Dum. We've just become good friends. That stinks."

"Yeah," agreed Brendan. "What about all the good times together? Toronto, yuck! Why there? Other than a good hockey team what else does it have?"

"And in Newburgh, you've got the sales barn," added Sneezy. "How can you leave that?"

"Don't worry guys. We're not going. We're going to tell The Old Man to get lost. We're staying here."

"What if he insists on going to Toronto?" argued Brendan. "What are you going to do then?"

"Then, we tell him to 'Go to Hell'. That's what we'll do."

"I don't know," said Sneezy. "I bet you go. That's just my luck."

"No we won't, Sneezy. You just wait and see."

"What a piss-off," said Brendan. "I can't even enjoy this sandwich now."

"No wonder," I replied. "How can you eat that shit?"

"It's great stuff. Isn't that right, Sneezy?"

"Me. I wouldn't walk across the street to the sales barn for that. It looks like something they feed the cows there."

And then the conversation resumed back to the usual taunts and insults. "I sure would miss these fools if I had to leave," I thought. "I wonder why Sneezy doesn't believe that we're staying put. I hope he's wrong. I know he's wrong."

The last few weeks of the summer vacation zoomed by. It went so fast that I was running and flipping just to keep up. Literally. One day while hitchhiking back from Napanee, Sean and I got a ride as far as Strathcona. We decided just to run the remaining two miles to Newburgh. In about fifteen minutes, we were running down the hill into the centre of town. We couldn't believe how quickly we covered the distance. Neither did Brendan, Sneezy, or anyone else for that matter. Also Sean taught me how to do front flips off the railing beside his house onto our lawn. I started to flip all over the place. I also won five dollars in a bet with Flip. He bet that I couldn't stand on my head (with no support) for one minute and I proved him wrong. When my feet were on the ground, I accomplished a lot in the last couple of weeks in August. I saw 'The Sound of Music' in Kingston with Brendan and one of his friends (the same one who introduced me to James Bond). I wasn't expecting much because I thought that I hated musicals. But it was rather good. I was so impressed that I went to another musical at the Napanee Drive-in with Bill and Malcolm King. It was called 'Help!'. We also went to Napanee to roller-skate one Sunday. I saw my former Science classmate Lois Branch and even got up enough nerve to ask her for one skate. We skated to the great new Stones song – '(I Can't Get No) Satisfaction'. I once more saw the dark-haired girl who smiled and said "Hi." I still didn't know her name. Neither did I know if she knew mine. "One day, I'll ask her to skate," I thought to myself. "And maybe I'll even ask what her name is. She might say no though."

One night after arriving home from one of these sources of entertainment, I walked into the living room to witness Ma, Bill, and Lily all sitting around looking rather serious. Aunt Becky had returned to Newfoundland by then and The Old Man was still in Toronto.

"What's up?" I asked.

"Your father called today," explained Ma. "He's got the job as the superintendent of the apartment. He also has another job lined up working for some electronics company."

"That's nice but what's that got to do with us?" I questioned.

"Let me finish, Benny. He wants us to move to Toronto at the end of September. That's when he takes over the apartment building."

"Didn't you tell him that we weren't leaving Newburgh?"

"I tried, Benny. I tried. Yes, I told him. He was really upset. He said that he was doing all of this for us. So that we could have a better life."

"And you bought all of that crap?"

"No, Benny, of course not. I'm not expecting anything to be better. That's not it. It's just that I've been thinking. I don't make enough money to keep you all in school, feed you, and pay the rent. We would have to move from this house. To where, I don't know. Some small dump in Napanee, I guess. Would you like that? We can't stay here, Benny. Anyway, I told The Old Man that we would talk about it. He's going to call back tomorrow. That's what we've been talking about."

"What do Bill and Lily say?" I looked at them both. "What do you say?"

"I agreed to go with Mom," Lily answered first. "We have no choice. Toronto won't be so bad. Mom also said that we could come back to Newburgh as much as we wanted to visit our friends. I don't want to go either. But I said OK."

"That's right. Benny," added Ma. "You're old enough now that you don't have to lose your friends. You can come back at Christmas and in the summer. You know, during school breaks. There's a bus that runs from Napanee to Toronto regularly. And as I've always said, when everyone is finished school then we'll say goodbye to The Old Man and go our own way. I promise."

I didn't say anything at first. I just looked at Bill. Finally I answered softly, "OK, Ma. Tell The Old Man we'll come with him. What about Bill?"

"I'm staying here, Benny," answered Bill. "I'm going to stay with Gord and Paula at their place. I already spoke to them about it. I'm sorry but I think you should go with Ma and Lily."

"I'm going wherever Ma goes. That's for sure. I just thought that we could all stay here."

"No Benny, we can't," Ma explained again. "I wish we could. But I thought about it. I haven't slept in weeks. We have to follow your father. He says, how can I break up the family? Let's tell him that we're going. OK?"

"Yes," I replied. "But how come Bill gets to stay behind?"

"He's older than you, Benny. He'll be twenty in October. You're still only sixteen."

"All right. Let's go. I'll miss Bill though."

"So will I," said Ma. "And Gordie too."

The next day, I broke the news to Brendan, Sneezy, and Flip.

"I knew it," exclaimed Sneezy. "I just knew it. Didn't I tell you?"

"You can stay at my place and visit as much and as long as you want," offered Brendan. "You'll come back, won't you?"

"Holy shit," said Flip. "Ain't that a bummer, Dummer?"

"Yes, yes, and yes," I replied.

That September was kind of weird. It was difficult to relax and enjoy myself knowing that I was soon leaving my friends for the cold, big city. Bill and I started back at school at N.R.H.S. both in Grade 12. Bill was in his last year of his four-year Business and Commerce course while I was enrolled in my penultimate year in the five-year Arts and Science program. Lily was continuing her education at the Newburgh Academy in Grade 7. Lily and I both wondered what we would learn in one month before switching schools and teachers. It was kind of hard to concentrate on the curriculum. I certainly had little interest in doing homework or studying. What were they going to do if I misbehaved – kick me out of school? Big deal! The whole month seemed like a waste. Well, not entirely. I arranged to be sitting beside Lois Branch in every class. That's not quite true. Lois actually sat right beside me in a few classes without my encouragement. That was a good sign, right? She also picked up every one of my textbooks and signed 'Lois Branch' in the front. Maybe she did like me too. Wouldn't you know it, just my luck, I'm leaving. I didn't even tell Lois until a few days after classes recommenced. She told me that she would miss me. As Sneezy said, "That stinks."

That year, we had a big corn roast at the dam. Most of the Newburgh clan was there. That included all the regular guys with their nicknames plus many of the Newburgh girls, most of whom I haven't told you much about. There was Peggy Day and Judy Winchester who I mentioned before and you might recall if you were paying attention. In addition there were others like Janet Washington, Jill Cox, and Margaret Forrest. Some gathered the corn by raiding a local farmer's field while others rounded up pots. We lit a large bonfire on the dam and we soon had a great roast on the go. I was told that they had done this before but I couldn't recall such an event. We all agreed that it was a huge success and should continue as an annual affair. After our feast was completed, I saw Sean grab a few stones. He looked at me and then whispered "Shhh." He went to the top of the dam and nonchalantly hurled one of the stones high in the air so that it returned a few yards from us.

"What the hell was that?" said Sean.

"It sounded like a rock hitting the dam," answered Peggy.

It was a dark night and only the fire provided any light, hence I was the only one that knew that Sean was the perpetrator of the seemingly hostile act. Sean then adeptly tossed another rock high in the air which landed even closer to our position. Sean again expressed surprise.

"There it is again! Somebody's throwing rocks at us!"

"I can't see anyone," said Jill.

"Look up there," said Sean pointing to the other side of the river. "I thought I saw someone moving."

"Come on Pooh," demanded Birdbrain. "Let's go see who these assholes are and beat the shit out of them."

Birdbrain, Pooh, Bill, and a few other boys then ran across the dam and up the adjacent bank. After about five minutes they returned and pronounced that whomever it was had long since gone. Things then returned to normal and before long most had decided that it was time to split. Shortly only Peggy, Jill, Margaret, Sean, Flip, and I were left standing on the dam. Then Sean threw another stone.

"Holy shit, they're back again," yelled Flip.

And then another stone crashed near us.

"I'd sure like to catch those bastards," advised Sean. "Wouldn't you, Dum Dum?"

"Sure thing, Sean." I didn't say much more. I was not a good liar and I was close to telling the girls and Flip the truth. But I decided to keep playing the game.

Anyways, after a couple more mysterious rock missiles, another fruitless chase, and continued outrage, it was decided to call it a night. As we were walking home, Sean smiled and winked.

The next day, Sean admitted to our friends what had happened. Most found it amusing in retrospect. Peggy didn't believe Sean. She was sure that someone was throwing stones at us. How could it have been Sean? He was standing beside us.

A week or so later, I was part of a trick that Sean played on Peggy again. There was this old story that went around Newburgh about 'The White Man'. He was this guy dressed all in white that would suddenly appear in the headlights of cars at night. He would appear at the side of the road and then float across the road in the path of the oncoming vehicle before disappearing who knows where. I thought the story sounded pretty fishy; however, everyone argued that it was a true story. He hadn't been seen for a few years, but 'The White Man' had made numerous appearances. And there had been several accounts of sightings from different normally reliable witnesses. I still didn't believe it. I didn't believe in ghosts in spite of my childhood experiences. I had stopped believing in the Easter Bunny, Santa Claus, the devil, and God, so how could I believe in ghosts. I didn't even believe in life after death. This story still inspired Sean. I met him one Sunday night (my last Sunday as a Newburgh resident) only to be surprised by his manner of dress. He was completely in white including some ugly white trench coat that I had never seen before.

"Come on, Dum Dum. Let's have some fun."

Sean knew that Peggy was arriving home at eleven. We waited behind some trees until we saw her car approaching. He then jumped out onto the road, waved his arms, and as quickly disappeared back into a bush. When the car stopped and I saw Peggy get out, Sean jumped out again. Only to vanish just as quickly. Peggy screamed and ran inside. For once in his life, I guess Sean felt guilty about his practical joke, because he walked towards the door and called me from my hiding place. We knocked on the door and called Peggy's name. She finally appeared and Sean confessed all.

"I almost had a heart attack, Sean. What are you two doing?"

"Just a little night stalking," said Sean.

"You're too much. I still don't believe that you threw those stones though."

"What stones?" asked Sean.

That night, I awoke in bed with a thought. Maybe that wasn't Sean's first nightly excursion. Maybe, Sean was 'The White Man'.

The next weekend, The Old Man came home and we all packed up and moved away. Ron Foot (of Fred and Them fame) came along as well. Ron was the driver of the rental moving truck. The Old Man drove his car. I found it very difficult to say goodbye to Bill. I was used to brothers getting older and leaving. But this was a first. I was leaving a brother. Now, there were only two – Lily and me. That would definitely feel strange. And there was another shock. We had to leave Pepper behind. The Old Man said that pets weren't allowed in the apartment. Nonetheless Lily told me that she was going to bring Pepper regardless of what The Old Man said. She arranged to go in the truck with Ron and smuggled on Pepper unbeknownst to The Old Man. The Old Man, Ma, and I were in the car. As we were driving up the hill, I saw Brendan, Sneezy and Flip in front of the Newburgh Lunch.

"Bye, Benny," shouted Brendan.
"Goodbye, Dummer," yelled Sneezy.
"See you soon, Dum Dum," exclaimed Flip.
Then they all waved; I waved back silently.

10 – Coal Man

When we arrived in Toronto, Lily stepped from the truck worried how The Old Man would react to the surprise presence of Pepper. She thought that she had Pepper well concealed from The Old Man's sight. However when he got out of the car, The Old Man addressed Lily right away.

"I see you brought the cat."

That was it. That's all he said. He then took us all on a tour of the apartment. A rather short tour. After all it was only a one-bedroom apartment. The building was situated in the Bathurst – St. Clair area of Toronto. Not that the location meant much to me. I didn't know one section of Toronto from another. The building was four stories high and our apartment was on the ground floor, which we were all glad to hear since there were no elevators. As we entered the apartment itself, we stepped into a small entrance-way. To the right, was a small, narrow kitchen. To the left, was a fair-sized living room. And straight ahead was the location of the best feature – a bathroom. It was small but it had a tub with a shower, a sink with running water, and a toilet that actually flushed! In short, it had all the modern conveniences. The one and only bedroom was accessed by a door at the other side of the living room. The bedroom looked big enough to hold only one bed – the double bed belonging to Ma and The Old Man. Ma walked through the apartment silently and only spoke after the tour was complete.

"How can we live here, Garf? We'll be on top of each other. The kids can't live like this. This apartment's hardly big enough to swing a cat. We shouldn't have come," Ma sobbed.

"Mary, don't cry," The Old Man pleaded. "It won't be so bad. You'll see. Besides, it's only temporary until we get onto our feet and I get more experience as a super. Then we can move to a bigger place. I promise. You'll make this place real comfy. No matter where we go, you always turn the place into home in no time. Lily can still have her cat too. Don't worry, everything will be OK."

The Old Man was right about Ma transforming any place into home, but she sure didn't have much to work with this time. As I surmised, the bedroom was stocked with my parents' bed and dresser. Somehow, Lily's dresser was also crammed into the room. Lily's bed was placed against the far wall in the living room. Then there was room for the living room furniture, TV, and my bedroom dresser. The dining room table was squeezed into the kitchen. My bed? It was the pullout bed in the chesterfield once again. The rest of our stuff was put into storage in the locker room. This time The Old Man didn't even hang up a blanket to separate Lily's 'room'. He said that he couldn't make any holes in the wall. We would just have to change in the bathroom or after the lights were switched off. Either that or just look the other direction.

At night and weekends, The Old Man acted as the building superintendent. It sure seemed weird when people addressed The Old Man as 'Super'. I couldn't see anything super about him. Perhaps, I was being too harsh. After all, he had quit drinking once more. And this time he said that he meant it. His daytime job was at an electronics firm in the city. I was going to say that I have no idea what he did there. But it just came to me. I think it was janitorial chores. Similar to what he had to do around the apartment building. All this by a man that had never raised a broom around our place before. Not to say that The Old Man wasn't a hard worker. He was. Just not at home.

My new school was about a fifteen-minute walk away. It was called Markham Avenue Collegiate Institute. I thought that Collegiate Institute was kind of a stuffy name for a High School. And I had always feared that I would end up in an institute one day. I walked to the school by myself the first Monday after our move. I spent a while in the office filling in forms before I was escorted to my first class by the Vice-Principal. The class (which was French) had already begun but the VP called the teacher out of the room to introduce her to the new student.

"This is a new student. A transfer from a town called Nab-a-knee. Down by Kingston."

"What's your name?" questioned the French teacher.

"Benny," I answered, "Benny Cooper."

"Benny," she replied. "I think you're getting a little too old for that. Don't you? We'll call you Ben. Is that OK, Ben Cooper?"

"OK," I responded although Ben didn't sound right to me. That was my late uncle's name. I didn't mention what I was called in Newburgh. I wasn't planning to tell anyone including my fellow classmates. That was my Newburgh name. I didn't want to be called 'Dum Dum' in Toronto. I didn't mind the name in Newburgh because it fit right in with the other names, but I thought it prudent to keep that a secret in my new surroundings. So when the French teacher brought me into the classroom, I was introduced as 'Ben'.

In my first few weeks of school, a few things became evident. The first was that at least eighty-five percent of the school population was Jewish. This meant that on Jewish holidays there were only five students left in our class. Which translated into some pretty lax study days during this period. The teachers didn't want to cover too much while the majority of the class was absent. The next thing that I became aware of was the fact that I was completely lost in Latin. I didn't realize that they spoke a different Latin language in Toronto. However, I discovered that they used different textbooks which had covered an altogether different vocabulary. Over night my best subject became my worst. On my first test I recorded a mark in the mid-forties. A fifty percentile drop. I couldn't believe it. I had a lot of catching up to do. The other class that I want to bring to your attention was swimming. Not only was that a new lesson for me, but the manner that it was taught seemed strange. We were all completely nude while the teacher instructed us from the diving board wearing swim trunks and a tee shirt. The idea behind the nudity supposedly had to do with hygiene and not having to worry about dirty swim trunks. I didn't get it. And this was no easy class. The teacher would drive us through an exercise-full hour. Many of the boys (oh yeah, I didn't mention that this class was segregated, naturally) were physically sick at the end of the lesson. The teacher would always keep us right to the bell, too. Then, you had a couple of minutes to throw up, shower, dry, get dressed, and run to the next class (which was French). The French teacher would give us a hard time about not getting to her class in time. We tried to explain the situation, but she wasn't very sympathetic. She wouldn't listen to any of our excuses.

Lily didn't have as far to walk to her school as I did. Hers was only a few blocks away, probably about a five-minute stroll. After a couple of days, Lily had already brought a new friend home from school with her. The Old Man commented to Ma, "See, Lily's fitting in already. I told you that everything would work out." As for me, I wasn't close to inviting anyone home after school. And I wasn't the recipient of any invitations either. And things hadn't changed after a couple of weeks. I had met some boys at school that I would sit with at lunch and hold some conversation. But I only remember a couple of those boys now. The most memorable was Noah Wayman. One time I answered a question from Noah by responding, "No – uh – way, man." He laughed and said that no one had said that to him before. I found that hard to believe. I figured that was as obvious as my relationship to Gary Cooper. I also got to know my fellow gentiles a little more because of the occasional extremely small classes. I was closest to a boy called Ron Baxter. But I hadn't met anybody that I could really call a friend. As soon as school ended, I would walk home by myself. I then spent my time at home doing my homework or watching TV. That was about it. I was lonely as hell to tell the truth. I missed hanging around with Brendan, Sneezy, Flip, and Dork. And I missed being called Dum Dum. And of course, I missed my brothers. It was very weird to be the only boy in the house. The good part was that it provided me the opportunity to spend more time with Lily. I remember that we went to a movie together. There was a theatre on St. Clair Avenue near Bathurst Street that used to show double features of second run movies at a good price. Lily and I went to see 'The Yellow Rolls-Royce' together. It wasn't too bad. I can't recall the other feature. The Old Man must have noticed that I was bored, as one day he brought me home a transistor radio from work.

"Here Benny. This is for you," he said.

"To keep?" I said surprised. "Thanks Dad."

I never had my own radio before. And it was portable. That was great. I would listen to CHUM when I did my homework at the kitchen table. There was no other place to do it. There were some great songs being played on the radio that fall. Songs like 'Get Off of My Cloud'. I loved that one. Or I could listen to people calling in to talk to Larry Solway. One time, someone called Larry to talk about how lonely it was to live in a city like Toronto. The caller explained that it was very hard to meet friends. The subject caught my attention and I listened intently. Larry Solway argued that he would much sooner be alone in a city than a small town. He said that nothing makes you feel more alone than being a stranger in a small town. At least in a city you can get lost in the crowd. You can go out and be entertained. In a town there was nothing – you are just alone.

"But Larry, you are only a stranger in a town for a couple of days," I shouted at the radio. "Then you meet lots of friends. You don't know what you are talking about."

But Larry didn't hear me and he continued on with his argument.

"Yeah," I continued, "in a city you can go to a movie by yourself. Bid deal. Isn't that exciting?"

It was about the end of October, when I arrived home from school to see my brother Bill sitting on the couch with Ma and Lily.

"Billy," I yelled. "How are you? What are you doing here?"

"Howdy Benny," responded Bill. "It's good to see you but I've got bad news for you."

"Bad news? Why, what's happened?"

"Nothing. Except now you have to share your bed with someone again. I'm back home for good."

"That's great!" I couldn't conceal my excitement. "You're welcome to share the chesterfield with me. There's lots of room in this place. Isn't that right, Ma?"

I then went over and gave Bill a big hug and said, "Welcome home. I missed you."

"I missed you all as well. Well, I didn't miss The Old Man. But you and Lily and Ma of course. I had to come home. It didn't really work out staying with Gord and Paula. But it's great to be home."

"Oh, by the way, my name's Ben now," I informed Bill.

"But I still call him Benny," said Ma.

"Me too," added Lily. "Ben doesn't sound right. Does it, dear little Benny?"

"That's right, Sissy," I replied.

Shortly after, I was informed that Bill wouldn't be attending Markham Avenue Collegiate Institute along with me. He would be enrolling at a technical school on Keele Street somewhere. Not really that close to where we lived. To get to his school, Bill would have to take the TTC (Toronto Transit Commission), which involved a streetcar ride and a couple of buses to arrive at his destination. Thus, I would still be making the solo trek to and from school each day. Anyway, having Bill home again, certainly would make my after school life a lot more interesting.

In early November – November 9th to be exact – Bill and I were sitting at the kitchen table doing our homework and listening to the radio. Ma, Lily, and The Old Man were watching something on the TV. Suddenly everything went black. And the radio went silent.

"Damn," said The Old Man, "I better go check the power. I wonder where I put that flashlight?"

"It's in the kitchen drawer at the far end," answered Ma.

The Old Man eventually found the flashlight and headed out into the hall. Bill and I sat and talked about nothing in particular while Lily complained about missing the end of the show. After a couple of minutes, The Old Man returned.

"There's nothing wrong in our apartment. The whole street is out. I looked both ways down the street and saw nothing but total darkness. Why don't you put on your transistor radio, Benny? I wonder if the power's out in this whole section of Toronto."

"I did have the radio on, Dad. It's gone out too."

"Are your batteries good?"

"Yeah, I just changed them yesterday. Maybe just CHUM went out. I'll try another station."

I twirled the tuning dial and continued to get nothing except static. "That's weird," I exclaimed. But suddenly the sound of a voice resumed on the radio.

"…power outage all over Toronto. We're not yet sure of all the areas affected. We'll try to find out and pass on the information as soon as we can. We lost power here at the station as well. We're now back on and stay tuned for further updates."

"All of Toronto," said The Old Man, "that's incredible. I never heard of anything like that."

"What can we do now," wondered Lily, "without a TV?"

"We used to live without power," The Old Man

111

responded. "Isn't that right, Benny? Do you remember that?"

"Yeah, a little bit."

"What did you do?" Lily asked. "That sounds real boring."

"We listened to the big battery radio or played games," I answered.

"Or we just talked," added The Old Man. "Isn't that right, Mary?"

"Yeah, that's right," said Ma hesitantly since she was unable to recall an occasion where we sat around and talked as a family with The Old Man.

"Do we have any candles?" Bill asked. "I have to finish this homework. And it doesn't sound like the lights will be back on real soon."

"Sure," said Ma, "I'll get them for you, Billy."

"Go look outside. It's right eerie. You can't see a light anywhere. Except for the cars of course."

"I think I saw this on The Twilight Zone," I noted. "An alien spacecraft sucked up all our power, I bet."

"Oh, you're just joking, Benny," said Lily. "You are, aren't you?"

"Yes Lily. I'm just kidding. If it were aliens the transistor wouldn't work either. Or the cars. I'm going outside. Who else is coming?"

So we all went out on the street along with quite a few other residents of the apartment. Everyone was talking about the power outage and sharing what information that they had gathered.

"I heard the power's out right down to Florida," said one of our neighbours. "It makes you think that we're being invaded. It reminds me of the blackouts during the war back home. I wonder what the hell is happening?"

What was happening was the great power blackout that affected most of central Canada and the Eastern seaboard of the United States. We listened in keen interest and wonder as the full extent of the outage was revealed. Bill and I completed our homework by candlelight while Lily decided to just go to bed. The next day at school the blackout was the discussion in every class. I was one of the few to have completed their assignments. I have to admit that I wouldn't have bothered if it wasn't for Bill. Funny, I couldn't recall him being all that studious before.

Later in November, Bill and I got a job. The Old Man told us that the manager of the building next door was looking for someone to help out. Bill and I got the job of shoveling the coal into the furnace to keep the fire going. As well we would do other chores like gathering the garbage and putting it out for collection. Bill and I decided to share the chores and the profits. We would take turns. The coal had to be stoked a few times a day. So we would alternate between shifts. The job allowed us to make a few extra dollars – at least enough to go to the local movie theatre or pay for bus fare. Bill thought that we should go to a Leaf game with our earnings; however, we soon discovered that getting tickets was an impossibility. So Bill came up with another plan. "Let's go see the Marlies." The Toronto Marlboros were the Junior 'A' team associated with the Leafs at the time. That turned out to be a great idea. We would attend the games on Sunday afternoons. My favourite Marlie was a young defenceman called Brian Glennie. His hits really packed a wallop. We also got to see Bobby Orr playing for the Oshawa Generals. It didn't take any hockey sense to realize that he was going to be a star for the Boston Bruins. I guess I should also disclose that the other part of the Marlie games that Bill and I enjoyed was the go-go dancer contests during intermission.

Another thing that we started to do a lot was to visit Fred and Them. Now they were only about a fifteen-minute bus ride away. So, we could easily go visit them for an evening with or without The Old Man. I should mention that The Old Man had once more resumed his drinking ways. I bet you didn't really believe that he would quit. So now when he got drunk and obnoxious we could head down to see Fred and Them. And if he was really obnoxious we could even stay overnight. But I 'm getting ahead of myself. That wasn't necessary – yet. One time, after returning from visiting Fred and Them (without The Old Man), Lily immediately noticed that Pepper was not in the apartment.

"Where's Pepper, Lily's cat?" Ma asked The Old Man. "You must have let him out, Garf?"

"How the hell would I know where the cat got? I haven't been watching it. I'm the super. I have to go in and out to do my chores. Maybe it ran out. I wouldn't know. That cat's the least of my worries."

"Well you must have seen it go out?" questioned Ma.

"Damn it, Mary! I told you. I haven't seen the fucking cat. Now leave me alone."

We searched every inch of the apartment but found no trace of Pepper. Lily, Bill, and I then went around the rest of the building calling Pepper. We also went outside in case he had somehow got out the main doors. We called and called but had no response. Eventually we started looking in places that he shouldn't have been able to get into – like the locker room. We decided to cover the whole building mainly because we couldn't think of any other options.

"Maybe he got out and one of the tenants took him," surmised Lily.

"Why would anyone take Pepper?" I asked. "I don't think anyone would do that."

"He's a good cat. Maybe someone took him for their kids or something."

"No, I don't think so. Let's keep looking. We can ask people tomorrow if they've seen him, if you like."

But that wasn't necessary. When we walked into the furnace room, Pepper was lying on the floor. He was not moving.

"Pepper!" Lily cried.

I felt a lump in my throat and my eyes began to water. Bill picked up Pepper, and informed Lily and me, that he was dead.

"Why?" Lily wept. "What happened? He looks OK. He's

114

not bleeding or anything."

"Maybe he ate something. Like his poor mother did," I conjectured.

"No," said Bill. "It's that bastard of a father of ours. He killed him just like he killed Poncho. I know it. He never wanted Pepper to come with us."

"Why do you say that?" I wondered.

"How would Pepper get in this room by himself? It's The Old Man all right."

"I wish we had never come to Toronto," cried Lily. "I want to go back to Newburgh."

"Me too," I agreed. "On the next bus."

The Old Man denied any involvement with either the disappearance or the demise of Pepper. He continued to swear that he had nothing to do with it. He had no explanation for how Pepper got in the furnace room.

"Maybe he followed me, I don't know. He must have eaten something poisonous. Or maybe he just died of old age. How can you blame me? I wouldn't do anything to hurt you, Lily and Benny. I know you loved that cat. I'm hurt that you think me capable of killing a poor defenceless cat. Please believe me. I don't know what happened. I'm sorry."

So that was the end of it. We were never really sure what happened. Just highly suspicious, that's all. And our family continued to shrink.

11 – Beware the Bat-Hooks

About a week after we found Pepper in the furnace room, The Old Man brought home a surprise for Lily. He had two small, gray kittens.

"Here Lily, these are for you. Aren't they cute? I just wanted to show you that I love you. I never hurt your cat. I don't care if you have a cat. See, I don't even care if you have two cats."

Whatever The Old Man's motives, Lily didn't care. She immediately fell in love with the two little rambunctious balls of fur. As did I and Bill. And Ma too. They sure were quite a handful in our small apartment. They could chase each other up and down and around while covering the entire place in seconds flat. Lily called one Smokey (yeah I know, not original) and the other was named Charley (short for Charcoal). Both Lily and I had told The Old Man earlier that we didn't want another cat. We just wanted Pepper back. But we were both glad that he hadn't listened to us.

In late November, Ma got tired of listening to me whine about missing Newburgh and suggested that I go down to visit Brendan and my other friends for the weekend.

"Just for the weekend?" I asked.

"Sure, why not?" responded Ma. "You can get the bus

116

down Friday night. And come back Sunday night. At least you'll have one full day with your friends."

I was quite pleased with Ma's suggestion. I had thought about going down myself but I figured that Ma would think I was crazy for going just for a weekend. And I was able to pay for the main part of the bus fare with my meagre earnings. So I called Brendan and he agreed that the impromptu visit was a great idea. And the next night, I was on the bus to Napanee. Brendan and Dork picked me up at the bus stop and drove me the seven miles to Newburgh. Brendan and I stayed up talking most of the night in his kitchen. We had a few good laughs talking about old times, music, politics, and everything else in the world that we had to catch up on. We slept in to about noon, until Brendan's mother decided it was time for us to get up. Brendan's two younger brothers even beat us up. I never mentioned them before, did I? They were all only a few years apart in age. Phillip Casey was the next in age after Brendan, while Jimmy was the youngest. It was Jimmy who first shortened the name Dum Dum into Dummer. And he still called me that. I loved it. It sounded warm and friendly after all those cold and unfriendly Ben's.

That day we spent hanging around the Newburgh Lunch with Flip and Sneezy. We couldn't find Dork. We did absolutely nothing and I had a ball. Soon it was after midnight on Saturday night and Brendan and I were the only ones left and we were still going strong. We were listening to my radio attempting to pick up some distant stations as opposed to the country songs on the Kingston stations. Actually there were two radio stations in Kingston at the time. One wasn't too bad some times of the day. The other was consistently hopeless. Anyway, we soon discovered that the best spot to place the radio to receive the optimum radio reception was on the window ledge of the barbershop. So that's where Brendan and I were sitting (on the step in front of the barbershop) when a police cruiser pulled up. We were listening to the new Bob Dylan song 'Like A Rolling Stone', which we both thought was amazing, when one of the two

117

constables stepped out of the car and came over to us.

"What are you two boys up to tonight?"

"Oh, nothing," answered Brendan. "Just listening to Bob Dylan."

"You're doing what?"

"Listening to the radio," clarified Brendan.

"Where did you get the radio?"

"It's mine," I replied.

"Can you prove that? Do you have a receipt?"

"No, I've had it for a while. It was a present from my father."

"I see. Can I see some identification?"

"I don't have any on me," Brendan responded. "My wallet is at home."

"I don't have any either," I added.

"Hmm. Where are you two boys from?"

"I live here in Newburgh at the top of the hill," said Brendan.

"What about you, son?" questioned the big police constable as he stared down at me.

"Toronto," I said.

"Toronto? What are you doing sitting here?"

"He's visiting me," replied Brendan.

"I'm not speaking to you," snapped the cop to Brendan before directing his attention back to me. "What are you doing here?"

"I'm visiting my friend."

"Why aren't you at school?"

"It's Saturday night."

"Don't get smart with me, boy. What's your name?"

"Uh ... Ben Cooper," I answered after a slight pause because I wasn't sure whether to say Bennett, Ben or Benny.

"You don't sound too sure what your name is."

"Yes, it's Ben Cooper."

"And who are you?" the interrogator asked Brendan.

"Brendan Casey. And that is Benny Cooper. He used to live here. He just moved to Toronto, didn't you Benny? Now he's come back to visit me for the weekend."

"All the way here just for the weekend? To do what?"

"Nothing," I said. "Just visit my friends."

"Hmm. And that's your radio? Why are you sitting here and not at your friends place?"

"Oh, we're just talking and here we get the best radio reception."

"What?"

"The best reception on the radio. It works better here in this window."

"That's right," said Brendan.

"Hmm. I think you two better get in the back of the cruiser."

"Why?" asked Brendan. "We didn't do anything."

"Shut up and get in the car! We're just going to call in and check out a few things."

Brendan and I looked at each other and climbed into the back seat. I had no idea what was going on. The constable spoke to the other uniformed occupant of the police car.

"Their story's pretty suspicious. We better check them out. The little one here is from Toronto. The other one says he lives in town." He then picked up his two-way radio and spoke to someone at the other end.

"I would like to do a check on a Ben Cooper of Toronto. Are there any prior records?"

"Oh shit," I thought. "They're going to find out about my previous life of crime during my smoking years. When they hear about that break-in, they'll assume that's what Brendan and I had planned to do – break into the barbershop. Ma won't let me come to Newburgh anymore. I go down for a weekend and I end up in jail. Maybe even in Kingston Pen. How could I explain this? What would The Old Man say and do? Would they come and bail me out? Would Lily still love me?"

"Okay, you're clean," the policeman said. I was so busy with my thoughts that I hadn't heard the original response from the station. "We're going to drive you back to Mr.

Casey's residence. Will anybody be there?"

"My Mom and my two brothers," said Brendan. "But they'll be in bed."

"As you two should be," said the other policeman speaking for the first time. "Don't you know that there is a town curfew?"

"No," said Brendan. "We didn't know."

"Well, there is for youngsters like you. Now direct us to your home."

I could tell that Brendan was pondering what his mother would say about her son and friend being driven home by two cops. If she was still up and looking out the window then she sure would wonder what the hell was going on. As we pulled into Brendan's driveway the house was in complete darkness.

"Okay, get out and go on in. We won't wake up your family this time. If there's a next time we'll take you to the station for questioning. Understand?"

"Yes," I said.

"Yes," said Brendan. "Thanks."

We went on into the house and turned on the living room light. We sat in silence until we saw the cruiser back out of the driveway and head up the remainder of the hill towards Napanee. Brendan was the first to speak.

"Dum Dum, the next time a cop asks you where you live, say Newburgh. OK?"

"Sure, I didn't realize that we Torontonians had such a bad reputation." That was the first time that I had called myself a Torontonian. Until then, I had still considered myself to be a Newburgher.

The next day my friends and I did the usual nothing, and I returned home on the bus which left Napanee at 6:00 p.m. The ride home was twice as long as the ride down because it stopped at every little town along Highway 2 during the trip. It was after midnight before I arrived home at our small apartment. But the trip was worth all the hassle. It sure felt good to experience friendship firsthand once more.

In December, I caught up on a few more movies. I saw my first restricted movie along with Bill and one of his school chums. I presented Bill's identification to prove that I was eighteen (I was only sixteen in reality). After watching the movie ('The Pumpkin Eater'), I couldn't understand what the fuss was all about. If that was all I was missing, then I could wait a couple more years without any trouble. Then all of us in the family went to see 'Cat Ballou'. Even The Old Man went. We all thought that the movie was great especially Lee Marvin. And Jane Fonda, of course. The family fun was short-lived though. The next day while Bill was out visiting a friend, The Old Man got drunk again. He was going in and out of the apartment and getting drunker by the minute. We eventually caught on that he must have had a stash of beer in the furnace room. The Old Man was out of the apartment when Lily suddenly noticed that one of the gray kittens was missing from the apartment. Charley was wandering around by himself looking for his brother Smokey. We had scoured every inch of the apartment when The Old Man returned once more. The Old Man noticed the sad look on everyone's face.

"What's wrong? What's wrong, sweetie?" he asked Lily.

"I can't find Smokey. One of the kittens. He's missing."

"Oh, is that all. I gave him to the Mitchell boy."

"You did what?" Ma exclaimed. "Go get him back. Who's the Mitchell boy?"

"The Mitchell boy. They live in 307; you know. He's a nice kid. I gave him the damn cat. Why do we need two? They were just driving us nuts chasing each other."

"I want Smokey back," demanded Lily. "He's my cat. You can't give him away."

"Well I did. And I'm not taking him back. I would break the little boy's heart. He loves him."

"You care more about some stranger than your own family," commented Ma.

"It's just a fucking cat. I brought it home and I can give it away. Lily's still got the other one. I could give that one away too if I wanted."

"Ma's right," I said. "You don't give a shit about us. All you care about is being the big man. You're a bastard," I continued surprising even myself.

"That gray-haired old bag is turning even you against me. Fuck you all!" shouted The Old Man as he left the apartment slamming the door behind him.

And that was that. We only saw Smokey a few more times whenever the young boy brought him out into the hall. Charley didn't seem to run near as much anymore. Lily thought that he looked really sad and I had to agree with her observation.

The other thing that I did in December was to start playing hockey again. I found out that there were weekly games being played after school. On the first day, I discovered that my stick didn't fit in my locker. So I just had to put it beside the locker against the wall. When I got to the rink, I found out that we only had forty-five minutes of ice-time including getting dressed and undressed. The game itself wasn't too bad although it was a bit unorganized. No one knew where to play. But I actually wasn't the worst player. I was probably in the middle somewhere as far as skill level went. Anyways, I did this a few times before coming to the conclusion that it wasn't worth it. I didn't know anyone that well and they all ignored me – even during the game. Some smart aleck kids hid my hockey stick one day. I had to carry all my equipment to and from school. And my heart was no longer in the game. So I called it quits and ended my hockey career then and there. I would just have to enjoy the game as a spectator from now on. Go Marlies Go!

That Christmas, I went to another movie with Bill and his friend. We went to the opening day of the latest James Bond film 'Thunderball'. It was pretty good but not up to 'Goldfinger'. The other thing that I did was return to Newburgh again. But this time I was able to spend close to a week there. Plus, I had time to visit Gordie. When the bus arrived in Napanee, I went straight to Gord and Paula's apartment. After our greetings, Gord, Paula, and I sat at the kitchen table and talked. I updated Gord on all the latest goings-on.

"What else is new, Benny?"

"Not much except my name is Ben now."

"Ben? Ma must hate that."

"Yeah, she does. She still calls me Benny."

"I think I will too."

"OK, Gordie."

"Oh, I hear you've got a radio. Did you bring it with you?"

"Here," I said picking up my transistor off the floor beside my suitcase. "What do you think this is – a hockey puck?" I then set it down on the floor and kicked it between the posts (legs) of a nearby chair. "He shoots! He scores!"

"I know it right now. It's a rabbit," exclaimed Gord.

"Aunt Becky's coming! Aunt Becky's coming!" I yelled.

Then we started laughing uncontrollably.

"What the hell's wrong with you two?" asked Paula. "You're like a couple of kids."

"I can't help it. I'm only nine," I replied.

"Are you an eight-day clock or a sewing machine?" Gord blurted out between fits of laughter.

"I told him Julie don't go!" I declared.

By this time, Gord and I were in hysterics and Paula had left the room. I surmised that she didn't appreciate the humour of Wayne and Schuster. Nor that of Benny and Gordie either, for that matter. She must have thought that we were off our rocker. I guess she wasn't that far off.

This visit, I had enough time to not only see Brendan, Sneezy, Flip, and Dork but the other regulars such as Birdbrain, Pooh, and Sean Becker. That reminds me that I met a girl that I hadn't seen before – an attractive blonde from Yarker. Her name was Wendy Becker. We talked a bit and she seemed quite friendly. When I mentioned her to Sean, I learned that they were cousins. I kidded Sean that there was certainly no resemblance – Wendy was good-looking. Other than that I did nothing and had a great time.

Very early in the New Year of 1966, Charley disappeared. We looked everywhere and knocked on every door. Bill and I also scouted out the apartment next door where we worked. But we never saw Charley again. We never knew what happened to him although we had a list of suspects with one name on it. This time Lily and I told The Old Man that we definitely didn't want another cat as long as we lived in Toronto. Ma also emphasized our wishes to The Old Man. And I got the feeling that he was only too willing to oblige.

That January, a new show started on TV that had a big impact on the conversation at Markham Avenue Collegiate and elsewhere in North America. It was Batman. Everyone would talk like Robin or Batman. This was especially prevalent during our swimming class. I'll give you an example.

"Holy ice cubes, Batman," I said to Ron Baxter one day after submerging myself in the pool. "This water is freezing."

"Beware the bat-hooks, Robin," stated Ron as he pointed to the hooks on the side of the pool. "You don't want to catch your Bat-balls on them."

"Holy scrotum, Batman. I'm glad you warned me. That would be painful."

"One must pay attention at all times, Robin. Safety at school is very important especially when it comes to your privates. Make sure you remember that, Robin."

"Holy castration, Batman. That's a valuable lesson."

"Indeed, Robin. Indeed."

"Come on you two, get swimming laps and shut up," shouted the instructor as he pulled us back to reality. "This is not drama class."

So we swam like maniacs, and this was one of those times that I had to place my head over the bat-bowl after class.

I remember a few more things about Markham Avenue Collegiate that winter and spring. Four of the school's students (including two from our class) appeared on the TV show 'Reach For The Top'. That was the one hosted by Alex Trebek which featured teams of different schools competing in answering skill-testing and knowledge questions. I think we won one week but lost the next week, but I'm not sure. Then there was English class. I was hopeless in it. I had pulled my socks up in Latin and now English was my worst subject. The teacher would read a word or two from a poem, short story, or novel and then lead a thirty minute discussion on why the author chose that particular word or words to use. She always seemed to ask me but I had no clue.

"Why do you think Blake used the word 'symmetry' here?" she asked one day. "Ben, what do you think?"

"Because he couldn't think of a better word to rhyme with 'eye' so he faked it," is what I thought.

"   ," is what I actually said.

That's right. I would just sit there and say nothing at all. I didn't even say, "I don't know." I just waited for something brilliant to come to me but it never did. It used to drive the teacher crazy. There were a few days that I actually enjoyed that class though. It was during one of the Jewish holidays when our class was down to only five students. Our lesson was on the play 'Zoo Story' by Edward Albee. I really enjoyed that diversion from the usual fare.

Another memory that I have is of one of the girls in another Grade 12 class. Her name was Alexandra and she was gorgeous. She actually won Queen of the Prom (or Queen of something or other). It was a well-deserved victory. I would think about Alexandra in English class whenever I got bored. But I never ever exchanged as much as a 'hello' with her. But I could dream. I was good at that. I wasn't the only one that dreamt about Alexandra though. I remember one of my male classmates staring at her as she walked by and then shaking before breaking into song. "Here it comes, here it comes, here comes my nineteenth nervous breakdown."

That spring, Bill and I continued going to Marlie games and also took in a few more movies. We saw 'A Man Could

Get Killed' starring James Garner and featuring the Frank Sinatra song 'Strangers In The Night'. Not a bad song for ol' blue-eyes. During the Easter break, I went to visit Brendan in Newburgh again. Not much exciting happened that trip, which I need to inform you about, except for seeing and conversing with Wendy Becker again. About a week after returning to Toronto, I arrived home from school to hear some surprising news from Ma.

"There's a letter for you, Benny. It's on the kitchen counter."

"And it looks like a girl's writing," Lily teased. "Benny has a girl-friend."

"I don't have a girlfriend. I have no idea who's writing me."

The letter was from Wendy Becker. She said how much she enjoyed my company and how she was looking forward to seeing me again in the summer. She was hoping that we could continue to write to each other on a regular basis. And she said that she missed me and some other stuff that I'm not going to tell you. I couldn't believe it. Maybe Lily was right. I also wondered how Wendy got my address. I thought that she must have liked me to go to the trouble of seeking out that information. I'd never had a letter from a girl before. Later Lily asked me who the letter was from. "Never mind," was all I replied.

12 – The Skunkmobile

The next day during study class – a break between two real lessons – I sat and wrote a return letter to Wendy Becker. I remember quite clearly where I was because the study class was in the cafeteria and I was sitting at a table with a girl I didn't know. The smell of her perfume was so strong that it was hard to concentrate on anything else. Before long my nose started to run and I began to sniffle because I didn't have any Kleenex on me. Just before the bell rang to signify the end of the class, the highly perfumed girl passed me a tissue and spoke for the first time.

"Here take this. Next time if you have a cold bring some Kleenex. It was disgusting listening to you."

"Thanks," was all I managed to reply but I felt like saying, "I don't have a cold. It's your bloody, strong, disgusting smelling perfume that's making me sniffle." But I felt that discretion was the better part of valour.

Anyway, I am getting sidetracked once again. I finished the letter to Wendy, put it in an envelope, took it home, and put it in the top drawer of my dresser. And there it sat. Don't ask me why I never mailed it. Maybe I wasn't ready for another relationship. I was still falling in love with every second girl that I met. How could I choose just one? Or perhaps, I didn't want a girlfriend to distract me from my main purpose for visiting Newburgh – to visit Brendan, Sneezy, Flip, Dork, Sean and all my other friends. After all I was only seventeen, and I had too much fun to experience yet to get tied down. Or then again, I was probably just too shy and embarrassed to put feelings to words and then actually send them to someone that I liked. So the letter just sat in my drawer gathering dust.

Later in the spring of '66, two things happened which shaped subsequent life directions and decisions. The first was my purchase of the Rolling Stones album 'Big Hits (High Tide & Green Grass)'. That event increased my appreciation of the Stones to a level higher than the Beatles and officially transformed me into a Stones fanatic. The second circumstance was the dismissal of The Old Man from the electronics company. That event officially transformed The Old Man into a full-time drunk. He only had an apartment to take care of now so what was to stop him from drinking twenty-four hours a day. I won't bore you with the details of any of his drunks at this point. But it is suffice to believe me when I say that his bouts of drunkenness and abusiveness increased dramatically. There was no boss around to watch his moves; he was his own master. And Hell just got hotter for us.

There was one other disturbing occurrence that spring. The Montreal Canadiens won the Stanley Cup. Again! Bill thought that was great and let me know it. And the last thing to tell you before the summer of '66 begins was that we all passed our grades. I somehow managed to squeak through English with a passing grade. I would be heading into Grade 13 the next year still with no idea what I wanted to be when I grew up. Bill had finished Grade 12 which was the furthest that he could go in his four-year course. So he was faced with a decision on his future. More about that later. Lily had just completed Grade 7 and thus would be entering Grade 8 in the fall. Boy, she was growing up fast.

It was now summer and time to head off again to you

know where – Newburgh. Now I could go for a couple of weeks at a time. You probably think that I must have been selfish to take off and leave Ma and Lily at home with The Old Man. Yes, Bill was still there then, but that's no excuse. Perhaps you're right. Maybe I was self-absorbed but Ma would have been the first to defend my excursions to our old hometown. She realized that I didn't have any true friends in Toronto and more than encouraged me to go. I guess I feel guilty about it now but Ma didn't want me to fret about it. That's just the way Ma was. She had explained why we couldn't leave The Old Man for good; nevertheless, she swore that having a drunken father wasn't going to prevent us kids from having a normal childhood. Well, at least as normal as possible in the situation. She certainly didn't want to see me sitting at home sulking. Ma also saw this as keeping up her part of the bargain that she made to us upon agreeing to go to Toronto in the first place. There, I feel a little better now that I got that off my chest.

So off I went to stay with Brendan again. Packing for Newburgh was fun. After I placed about twenty-five record albums in my suitcase, there wasn't much room for other luxuries such as underwear and socks. But I still managed to fit all the necessities into my case.

Upon arrival, one noticeable change to Newburgh was the creation of a new park. It was located back behind Dorchester's garage along the flat part of the river. It was situated where no one ever went except in the winter to skate, or on Halloween when being pursued by police. None of us could understand why the town had built a park there; we all thought that it should have been located at the dam. After all that's where everyone spent hot summer days. So about twenty to thirty of us boys and girls spent one day cleaning up the whole area around the dam. We cleared out brush, fallen trees, garbage, and other unsightly objects. The dam area had never looked better. Then someone made a small wooden sign which we hung from one of the trees close to the river. It read, 'Great Elk Park'. No one would ever use the official town park except for tourists, and there were none of those in Newburgh. Why would there be?

A few days after arriving, Sneezy, Brendan and I were sitting in front of the Newburgh Lunch when I saw Wendy Becker walk around the corner from Water Street. She was with Kelly Weston a friend of Lily's who lived further down our old street. They walked by and we all said hello to the two girls. Kelly said, "Hello Benny, how are you? How's Lily?" Wendy never said a word. She never even acknowledged me. I guess she was pissed off at me for ignoring her letter. And who could blame her. I certainly didn't, so I didn't attempt to offer an explanation. I didn't have one anyway. We never spoke again. I looked at Wendy and thought what an idiot I am. She was as pretty as ever. I also noticed something else. Kelly was growing into an attractive girl as well.

I soon erased my doubts about not wanting to go steady with one girl by dancing my qualms away. One day a couple of girls came to Brendan's place to listen to records. And to my surprise we all started dancing. The girls were Jill Cox and Janet Washington who I have only mentioned in passing before. Jill lived next door to Brendan while Janet lived at the other end of town near to our first Newburgh residence – Chance's Place. Jill was about my age while Janet was Brendan's age. In other words a year or two younger. First we danced to fast songs like 'Hanky Panky' and then the proceedings got slower with 'Pretty Flamingo'. When I danced with Jill I thought that I really liked her. And then I danced with Janet and I liked her. At the end of the day I danced more with Janet and Brendan kicked up his heels with Jill. I thought that it was a great time even if Brendan's brothers Philip and Jimmy were sitting there watching us and making snide remarks. And Brendan's mother (named Mary like Ma) was there too but she didn't pick on us near as much.

After we got dance fever, we started attending the barn dances which happened about a mile out of town. They were always well attended and the parking lot would be full of cars.

A live band would play. Most of what they played was country but they would play the odd rock song as well. Not really my first choice of music but it was fine for dancing with Janet Washington. There was also another girl that I danced with quite a bit. She was from Sudbury and was only visiting Newburgh for the summer. Her name was Beverly Coleman. I couldn't understand what a girl from Sudbury was doing in Newburgh for the summer; I guess she couldn't understand a boy from Toronto vacationing there either. A lot of the boys had a crush on Beverly including Pooh who made it obvious.

The funny part about the barn dances was watching the mass exodus of all the boys whenever a square dance commenced. We would all head outside and have a drink of beer that someone had brought in the trunk of their car or else we would steal a swig of rye from a mickey hidden in the inside pockets of our jackets. When the square dance ended everyone would make their way back inside to continue their dancing ways. I have to admit, that a few times I let Janet, Beverly, or some other girl grab me and force me to participate in the rectangular dance ritual. I never understood what the caller was saying, hence I followed the lead of others. I guess there were worse fates to suffer than being swung around the floor by four different girls in one dance. I still preferred to escape outside for a drink though. Depending on how many times I made it outside previously during the night, my desire to remain for the hoofing could increase.

That was about it as far as highlights for that trip. When I got back to Toronto, it was time for two more surprises. We were moving again and Bill was leaving home to join the army. Where we moved was further up Bathurst Street around Finch Avenue. The Old Man got a job as a superintendent of a bigger apartment up there. This one was big enough – about a dozen stories, I think – that The Old Man didn't require any other occupation. He would now be a full-time super guy. That wasn't exactly good news. But there were some good points about the move. We now had a two-bedroom apartment (I think it was on the sixth floor) which meant that Lily got her own room. The master bedroom was large so my bed was placed in the same room and only a few feet away from that of Ma and The Old Man. If that sounds weird to you, I agree. That's what I thought too. I knew that the bed placement was going to lead to some uncomfortable situations. The apartment setup was pretty standard with a fair-sized living room shaped like the letter 'L' so that the one area was the dining room. The kitchen was quite a bit bigger than that in our other apartment. The other good feature was a swimming pool. It actually was behind the neighbouring building, but it was shared between the two. The Old Man and the other superintendent also shared the duties of caring for the pool. I had never lived where there was a pool before. I thought that was pretty cool.

As I mentioned, Bill did not move with us. I found myself once more having to face the difficult task of saying goodbye to Bill. Except this time I knew I wouldn't be seeing him again real soon. He was heading out to Alberta for his training. It was a sad day for all of us – but especially for Ma – when we watched Bill pull away in some friend's car. We were now a very small family. Lily and I didn't even have any pets to keep us company. It was going to seem awful quiet. On second thought, I guess The Old Man would ensure that that wouldn't be the case.

After the move, I decided to determine how many places that I had lived in my life. It worked out to seventeen. The same as my age and also my lucky number. Seventeen different domiciles in seventeen years. It was hard to believe. But figure it out; it was true.

After a few days, The Old Man introduced me to a young couple who were new tenants in the building.

"Hey Benny, you should talk to Mark and Sylvia here. They know the Beatles."

"Is that right?" I asked.

"Well," not quite right answered the young woman whom I conjectured was Sylvia. "We're from Liverpool and we know friends who have met them. They say they're nice young lads."

I now recognized the Liverpudlian accent as I continued to question them, "Have you ever seen them play live?"

"No, we haven't," continued Sylvia, "but we know lots of people that saw them at the Cavern. You know, before they made it big."

"That's great," I commented.

"The music scene is quite exciting there now," added Mark. "There's also Gerry and the Pacemakers, the Dave Clark Five, and many more."

"What about the Rolling Stones?" I asked.

"Oh, they're from London," answered Sylvia. "But they're pretty good too. Do you like them?"

"Yeah, they're my favourite group. What about the Animals?"

"Oh, you don't like that dirty, shaggy lot, do you?" replied Sylvia. "They're from up North – Newcastle, I think."

"Yeah, I don't mind them but the Rolling Stones are my favourite."

"The Stones are OK, but the Animals are just that," commented Sylvia. "But the Beatles are the best."

"They're great too," I agreed.

On the first sunny, hot day I headed downstairs with Lily to check out the pool. It was great. I did flips off the diving board – frontwards and backwards. It was a ball. I also noticed two girls by the poolside. One was a blonde in a green striped bikini and the other was a dark-haired girl in a one-piece suit. I fell for the blonde but they were both attractive. I couldn't believe it when they came over and introduced themselves. They welcomed us to the building and said that they hoped to see us around lots. The blonde's name was Lynne (I can't recall her last name); the brunette was called Sandra Sanderson. You can see why I can remember her entire name. They even invited us to go to Yorkdale Shopping Mall with them and some of their friends the next night. I already much preferred my new home to my previous one.

Also at this time, my brother Ernie and his wife Ruth were now living in an apartment in Brampton, and with us now located in northern Toronto (or Willowdale to be exact), we weren't really that far apart. That meant that Ernie and Ruth would be able to come for dinner almost every Sunday evening. And with the Brewers' Retail and the Liquor Control Commission closed on Sunday, we could usually count on The Old Man being sober that night of the week. No matter how much he bought on Saturday, it would most likely be all consumed by Sunday. So all in all, Sunday evenings were something to look forward to. Seeing Ernie on a regular basis partially compensated for the fact that our at-home family had shrunk in size.

I'm not sure if I mentioned earlier that Ernie was in the militia attached to an artillery regiment. Now with Bill in the Army and Brad formerly of the Air Force, it seemed only logical that I follow in their footsteps. At least, that's what Ernie thought. I wasn't so sure. He argued that I could then attend university and have the government pay for my way. He suggested that I attend RMC (Royal Military College) in Kingston, get my education, and spend a few years in the forces. I had nothing to lose. I could always get out later, if it wasn't for me. So I began to give the idea some serious thought. It did make sense. I could never afford to attend university on The Old Man's salary. And I couldn't think of anything else that jumped out at me. I didn't favour law because I never liked to argue. I was barely capable of expressing my opinions. Medicine had no appeal to me at all. Just thinking about the sight of a skinned rabbit hanging in our back shed one time in Hillsburgh made me feel queasy. I didn't even want to imagine what it would be like to operate on a human being. Many other careers I was too short for and then there was business. That sounded nauseating. So eventually, Ernie won me over to the possibilities of RMC. But I still wasn't really convinced it was what I really wanted to do. I mean for me, the best reason was still the fact that I would be in Kingston – close to Newburgh. Not really the best criteria for choosing my future.

I decided to put off the decision-making for a while, because in August it was time to go to Newburgh again for a few weeks before school resumed. Brendan and Dork picked me up at the bus depot in Napanee. Dork was driving a white car that looked vaguely familiar.

"Whose car is this?" I asked Dork.

"It's mine," said Dork. "I bought it from Sledgehammer." That was the mechanic at Dorchester's Garage. "I got it real cheap," added Dork with a grin.

I then climbed into the back seat of the car at the same time that Dork and Brendan got into the front.

"Whoa," I exclaimed, "what the hell is that smell? It smells like a dead skunk."

"Close," answered Dork. "My dog got sprayed by a skunk and then jumped into Sledgehammer's car. He tried everything to get rid of the smell. Without much luck."

"I can see, I mean smell, that."

"Now you know why Dork got the car cheap, eh Benny?"

"It's not so bad," I lied. "At least you have your own wheels. Your very own Skunkmobile."

"The Skunkmobile," that's perfect laughed Dork along with Brendan.

"Holy stench, Dork," I replied. "This Skunkmobile's great."

"Perhaps you should paint a black strip down the middle," deadpanned Brendan. "What do you think, Dork?"

"That's not a bad idea, maybe I will."

That night, Brendan and I stayed up half the night as usual listening to each other's latest additions to our record collection. I had brought about 30 albums (and less socks) with me this time. We finally settled into the single beds which were normally occupied by Brendan's brothers. Jimmy was in Brendan's bed while Phillip was away somewhere.

"The Stones are my favourite group now," I

commented.

"The Beatles are better," Brendan retorted.

"The Stones are better," I shot back.

"The Beatles."

"The Stones."

"Mick Jagger couldn't carry John Lennon's guitar."

"Paul McCartney couldn't carry Brian Jones' guitar. Or Mick Jagger's harmonica."

"The Toronto smog has destroyed your taste."

"You've spent too much time in the Skunkmobile. The smell has ate your brain."

"The Beatles are better and that's that. Now let's go to sleep."

"The Stones are better."

"The Beatles."

"The Stones."

"The Beatles."

"The Stones."

"You want to fight over it?"

"Sure," Brendan said as he jumped onto my bed and started pounding my body with his fists.

I swung back while yelling and laughing at the same time, "The Stones are still better."

"Shut up and go to sleep," yelled Mary Casey. "If you don't go right to sleep now, you'll wish that you never heard of either group. You hear me, Brendan Thomas Casey?"

"Yes, mother. We're going to sleep now." Brendan then climbed back into his own bed.

Neither one of us could stop laughing. Moments later, I finally got control of myself and restrained from giggling. The night was once again silent.

"The Beatles," whispered Brendan.

The next day, we asked Sneezy to settle the argument.

"The Beatles or the Stones? Are you two crazy? I wouldn't walk across the street to the sales barn to see either one. Give me good music like Billy Joe Royal or Neil Diamond. Now that's real music."

"Down in the boondocks! Down in the boondocks! People put me down 'cause that's the side of town I was born in," we all sang in unison.

After a few days, the three of us were chauffeured to Beaver Lake by Dork. It was time to reestablish the Republic of Dorchestershire. It was pretty much a repeat of last summer's adventure. That is, some water skiing, some beer, some music, and a lot of laughs. My water skiing skills had even improved from the previous year. We met some girls from the southern United States who were even impressed by the way I rode the waves. That was a first – having a girl compliment me on my athletic abilities. In retrospect though, these were the same girls who wondered where they could go downhill skiing. Anyway after witnessing Dork slalom around on one ski, my small feat didn't seem near as dazzling. Dork did teach me a new trick though. I rode on this circular board as a replacement for the skis. I was able to manage rotating turns and everything. I felt like a water-show star. Another new addition to Dorchestershire, was this large motorized raft on pontoons. That was fun for cruising around the lake, having a beer (or two), and listening to the latest songs like 'Red Rubber Ball', 'Paint It Black', and 'Paperback Writer'. Of course, I told Brendan that 'Paint It Black' was better.

Upon our return to dry land in the village of Newburgh, we told Flip the Sausage the complete details about all the fun that he had missed. In order to make him feel better, we decided to party some more. We were sitting at the far end of town around the post office when Flip came up with one of his great lines.

"Wouldn't it be awful," he stated, "if you woke up and discovered that the entire world was covered in shit. You know, like three feet deep. Just shit everywhere. And you had to walk in it. Wouldn't that be a drag?"

We all looked at Flip like he had lost his mind and then fell on the ground in hysterics.

"How do you come up with this shit? Pardon the expression," said Sneezy. "You are a complete idiot, Flip."

137

"Why? Don't you think that would be a pain? Having to wade around in shit up to your neck."

"There's no hope for you, Flip," I commented. "No hope at all."

Another source of entertainment that summer was cruising the streets of Napanee. We would sit in somebody's car from Newburgh and just ride up and down the main street looking cool. We might even lay some rubber down. We must have impressed a lot of girls. Don't you think?

13 – Oh Christmas Tree

September came before I knew it and it was time to start Grade 13 and another new school. The school – Northern Hills Secondary School – was only a five-minute walk away from our apartment building. Lily's school (where she would be attending Grade 8) was a little further but not by much. Hey, now it doesn't take near as long to disclose everyone's grade level, does it? As a fresh new look for the new school year, I decided that it was time to change my hairstyle. Gone was the Elvis Presley look and the Brylcreem. Enter the Beatles look. Or should I say the Rolling Stones look. I didn't grow my hair much longer. All I did was stop combing my hair back in a ducktail and started combing it down so that I had bangs covering my forehead. And no more wet head. Picture Charlie Watts on the Stones '12 X 5' album. That's the appearance that I was going for. I wasn't quite ready for the Brian Jones style just yet. Nor probably was the school. They certainly frowned on long hair. The definition of long hair: when one's hair is touching their ears or collar. As far as the dress code went, jeans were a definite no-no. That wasn't unusual. That was probably true for all Ontario schools in 1966. That year I only had to enroll in five subjects. They consisted of Physics, Chemistry, Math A, Math B, and (ugh!)

English. No choice on that one. I was just as hopeless as ever. But it was farewell to all other languages and Physical Education. No more learning how to skinny-dip.

Stardate: 1513.1 or September 8, 1966 (to the unconverted), Star Trek debuted on television. I was hooked on the missions of the U.S.S. Enterprise and its captain James T. Kirk right from the opening scenes of the first episode 'The Man Trap'. I was enthralled by the fact that their uniforms looked so much like the pyjamas that we used to wear many years before. Were us Coopers ahead of our time? Now I had to fight to gain control of the TV from Lily and Ma on Friday nights. No mean task. They didn't want to miss Bewitched or My Three Sons. Luckily, in Toronto the same shows were often shown at different days and times. Once on the U.S. network station and another time (usually before) on the Canadian network or local station. That helped avoid a lot of hostile confrontations. Now all I needed was a colour television.

Later that fall, I finally came to the conclusion that I would accept Ernie's advice and attend Royal Military College. At least that's what I confided to Ernie one Sunday after dinner. However, I left my options open and prepared applications for the University of Toronto and Queen's University (in Kingston). I decided to even apply for Architecture at U of T. I hadn't forgotten that long ago ambition. In other words, I still wasn't really convinced by Ernie's persuasive arguments. I had gone back to Markham Avenue Collegiate Institute one evening to attend my Grade 12 graduation. I couldn't understand that. I didn't feel like I was graduating from anything just yet. I had just changed schools; that's all. Nothing new or exciting about that. But Ma, Lily, and The Old Man still came to watch me accept my Grade 12 diploma. And Ma was still as proud as punch. Anyway the purpose of relating this episode was to tell you that I witnessed a former classmate, and current RMC cadet, accept his diploma. He was wearing a bright red uniform topped by a pillbox shaped red hat resting sideways on his head which was sporting a closely-cropped brush cut. I thought, "Do I really want to look like that? What am I doing? Well, I guess it's only a haircut. It won't change my personality. Will it? Can I look like that and still listen to the Stones? Oh well, I'll get my education that's the important thing."

When we said our goodbyes to Bill, I feared that we were losing our protector. That The Old Man would take the opportunity to be more obnoxious and dangerous than ever. I was right. I assume Ma had the same fears. I wasn't ready to replace Bill and fight back against The Old Man. I don't know why, I just couldn't. Neither physically nor verbally. I was always paralyzed into numbness. I never knew what to say other than the occasional pleadings, "Leave Mom alone." I guess the exception was when The Old Man would start on Lily. That would make me lose control and I might say things like, "Shut the fuck up, you goddamned stinking, lousy excuse for a father." When things got to that point, we would usually vacate the premises and go visit Fred and Them. If it was the middle of the night, then that was a different story.

One night, I was lying in my bed attempting to sleep. Ma was in her bed a few feet away. I wasn't sure if she was asleep but I doubted it. I could hear The Old Man in the living room. The television was blaring some late night movie but even that couldn't drown out the curses coming from the bastard.

"Jesus fucking Christ! Where the fuck is that gray-haired old cunt. I want something to eat. Where am I, in a fucking whorehouse? That's all she cares about – fucking all day and all night and with anything that moves. I'd like to take a fucking knife to that whore and do the whole world a favour. Goddamn it! That's just what I'll do."

I sat up. I was shaking. I listened but I couldn't hear The Old Man moving, however he kept up the rant. Eventually I laid back down with my eyes and ears wide open.

"The knife is not good enough for that gray-haired, old bag. She needs to learn what a cunt she is. I still need my

141

fucking dinner though. Mary! Can you get me something to eat, dear? I'm starving. Please, Mary?"

Ma didn't answer but I knew she wasn't asleep. How could she be? Suddenly the bedroom door swung open wide. The Old Man pulled all the bed covers off of Ma within a second of entering the room.

"Get up you lazy bitch. Get me something to eat, will you!"

"Don't Garf!" shouted Ma. "Give me back the covers. I'm trying to sleep. It's three in the morning. You can get your own food. Benny's in the next bed. He's trying to sleep too."

"Benny? Benny? What the fuck do I care about him for? He's turned against me just like the rest of you. You made sure of that, you gray-haired, old bag. He can rot in hell as far as I care. Now, get up!"

The Old Man then quickly grabbed one of Ma's legs and started to twist it as he pulled Ma down and half-off the end of the bed. I had finally seen and heard enough.

"Let go of Mom, you bastard!" I screamed as I jumped at the assailant.

"Garf, you're hurting me," cried Ma.

"I'll give you something that hurts, you…."

I hit The Old Man in the chest with the full force of my shoulder after a running, jumping assault. He fell backwards stunned and out of breath.

"Get the hell out of this room!" I screamed. I noticed that Lily was standing outside the door as I continued to direct my attention to The Old Man. "You leave Mom alone or I'll … Get out!"

When The Old Man regained his balance, I pushed him out the door. Lily sidestepped away just in time and then entered the bedroom. I slammed the door shut and stood with my body pressed against the door with all the force that I could muster. I doubted though that I was strong enough to hold off The Old Man.

"Goddamn you all!" we heard through the door. "I don't

need any of you."

We then heard steps towards the door into the hallway. And then there was the loud noise of a door slamming.

"Are you OK, Mom?" asked Lily. "The bastard hurt you, didn't he?"

"My leg hurts some, Lily dear. Could you please pass me the covers from the floor? Turn on the light, Benny. I want to see what he did to my leg." I turned on the light as Ma requested. "I think it's OK. Just a little red. You can see The Old Man's fingerprints on my leg. Look. But I think I'll be OK. Let's go to sleep." I flicked the light switch back off. "Come lie down with me, Lily. I don't want you in your own room. I don't trust what your father will do next. He's getting worse all the time. He keeps threatening to kill me now. I'm afraid that..." Ma could not finish the thought. "Why don't you go back to bed, Benny?"

"No, Ma. I'm going to guard the door for a while. You and Lily go to sleep. I'm OK."

"I hate The Old Man," stated Lily. "I hate him."

"Me too," I responded. "Me too."

Then Ma broke into tears. I stood by the door as Lily and Ma exchanged hugs and tears.

"I promise that we'll leave him one day," Ma said. "Somehow we'll manage."

I stood by the door for about a half of an hour. I heard no sounds other than the sobs of Lily and Ma. And the beating of my own heart. I eventually crawled back into my bed shaking and then burst into tears.

I was looking forward to Christmas Day with great anticipation. Our tree (a real one as always) was up and carefully decorated by Ma, Lily, and me with all our lights, bulbs, and other ornaments. Many of the decorations were older than Lily and others had been accumulated over the years since the beginning of this saga. On Christmas Eve, various presents were deposited under the tree. And some had intrigued me with what their contents could be. We were all ready for bed around midnight but there was no sign of

The Old Man. He had disappeared sometime in the afternoon. Many of the tenants had given The Old Man decorated bags that suspiciously appeared to contain either wine or liquor. As well The Old Man had purchased beer earlier. So we had a notion what The Old Man could have been up to. Regardless, we headed off to bed and hoped for the best – that The Old Man was passed out cold and would reappear tomorrow morning sick as a dog. Then he would be in his conciliatory mood for Christmas dinner when Ernie and Ruth arrived. And that was the other reason that I had been looking forward to Christmas Day – to see Ernie and Ruth. It was quite a long time before I finally was able to enter the land of slumber. I was sound asleep when I was awoken by a loud thud – a sound like someone falling.

"Whoa, Jesus. Mary! Mary, I'm drunk again. I just fell down. I'm so drunk. It's the whiskey I guess. I better have a beer instead. Where is everyone? It's Christmas! Why aren't the lights on? The tree lights should be on. It's Christmas. What do they think this is? A cat-house? Why aren't the fucking lights on? I'll put them on." There was a pause for a minute. "There. That's better. Where the fuck did I put my beer?"

The next sound I heard was the television. The Old man continued to talk to himself but somehow I went to sleep. When I awoke again, the house was quiet. I then heard Ma moving in her bed. I looked across to see that Ma was the only occupant of the bed.

"What time is it, Ma?"

"Just shortly after six, Benny."

"Has The Old Man passed out?"

"I think so, I haven't heard him for a while."

"Did you sleep at all? I slept better than I thought I would."

"No, I've been awake all night. I'm glad that you were able to sleep though. I wonder if Lily slept. Let's lie for a bit longer. I'll get up around seven. OK, dear?"

"Sure Ma. That's fine with me."

At seven o'clock, I got up along with Ma and headed into the living room. I didn't bother to get dressed yet. I just put my housecoat on. When we stepped into the living room, Ma and I were both in for a surprise. The Old Man was sitting up on the couch with a bottle of beer in his hand and an empty rye bottle sitting on the coffee table in front of him. His eyes were wide open.

"What the fuck are you two staring at? Can't a man drink in peace in his own house? You goddamned, fucking, old bag. Leave me the fuck alone!"

"I didn't say a word," answered Ma. "I was just hoping that we could have had a peaceful Christmas. You know that Ernie and Ruth are coming later today."

"Christmas? That's just a load of shit. Don't talk to me about Christmas for Christ's sake. What the fuck do I care about Christmas? And Ernie and Ruth. Who gives a fuck? You goddamned, gray-haired, old bag. Don't tell me what to do in my own goddamned place. I do all the work around here while the rest of you sit on your ass watching TV. Or you're out fucking someone's dog. And that fucking daughter of yours is just as bad. Fuck you all!"

"Merry Christmas to you too," I said.

The Old Man then slammed his beer bottle down upon the coffee table and sent the whiskey bottle flying across the room and under the tree. He then jumped to his feet. I was surprised that he could still stand.

"Christmas! I'll show you what I think about Christmas."

The Old Man then grabbed a string of lights and started to pull them from the tree. The tree started leaning over towards the direction that he was pulling.

"Be careful," advised Ma. "You'll pull the tree down!"

The Old Man then yanked harder on the lights and then grabbed a tree branch and pulled the Christmas tree to the floor. The Old Man then grabbed one of the bulbs and threw it with all of his force to the hardwood floor. It smashed into pieces. Ma and I both watched as The Old Man continued his attack.

"Please Dad, don't," I pleaded.

But he just kept the assault up as he mumbled and swore. Three more ornaments had met their demise.

"Come on, Benny. Let's grab the presents and get out of here."

"I'll help," It was Lily – fully dressed. "Let's go, Mom. Let's go to Fred and Them's place."

"That's a good idea, Lily. Benny, get dressed. We're going."

"If you go," The Old Man threatened, "There won't be a tree left. There won't be anything left. I'll smash every fucking thing in this house."

"Go ahead," said Ma calmly. "We're not staying. You've already ruined everybody's Christmas already."

"And it's not a house. It's an apartment," I added sarcastically.

"Goddamn it!" shouted The Old Man. "You're all dirt. Dirt under my feet!"

He then started jumping up and down on a string of lights splintering the bulbs into tiny pieces. By this time I was already dressed and Ma and Lily had all the presents in a bag. We then went out the door as quick as we could. We went down the stairs rather than taking the time to stand and wait for an elevator. We were all worried that The Old Man might appear as we stood by the bus stop but fortunately a Bathurst bus arrived soon after.

"What about Ernie and Ruth?" I asked Ma after we were seated on the bus.

"I'll call them from Fred and Them's place. Maybe they can come for dinner another night."

I then sat in silence for the rest of the bus trip. The bus was almost empty. Everyone else was at home opening their presents, or sleeping, or just living a normal life. Me? I was tired, angry, depressed, and confused. I wished that my father would die. And I was willing to assist.

Although Fred and Them made us feel at home, none of us could relax and enjoy the festivities. I can't even recall what our presents were. I had other things on my mind at the time. We decided to spend our Christmas night at Fred and Them's and then we hesitantly returned home the next day. We entered the apartment not quite sure what to expect. There was absolutely nothing left on the tree. There was not one ornament intact. Even the non-breakable ones were ripped apart; the garland was shredded, and every single light was demolished. The good news was that there was no other visible damage elsewhere. And The Old Man was passed out on the bed with every bottle in the place empty. None of us could hide our tears as we started to pick up and sweep up the damaged decorations. Suddenly Lily found one glass ornament that somehow had managed to evade the wrath of The Old Man.

"Look Mom, this one got away," said Lily, almost bringing a smile to Ma's face.

It was a New Year – 1967 – a year to celebrate in Canada. Our country was a hundred years old and nationalism seemed to be at an all-time high. Centennial celebrations were planned and the World's Fair was going to be in Montreal that summer. Myself, I was just looking for a change in my life. A change that preferably removed The Old Man from the picture. I thought about RMC in the fall. That would take me far away but what would happen to Ma and Lily? They needed an escape route as well. I feared what would happen to them when I left home. I needed to find a way to make some money and then we could all leave The Old Man to cook in his own stew. I told this to Ma one day while she was adding the latest clippings to her scrapbook. The latest was a picture of Ernie from the Guelph paper. He was in his army uniform with some other artillery officers.

"I guess you'll have to do something to make a lot of money," said Ma, "and become famous."

"Yeah," I answered, "I noticed that there's hardly anything about me in the scrapbook. Other than in class graduation lists and a hockey summary of a goal where I still haven't touched the puck. I'll have to do something to get my picture in the paper like Ernie and Brad."

"Just don't rob a bank," laughed Ma.

"No, I gave that up when I stopped playing cowboys with Sammy."

A few days later, I did have my name on a school program, though. I received an Honours Pin for my marks during the first term. The presentation was during the school day so Ma didn't get to see it. I wore a bright purple shirt with a high-collar and black pants with no jacket or tie. My hair was getting longer – more like Charlie Watts on 'Aftermath' now. My hair was definitely touching my collar when I wore my purple shirt. All the other honour students were dressed up. The boys in jackets and ties, and the girls in long dresses. More than one boy commented on my attire. I remember one who thought I was appropriately outfitted though. His name was Dennis Webster. Dennis had the longest hair in the class. So long that a few days later he was sent home and told not to come back until he had got it cut. Dennis returned the next day looking pretty much the same swearing that he did get a haircut. After the homeroom teacher questioned which hair he got cut, Dennis was sent home again. He stayed away for two more days before returning with sufficiently shorter hair. When Dennis was first expelled, I made sure that the hair on the side of my head wasn't over my ears and tucked it behind them. And then after a few days I decided to break down and get a haircut too. Well, at least a trim.

On the morning of February 2nd, I was ready to head out the door and off to school when The Old Man spoke.

"Are you going to come with me tonight, Benny? I'm going to go get a colour TV."

"That sounds great, Dad. Where are we going?"

"Just to the corner, but I want you to help me pick the best one. OK?"

"Sure," I replied with visions of finally seeing what colour Kirk and Spock's uniforms were. "Bye, I've got to go. Bye Ma, I'll see you next week."

"Next week?" questioned Ma.

"Oh, I'm just joking. I'll see you right after school. I have to study for a Chemistry test tomorrow."

"Don't even joke about something like that. Now, what if something terrible was to happen. How would you feel?"

"If I was killed I wouldn't feel a thing. Sorry Ma, just joking again. Anyway I have clean underwear on."

"Come here Benny, so that I can slap you across the ears," joked Ma.

I laughed and went out the door quickly before Ma could catch me to give me a cuff. "Bye Ma, see you tomorrow," I yelled through the door.

14 – Zapped

I was lying down. I looked up and saw a white ceiling. I heard people around me. Then I saw that Ma was standing beside me.

"Where am I, Ma?"

"Oh, Benny. It's so good to hear you. You're in the hospital."

"What? What am I doing here?"

"There was an accident at the school. Do you remember?"

"No, did I get hit by a car on the way to school?"

"No, Benny. It happened at school. A terrible accident. I'll tell you later. Just rest, dear. You were electrocuted." And then Ma started crying.

"I'll be fine, Ma. But I guess I'll miss that Chemistry test."

I looked up and saw a bright light above me. There were many people dressed in white all around me. Someone was holding my hand. It was Ma. Lily was standing beside her. I was in a different room.

"Hello Benny," said a voice from the other side of the bed. It was The Old Man. "I guess the colour TV will just have to wait until you get better. How are you feeling?"

"I'm fine. Where am I?"

"In Camden Hospital, Benny," The Old Man replied.

"In an Intensive Care room," added Lily.

"What am I doing here? I'm fine. Can I go home soon?"

"Benny," said Ma, as she squeezed my hand. "You are very, very sick. You have burns on your head, your neck, and your feet. Your feet are…" continued Ma attempting to finish the sentence, but I couldn't understand her between the sobs.

"Don't worry, Ma. I'll be fine."

The next time that I opened my eyes, the scenery had changed again. I glanced around and saw that I was in a room with only one bed. There were two people sitting in the room with me. They both were wearing white hospital gowns and surgical masks. They looked like two doctors ready for an operation.

"Hello Benny," said Ma through the mask as she held my hand once more. "How do you feel now?"

"Fine. My feet hurt a bit though. Where's Lily and Dad?"

"They went home to get some sleep. It's the middle of the night. Ernie is there too. He was here earlier. I guess you didn't see him."

"No, you should have woke me up. Oh, my head hurts too. Ma, my feet really hurt."

"I'll check your medication," said the other masked occupant of the room. "I'll be right back."

"Who's that?" I asked.

"A nurse, dear. There will be someone here with you all day and night."

"Then you should go home, Ma. And get some rest."

"No, dear. I won't be able to sleep anyways. I feel better just sitting here holding your hand. Is that OK, Benny?"

"Sure Ma. It feels nice."

I looked up. Ma was gone. There was someone sitting in a chair near the bed. I didn't recognize who it was behind the mask. I guessed it was a different nurse. I knew it wasn't Ma. Not unless she had changed her hair and skin colour recently.

"Good morning, Benny. How are you today?" said The Old Man from a chair at the end of the bed.

"Oh, hi Dad. I didn't see you there. How long have you been here?"

"Just a few minutes. It's seven in the morning. I sent your mother home to get some sleep."

"Will she be back later?"

"Of course, Benny. You're going to have lots of visitors later," continued The Old Man as he moved to stand on the left side of the bed. "Ernie will be here and Gordie. And Lily, of course. Claudia will be up tomorrow or the next day too."

"Why is everybody coming? It's not like I'm on my deathbed or anything?"

"Ernie called everyone last night. They are very worried about you. You had a serious accident, Benny. Billy and Brad would come too, if they could. We'll just call them again and let them know how you are doing. Your mother will call Aunt Becky today. You are famous now, Benny. Your picture is all over the papers – the front page in every paper."

"What happened, Dad? I don't know what happened to me."

"You don't remember anything?"

"No, the last thing that I remember was when I left for school. Did the accident happen before school?"

"No, Benny. The school was putting up this big balloon for the Centennial or something."

"Yeah, they were supposed to be letting a balloon go with free tickets in it. It was for the school's tenth anniversary. I remember that. They told us that they were going to be doing that. They told us that last week."

"Well for some reason they tied a wire to the balloon," explained The Old Man. "Some stupid idiot, I don't believe it; you learn this in grade school. Some stupid idiot decided to tie a copper wire to the balloon. A baby would know better. It hit the hydro lines – 27,000 volts according to the papers – and then you and another boy in the crowd. The boy that was holding the line was hurt too, but you were hurt the worse."

"Wow, 27,000 volts. How come I'm not dead?"

"Yes, you are a very lucky boy, Benny. I have to go soon. I won't come tonight. You'll have enough company then. There are only supposed to be two visitors at a time. I'll come again tomorrow morning. Is that OK?"

"Sure, Dad. That would be good."

"I love you, Benny. Get well soon. We all miss you."

"Bye, Dad. See you tomorrow."

I couldn't believe it. That was the best conversation that I had with The Old Man since who knows when. I was actually looking forward to his next visit. I then took the time to survey the scene and the damage. I was hooked up by needles to bags hanging from a couple of poles. I recognized the contents of the bags as blood, I.V., and unknown drugs. I felt that my head was wrapped in a large gauze bandage. Another was wrapped around my neck. Both of my legs were also covered in bandages from just below my knees to down and around my feet. A tent type structure had been placed on the bottom half of the bed in order to keep the weight of the blankets from pressing down on them. My head started to throb.

"You better lie back down," warned the nurse. "You've had enough excitement for this morning. It's time to get some rest."

"OK," I agreed.

After what seemed like only a few minutes, I awoke to see Ma sitting beside me once more. And Lily was with her again.

"Hi Ma. Hi Lily. How are you doing?"

"Hi Benny," said Lily.

"I'm doing OK, Benny. Considering," answered Ma. "How are you?"

"I'm fine. You look tired Ma."

"I guess I am, Benny. I was just talking to the doctor. They will be taking you to the operating room again in a few days – to look at your burns."

"I'll be fine, Ma. Don't worry," I said attempting to

comfort Ma before changing the subject. "I understand that I'm famous now. I finally got a story for your scrapbook."

"This is not quite what I had in mind, dear. Couldn't you have found another way? Do you remember what happened?"

"No, nothing, nothing at all. But Dad told me what happened. I was trying to be Benjamin Franklin, I understand. I was looking for electricity."

"It was awful what happened, Benny," advised Lily. "You should see the pictures. You look like you're dead."

"That's right," sighed Ma. "We shouldn't joke about it."

"Can I see the newspapers? I would like to read about it and see what they say. I can't remember anything."

"OK, dear," said Ma. "I'll bring them tomorrow."

"Thanks, Ma."

Soon Gordie was standing beside me. He like everyone else was wearing a white gown and a surgical mask.

"Trying to outdo me. Were you, Benny? There must be easier ways to get your picture and story in the paper."

Before long, Ernie and Ruth were visiting me.

"Hello Benny," said Ernie. "I only got hit by a train. Your story beats mine."

That's about the extent of what I recall from the first day and a half in the hospital. My mind wasn't too coherent. The next day, Ma brought in the stories from the Telegram and the Star. They differed slightly on the voltage. But the story that The Old Man told me was what was reported in the papers. Except the paper didn't mention that the wire was copper. There was a picture of me lying on the ground with the snow melted in a large circle around me. Lily was right. I looked deader than a doornail. The other boy – Rick Field – was also pictured similarly. The third boy – the one that was holding the wire to begin with – was let out of the hospital the same day. He was the lucky one. Rick Field was now in the next room. But Ma repeated what The Old Man had told me. That I was the one in the most serious condition. I started to read the stories.

"It says here that I am in extremely serious condition," I laughed. "They make it sound so dramatic."

"But you are in serious condition, Benny," argued Ma. "You're lucky to be alive. They still don't even know how badly you are hurt yet. They have to wait a few more days. You almost died."

"Oh," I said sheepishly. "I didn't know."

I then read the whole story about how the balloon crossed the road and made contact with the high-tension wires. They were 24,000 to 27,000 volts depending on which paper you believed. The third student who had been holding the wire let it go and it swung through the crowd striking me and Rick Field. The balloon was being hoisted to commemorate the school's tenth anniversary, just like I had thought. There was to be a Homecoming in a week or so and former Prime Minister John Diefenbaker was the main guest speaker. The weather balloon was originally going to be let loose but another course of action was taken when fears of it being sucked into the engine of an airplane were raised. There were a few different theories on why Rick and I had survived. Perhaps a first shock had stopped our hearts and a second one started them up again. Or maybe it was the fact that the wire crossed two different lines of different voltage causing it to snap in two and saving us from experiencing the full extent of the shock of the electricity. I had no theories. I figured that I just wasn't ready to die yet. Another point in our favour was the fact that Camden Hospital was just across the street from Northern Hills. I also read how I might have been saved by the rubber boots that I was wearing.

"What happened to my boots?" I asked Ma.

"There was nothing left of them, dear. They burnt right off your feet. I never saw them after. I don't know what they did with them."

"I liked those boots."

I then read how I was concerned that I was going to miss my exams.

"That's not what I said. I said that I guess I would miss

my Chemistry test. No big deal. I wasn't concerned. They make me sound like a brown-noser. The press are funny."

I continued to read the descriptions of the flash, the sparks, and how my face appeared to be on fire. One story explained how one student had given me mouth-to-mouth resuscitation. Another had a picture of Ma sitting in the emergency department of the hospital looking like a ghost. I chuckled when I read the caption – 'Mrs. Bennett Cooper'. And then I groaned when I read that they thought that I could be in the hospital for three to four weeks. When I expressed this to Ma she didn't say too much, but I guessed that she thought that was an optimistic estimate. It was not until later that night that the severity of the situation finally hit me. I was still covered in bandages and they were afraid to look under them. I just had to be patient and wait. I felt fear starting to rise within me but I quickly dismissed it.

"I'll be fine," I thought. "Just fine."

Because I was drugged and semi-conscious a lot of the time, I am not sure of the exact order of things during the next week. One day, Ma had thought that she had entered the wrong room. My face had swollen up so much that you couldn't distinguish any facial features – such as my nose. And I had turned black from the burns. Ma took one look at me and burst into tears. I remember Claudia coming to visit me and then immediately leaving the room. She came back in after a few minutes. Ma later explained to me that Claudia was very upset when she first saw me.

"That's not the dear little Benny that I remember," she had told Ma. "That poor boy."

"I'm fine," I had told Claudia.

The Old Man (or should I say Dad) never failed to visit me each morning. We would have conversations and laugh and even share our love. I had almost forgotten the fact that I hated him. Towards the end of the first week, I went back and forth to the operating room a few times so that the doctors could assess the damage. After a while, Ma finally told me what was wrong with her the day that I said she looked so tired.

"I spoke to Dr. Brown that day. I don't like him. He said that you might lose one or both of your feet. I tell you now because they have since told me that they think you won't lose them. You just need lots of skin grafts and time. Anyways, Dr. Brown told me that you may lose your feet and I said, 'Can't you save them, doctor. He's still a young boy.' And he just snapped at me. 'Don't worry about his feet; we don't even know if he's going to live yet.' That's what he said and just like that. I was shocked. It was like someone kicked me in the stomach. I thought that I was going to faint. I am so worried about you, Benny. What would I do without you?" Ma started to cry.

"Oh Ma, don't cry. I'll be fine. You'll see. I'm not going to die. And I'll be walking out of here before you know it. You just wait and see."

"I hope so, Benny. I love you."

"I love you too, Ma."

At some point, another bed was moved into my room. It belonged to Rick Field. We were to be roommates. And then John Diefenbaker came to visit us. The new principal of the school – Ted Connors – escorted him over. I think my head must have been a bit fuzzy at the time because I can't recall too much of the visit. I do know though that I didn't tell 'Dief' that I was a Lester B. fan. I don't think that I said much of anything. Did Diefenbaker wear a surgical mask? I really don't recollect. That necessity stopped somewhere around that time. A week or two later, Rick and I both received a nice letter from John Diefenbaker telling us what brave boys we were. And how we had demonstrated great courage. I didn't remember demonstrating anything. I thought that I just laid there like a log. I probably said, "I'm fine." That would have been about it.

Having a roommate was great. We had someone to share each other's pains and complaints with. And we would make each other laugh. Not such a good idea when your head is swathed in bandages. Let me tell you. I found out that Rick was in Grade 11 and was the world's biggest Elvis Presley fan. I didn't mind Elvis but you know who I liked better. Rick had seen every Elvis movie that had ever been made. I had seen a few but Love Me Tender was the only one that stood out for me. The others were just good drive-in fodder. But I told Rick that I liked them all. Not a lie but not exactly the truth.

Eventually, my skin started to peel exposing a bright pink layer underneath. Ma said that it looked like a new baby's skin. Dad said that maybe I wouldn't have to shave. I would have baby skin forever. I didn't like the sound of that. The old skin didn't come off easy though. And the new skin was sore. I went into surgery and had a few skin grafts on my neck and my feet – on both ankles. My head was still covered in bandages. The worst part about the grafting was the pain where the skin was taken. I didn't feel anything on my feet but my thighs hurt like hell. I needed lots of drugs to get me through the next few days. I screamed in agony a few times.

The newspapers reported that Rick and I were slowly recovering and improving. I read how our condition had been upgraded to satisfactory. However, it didn't feel 'satisfactory' to me. Lily would visit at least once a day while Ma kept coming two or three times a day. And I always told her that things were going well. In all seriousness, that's what I felt. I never doubted that I wasn't going to be walking home before long. I planned to water-ski at Beaver Lake that summer and attend RMC in the fall. I placed my full faith in the doctors. After all, the plastic surgeon's name was Dr. McCoy. How could I not trust 'Bones'?

When they finally removed the bandages from my head, I felt like Claude Rains in 'The Invisible Man'. What secrets would lie beneath those strips of cloth? Just a matted mess of hair and burnt flesh, as it turned out. Time for another operation to cleanse the wound. Later one of the nurses told me that she could see my brain through the hole in the top of my head. She almost had me believing her. I wondered what Gordie would say to me next time that he was up. He always thought that I had a hole in my head. Then it was time for an operation to place a small bit of skin over the wound. This one wasn't near as bad. They didn't take as much from my thighs as last time. I slowly lost the various tubes and such which were connected to my body and I could actually eat again. That was good news and bad news. Good news: Dad would bring me a small container of ice cream every morning. Bad news: the food at Camden Hospital (don't ever try one of their Veggie Burgers). Worse news: Bedpans. I was still confined to bed while my feet remained covered.

A month passed and I had not yet got out of bed. The highlight was one day when I slid into a chair so that they could make my bed. The look on Ma's face when she saw me sitting up in a chair was priceless. She was beaming. My feet were aching though and I was soon back in bed exhausted from the workout. At the beginning of March, I had an early birthday present. Ron Ellis came to visit me. For those who don't know – he was a Toronto Maple Leaf and a very good one. One of my favourite players. The school principal, Mr. Connors – had arranged it. He knew Ron Ellis from some other connection. Anyways, Ron came into the room and spoke to Rick and me, and gave us both autographed hockey sticks. My stick had belonged to Larry Hillman and it was signed by every current member of the Maple Leafs. I eventually deciphered every signature. Eddie Shack's name was in big, bold letters and was the most noticeable. I finally found Dave Keon's name. Ron Ellis also told us that he would give us tickets to a game when we got out of the hospital. He hoped it was during the playoffs when they were going for the Stanley Cup. During the next game, Ron Ellis scored a goal.

"He scored it for you, Benny," said Dad. "He said that he would score for you."

Funny, I didn't remember him saying that.

15 – A Learning Experience

I spent my eighteenth birthday in the hospital still confined to my bed. I had a load of visitors including Ma, Dad, Lily, Ernie, and Ruth. The nurses ignored the fact that the count was slightly higher than the limit of two. I received the new Rolling Stones album 'Between The Buttons' from Ma and the Eric Burdon and the Animals album 'Eric Is Here' from Lily. I was thrilled and requested that they bring in my record player and my radio. Dad also told me that he would rent a TV for me in the room. That was great because now I could watch Star Trek and Hockey Night In Canada again. I was getting kind of bored just sitting there doing nothing. When I looked at my legs, I noticed that they resembled toothpicks. I wasn't sure what I weighed but I knew that I had lost quite a few pounds. I wasn't getting much exercise. Physical activity at that point consisted of squeezing an orange or a ball in order to develop strength back in my hands. The electricity had affected my fine motor functions, so I had a lot of trouble even managing that routine.

During one of their visits, Lily and Ma mentioned that they were looking at all the get well cards that I had received. I had forgotten all about them. They were around the room when I wasn't too aware of anything. So I asked Ma to bring them in so that I could see them again. I was amazed at how many there were. Not just from my family but also from my Newburgh friends, classmates, Sandra Sanderson, Sammy Smale, Fred and Them, and some from people that I had no idea who they were. I assumed that many were students at Northern Hills that I didn't know. One card stood out. It was signed, "I miss you. Get well soon. Love from Your Secret Admirer." To this day, I have no idea who sent me that card. Lily teased me about it to no end.

As well as having my family visit daily, there were others that would call on me. Sandra Sanderson came to see me a few times. Some of my classmates would drop by too. And then there was Mr. Connors. He became a regular visitor. He even brought me a birthday present – 'The Temptations Greatest Hits'. And even my first girlfriend, Wendy Monahan visited one day. Ruth arranged that. I wished that I could have got out of bed that day. The other main visitors were three teachers. Now that I was feeling better, Mr. Connors thought that it was time for me to continue my education. And who was I to argue. He had arranged that teachers would come to the hospital once or twice a week in order to instruct me in Math A, Math B, and Physics. For some reason (that I didn't complain about), English lessons were not included in the package. Chemistry was left out for the obvious reason that much of the classroom studies required them to take place in a laboratory. And then there was another regular that would appear in my room – The Vampire. In reality, that was a young nurse that would come to extract blood samples from my arm. Whenever I saw her coming, I would say, "Here comes The Vampire again. She wants my blood!" She seemed to take the ribbing well. Speaking of nurses, I had become pretty friendly with most of them. Rick and I were old regulars who didn't give them too hard of a time. I especially looked forward to Sundays. That's when the student nurses would come by. They were closer to my age. And many were eager to demonstrate their new skills – such as back rubbing. Whenever a student nurse asked if I minded if they gave me a backrub, I did not protest too much. After all, I was bedridden and needed to keep my muscles active. And then there were the candy stripers. They could cheer a fellow up on a gloomy day. Also there was someone else that came to see me – the hospital chaplain.

"Hello son. How are you today?" he asked.

"Fine," I replied.

"You're a brave boy. You've gone through a lot." I nodded but said nothing. "You must feel a lot of resentment about everything that has happened to you."

"No, not really."

"But don't you wonder, 'Why me? Why was I chosen to be hurt like this? What did I do to deserve this?'"

"No, I feel I was just standing in the wrong place at the wrong time."

"You are a brave boy! You must have a lot of faith." Again I remained silent. "Then for sure, you must ask yourself, 'Why did the Lord reach out and save me? I must be a lucky lad.' Isn't that true?"

"No, not really. If I was lucky then I wouldn't have got electrocuted in the first place." I also wondered if the Lord could step in to save my life why didn't he interfere a minute earlier and make the cable miss the high-tension wires.

"But don't you feel that the Lord must have saved you for a bigger purpose? That he knew that Benny Cooper still had something to accomplish in this world. He gave you a gift. A gift of your life. You should feel special." I said nothing even though there was a long uncomfortable pause in the conversation. "I am so glad that you don't feel any bitterness towards God. You don't, do you?"

"No," I said without expounding any further.

"That's wonderful! You have a good attitude towards your misfortune. You know that God is looking after you and that he saved your life. That's the right way to look at it. You will do fine."

"I'm fine," I replied.

"Great! Listen, I've got to go. Do you mind if I say a

prayer for you?"

"No," I answered.

Why should I have argued against it if it made the minister feel better? It wouldn't hurt. So the chaplain said his prayer and went on his way. And I went back to sleep.

One morning when Dad came to visit, he brought along a stranger. It turned out that he was a lawyer that also was a tenant of our building. Dad had retained him to represent us in a lawsuit against the school board, the school, and a teacher. The lawyer said that I had a very good case to receive significant compensation for my hardships and pain. Even though I had told the minister that I didn't feel any resentment towards anyone, I still had to agree with this decision. I had suffered a lot of pain over an unfortunate but avoidable incident. And so had the family, especially Ma. "Let's make the devils pay!" I thought.

In late March, I made my first sojourn out of the room without being on a gurney. I slowly edged myself into a wheelchair with assistance from a nurse. And then Lily pushed me around the hall while Ma walked beside the chair. It was like being released from prison. At least that's what I thought. I didn't have any first-hand experience to validate the comparison. My feet were sticking straight out and my head was still covered in gauze. My neck was finally exposed since that graft had now healed. My newfound mobility changed the flavour of the visitations. I now wanted to be escorted up and down the halls. I would speak to all the nurses who would comment on how good it was to see that I was finally out of bed. We would also pass Rick who was now walking up and down the hall with his parents. I never doubted that I would soon be joining him. But first things first. The next step was to manoeuvre the wheelchair by myself. At first, I went very slow. I didn't have the strength in my hands or my arms to get much movement out of the large wheels. However, within a week I was motoring up and down the halls. I was becoming an expert and soon challenged other patients to drag races. I even won a few.

Then came the next step – walking. I was assigned to this large walker. It looked like a baby crib with the springs and mattress removed. I would swing myself out of bed and lower myself by my arms into a seat inside the walker. Then came the hard part – standing up. The seat could be raised but I left it down just in case. I forced myself to take one step while the walker moved forward on its wheels. Pain shot from my feet. It felt like someone had hit them with a sledgehammer. I sat back down. I was exhausted.

"Come on," said the physiotherapist. "You can do better than that."

"It hurts," I cried. "My feet hurt. And my legs are too weak. I can't do it."

"What do you mean you can't do it? You haven't tried it yet. Let's go again."

"OK," I said. "Here I go."

I then took two steps. I hated the therapist. I then took three steps. And then four. And then five. I loved the therapist. I couldn't wait until Ma and Lily arrived later so that I could demonstrate my new skills.

Both Ma and Lily were ecstatic about my progress. They walked with me and I made it all the way to the nurses' station and back. The next day I went further. And on the third day, I went all the way around the section floor. Now they were trying to slow me down. They didn't want me to take it too fast and injure my ankles or tire myself out. So at night I would revert back to the wheelchair and zoom around the floor. I was a speed demon.

One day, I mentioned that I found the TV not as clear as usual. Anyway, they decided to send in an eye specialist to see me. He was an eye surgeon named Dr. Curzon. The examination revealed that I was slowly developing a cataract on one of my eyes. Dr. Curzon referred to it as an 'electric cataract'. In other words, it was caused by the electric shock. He said it was not yet too bad; however, I was advised that I should go to him for regular checkups so that they could monitor the situation. If it got worse, then he would eventually have to operate on my eye. So far, I couldn't really notice a lot of difference. My sight was just a bit misty through the one eye but not enough to even think about most times. So I was not too concerned. And it soon left my conscious thoughts. Speaking of consciousness, it was interesting that my accident still hadn't reached into my dreams. Ever since I had been in the hospital, my dreams would involve me walking normally like I always had. I would run, dance, do handstands, swim, complete flips, water ski, and all the other things that I enjoyed. Never once was I lying in a bed. I guess my subconscious still hadn't accepted my condition.

About mid-April, Rick was released from the hospital and I was alone in the room. I missed Rick but being alone didn't bother me too much. I still had lots of visitors, teachers, nurses, student nurses, candy stripers, and The Vampire to keep me company. As well, I could get out and visit other patients. I was having a ball. I would even go to the lounge at night in my wheelchair and bring my radio along. I would rest the radio in the window (where the best reception was) and listen to the latest songs. There was a show that came on Sunday nights that played the hits from England that hadn't hit North America yet. One night, I heard a new song that was currently number one in England. It was predicted to be a big hit in Canada as well. It was 'Whiter Shade of Pale' by Procol Harum. I loved it!

Just after Rick was discharged from the hospital, Dad informed me that he had talked to Mr. Field about their lawyer and he had decided to switch to the same firm as they were using. My lawyer would be from one of the well-known downtown law firms located at the Richmond-Adelaide Centre. That sounded good to me.

As April moved along, I felt that I was making great progress and expected to be going home soon. When Dr. McCoy checked me the next time, I asked him about the probability of being able to attend RMC in the fall. To be able to run and jump and climb and who knows what else.

"We'll have to take it slow," he said. "It's hard to tell. This will be a long process."

I knew what that really meant, "No damn way. So get that crazy idea out of your head."

At first I was upset. But I soon accepted that I would have to develop another plan. And before long, I thought that it was probably for the best. And eventually I came to the conclusion that I never wanted to go to RMC in the first place. That was Ernie's idea, not mine.

When I stopped having to wear the head bandage, I looked at myself in the mirror. I was shocked. I looked ridiculous. I hadn't had a haircut and my hair completely covered my ears and came down almost to my shoulders. Except for the top of my head which was nearly bald. It was shaven clean from the last operation. And then there was a large missing chunk out of the right side of my head covered only by a small bandage. I didn't want to leave the room. But Ma told me that I looked good. Lily said that I looked like Benjamin Franklin. So I forced myself to venture out into the halls once more. However, within a couple of days, I had arranged for a barber to come and cut my hair very short all over. I didn't like it but at least it looked better than having two different hair lengths.

On April 6th the Stanley Cup playoffs had begun. The Leafs were playing Chicago while Montreal was matched against the Rangers. And both Montreal and Toronto won their series. So the Leafs were going to play the Habs for the Cup. I knew one of the nurses was a huge Montreal fan, so I bet her ten dollars that the Leafs would win the Cup. She thought that the Canadiens were a shoo-in so she readily agreed to the wager. The finals began on Lily's birthday. I was excited about watching the finals on TV even if I was in the hospital. The only bad part was that I wouldn't be able to take advantage of the offer of tickets from Ron Ellis. That would have been amazing if I could have attended a Leafs – Canadiens Stanley Cup playoff final. But it was not to be, so I just sat back and enjoyed the action. On May 2nd I collected my ten dollars when Toronto won game six by a score of 3-1. They probably heard my cheers all over the hospital.

I've got so wrapped up in the Leafs that I've failed to mention that I progressed along with my favourite team. I was a walking maniac. Soon after the playoffs ended in celebration, I said goodbye to my faithful walker and switched to crutches. And on May 22nd, Dr. McCoy caught me by surprise when he said that I would soon be able to go home. He felt that I was doing really well and that I could complete my recovery better at home. I would finally be going home. This was what I was waiting for. Or so I had thought. But now I wasn't so sure. I enjoyed my stay at Camden Hospital. I had met a lot of new friends including one particular student nurse. And I would miss the backrubs. Sure I was happy to be going home and to be with Lily and Ma again. But there was the one thing that I dreaded. The one thing that made me nervous. Dad would become The Old Man again. He had been like a real father for the last three to four months. I didn't want to see that end. Or more to the point, I didn't want to see The Old Man return. But I knew he would. For Ma and Lily, he had never left. They just kept any incidents to themselves so that I wouldn't be worried. I did want to go home though. Anyway I didn't have time to mull over it because the next afternoon, Dr. McCoy discharged me from the hospital. I went downstairs in a wheelchair and walked out the front door on crutches. I didn't even have time to say goodbye to all my favourite nurses.

16 – The Rope Broke

Perhaps I should explain the extent of my injuries a little more so that you can have a better appreciation of my condition upon release. The top of my head on the right-hand side had been burnt right through the scalp and into the skull. The dead tissue and bone had been removed and new skin was grafted over the hole. So I was being literal when I said that I had a hole in my head. When I left the hospital, I had a dressing over the pothole in my head that had to be changed daily. Ma was selected as the lucky person to perform that daily chore. On my neck there was a large pinkish skin graft which had been transplanted from just below my chin to just above my Adam's apple. It stretched across the entire front of my neck. It did not bother me too much except for getting very itchy at times. On my right foot there was a skin graft located over my ankle. This was healing nicely and wasn't causing any trouble. There was a graft on my left ankle as well. But it was much bigger and the internal damage was a lot deeper. One of my tendons had been severed causing my left foot to tilt outwards on its side. Also my toe beside the big toe (what do you call that toe except for the little pig that had none?) was bent down in a hook and wouldn't straighten up. There was also a small graft on the bottom of my left heel that would become tender if I walked on it too much. Oh, I almost forgot the scars on my thighs where all the aforementioned skin had been confiscated. They were healing well and only tended to be itchy once in a while. All of these wounds make sense when you realize that the electrified wire hit me on the top of the head and then the electric current escaped out through my feet. I was wearing a turtleneck sweater at the time so maybe that had something to do with the location of the neck burn. That completes the description of my visible scars. Then there was the effect of the electrical shock on my nervous system. As I had mentioned earlier some of my fine motor skills needed to be put back into shape. That had progressed well but I still found myself going into uncontrollable shakes ever so often. Especially in my legs. And my equilibrium wasn't back to normal. In other words, I had trouble with my balance. Because of all of this, I was instructed to walk with crutches, and then to slowly move to two canes, and eventually to only one cane. In the apartment I could use one cane because I had the walls to bounce off and help keep me perpendicular. If I ventured outside of our domain then I was to use the crutches. I say 'was' because I didn't exactly follow doctor's orders.

How many of you out there remember the 1956 movie 'Reach for the Sky', the true story of Douglas Bader? I had seen it several times. Bader joined the RAF in 1930 and then lost both of his legs in a plane crash in 1931. He was told that his flying and walking days were over. However, he didn't listen. He was fitted with artificial legs and rejoined the RAF. He then achieved a series of aerial victories during the war and was promoted to Wing Commander before eventually being shot down and captured. But what I remember most about the movie was Douglas Bader playing golf. On each swing he would fall down and then he would get up and try it again until he had mastered it successfully. I never forgot that part. So I went outside with my one cane and that was all. I didn't have any use for the crutches; they hurt my arms. I don't remember falling but I certainly didn't walk a straight line. If I was coming down the sidewalk, you would have been advised to move out of the way. Because I needed all of it. Ma was worried whenever I ventured out the door. She pleaded with me to use the crutches but I declined.

"Don't worry, Ma. I'll be OK. I'm fine."

One day I even walked as far as Camden Hospital to visit the nurses. I don't think I told Ma about that.

I guess I was quite a sight. Strangers would regularly walk up to me and ask what had happened to me. At first I was really polite and would explain the entire episode. But this always led to more questions and the need to describe the event in detail. Before long the constant explanations got a little tiresome. So sometimes I would just answer, "I got zapped." It would depend on who was asking and how they asked. If the question implied genuine concern as opposed to ghoulish curiosity then I wouldn't be so flippant. However, one day I was in a record store at Yorkdale Mall with Sandra Sanderson, Lily, and some others when this guy walked right up to me and stared at my neck. I had a hat on or else I guess he would have gawked at the hole in my head instead.

"What the hell happened to you?" he asked.

"They tried to hang me," I answered, "but the rope broke." I then walked away and left the inquisitor to mull over that reply.

There was another obvious change in my appearance. I had grown by at least six inches since the accident. The Old Man kidded me that the electricity must have given me a growth spurt but I figure that I was just following the regular Cooper growing schedule. Don't grow until you are seventeen to eighteen, then grow a foot, and then stop. I was now close to five feet seven inches which I figured would be my final height.

My school tutoring continued at home and even increased in frequency. In early June it was time to write my exams. I wrote the three examinations in the office of the apartment building. A teacher sat outside the office to monitor that I didn't have any guests while I sat inside and wrote. It certainly felt weird to be writing the exams outside of the school and alone. However I thought that they went fairly well but I couldn't be sure.

That June, Lily thought that the Cooper household had gone long enough without a pet and obtained approval to acquire a budgie bird. Ma, Lily, and I went to a pet store and saw these two blue budgies sitting together in a cage. One was male and the other was female. We didn't have the heart to separate them, so we got them both. Lily called them Corey and Candy. They weren't exactly a suitable replacement for cats but their songs still seemed to liven up the living room.

That June, I went to see Fred and Them a few times. One time I was supposed to baby-sit for Lucy and Tom. Everyone was going out except for the kids – Lizzie, April, and Matthew. However, when I arrived, I discovered that a daughter of one of the neighbours was visiting Lizzie. And she had babysitting experience. So I stayed and kept the girls and Matthew company. The girl's name was Diana Ronson and I took a liking to her right away. So what, if she was a few years younger than me. I could live with that. We talked a lot that night and I appreciated the fact that she didn't interrogate me about my injuries. It didn't seem to be a big deal to Diana. This lifted my spirits because I figured that I looked kind of like a freak. And I wondered who would be interested in a boy that walked with a cane. I had become pretty self-conscious about the nasty looking wound on the top of my head. Lily had bought me a paisley cap that I took to wearing twenty-four hours a day to cover it up. But Diana told me that I needn't feel embarrassed. She even said that I was sexy-looking. Thus I removed the cap and Diana didn't even throw up. When I rode the bus home that night, I was on a high.

The next day, Diana called me and came to visit. I introduced her to Lily and Ma before we went for a walk. I sensed that Ma and Lily were less than impressed with Diana.

I wasn't sure if it had to do with her age (not that much older than Lily) or her effervescent personality. Most definitely the opposite of me. I figured that Ma was mainly worried about my health and was concerned that I should just rest at home. Anyways, everyone was civil and friendly and Diana and I went out for a walk. After our walk, we said goodbye at the bus stop while kissing and watching two buses go by. During our first kiss, Diana told me that I wasn't doing it right. She then taught me how it was done. After Diana finally climbed aboard the third bus, I was flying high when I went back into the apartment. Ma just looked at the silly grin on my face and smiled.

It was getting more difficult to see straight. Oh, I am not talking about my light-headed condition brought on by being with Diana. I mean my actual eyesight. The vision in my left eye was deteriorating although my right one still seemed to be OK. Having a cataract is sort of like looking through a frosted car windshield. And the frost was slowly getting thicker. I went to see Dr. Curzon and he advised that I would probably need an operation at a later date. But he recommended that we leave it for now. It looked like I would be having the operation the next summer. But first there was this summer. I went back into the hospital at the end of June to get rid of the hole in my head. At first Dr. McCoy advised that he would be inserting a plastic plate into my skull to compensate for the missing bone. And then he decided against that approach – at least for now. The operation consisted of folding a large flap of skin and flesh from the left side of my head in order to cover the hole on the right side. Once again I had the top of my head shaved in order to prepare for the procedure. I was embarrassed when Diana came to see me the day before the operation but she didn't make any disparaging comments about my appearance. I kissed her goodbye by the elevator. Now, I was embarrassed! All my nurse friends could see us. I wondered what they would think.

When I awoke after the operation, my head hurt worse

than ever before. But now it was the previously good side of my head that was in such pain. My roommate had a heart operation on the same day. He was quite a kidder. He would make me laugh until I yelled, "Ow, that hurts. Don't make me laugh." Then I would say something else funny in response to his comments. "Ow, my chest hurts," he would say. We were quite a pair. While I was in the hospital, there was a story about Rick Field and me in the local Willowdale paper again. It basically detailed our medical progress six months after the accident. It said that I was going to get a plastic plate inserted in my skull. And there was a picture of me that had been taken just before I went back into the hospital. Ma added the story and pictures to her scrapbook. After three to four weeks, I was released to Ma's care once more. Hair was starting to grow where the hole had been, but now there was a large triangular-shaped bald spot on the left side of my head. I wore bandages around my head for about a week more, before switching to small gauze dressings under my paisley cap.

Towards the end of July, I eventually convinced Ma to let me go to Newburgh to visit Brendan and my other friends. She was naturally concerned whether I was up to it.

"You better take the crutches, Benny."

"The crutches? I haven't used them for two months."

"Take two canes then."

"One is enough, Ma. That's all I use outside now. I don't use any in the apartment now. I'll take my cane. OK, Ma?"

"All right, I guess. But you be careful, especially by the dam."

"I will, Ma. Don't worry. Brendan will take care of me."

"OK, dear. But I'm still worried."

"Oh, Ma."

Before I left, I phoned Diana to let her know that I was going away for a few weeks. But she wasn't home so I just left a message with someone in her family. I then packed up my suitcase containing fifty record albums and off I went. When I arrived in Napanee, I had a few hours to visit Gord and Paula before Dork and Brendan were to meet me. Gord and I talked about old times and listened to Gord's new Donovan album. Gord informed me that he had talked to Ma on the phone earlier and how she had expressed great reservations about me going away by myself. And with only one cane. Before long, the Skunkmobile arrived to take me to Newburgh. Both Dork and Brendan said that I looked great. But I knew that they were both at first shocked by my sight.

"I didn't realize that you needed a cane to walk," Brendan stated.

"I don't," I replied, "but I promised Ma that I would use it."

"You don't look too steady on your feet," commented Brendan.

"I'm fine. I just need things to bounce off of. That's all."

"I don't know if I should tell you this," said Brendan, "but when we first heard about your accident, Sneezy and I were talking. And he says, if Benny dies, I guess we should go to Toronto for the funeral."

"That's terrible, Dickman," said Dork.

"No," I corrected, "that just means that they were thinking of me. I have no problem with that. What's with Dickman?"

"That's my new nickname, Dum Dum," Brendan informed. "It came about because someone said that I looked like Gordon Dickman. He lives in Moscow."

"Gordon Dickman?" I said. "I don't think I know him."

"It's not a compliment to look like Gordon Dickman," said Dork. "He's also not too bright."

"I detect the work of Birdbrain. Did he call you Dickman first?" I asked Brendan.

"You got it, Dum Dum."

"I'm not sure that I'll get used to that name. I'm too used to Brendan."

When we arrived at the Casey household, Brendan's younger brother Jimmy met us at the door.

"Hey, Dummer! How the hell are you doing? And how's

my big brother, Peckerboy?"

"Peckerboy?" I questioned Brendan, "Oh, I get it. Dickman, Peckerboy. On second thought, I'll most definitely just stick to Brendan."

"Thanks, Dum Dum. I mean, Benny."

The next day, we went out the front door of Brendan's house and headed down the hill to see Sneezy and Flip.

"Hey," warned Brendan, "you forgot your cane, Benny."

"Oh well. It can stay in your room. I don't really need it," I stated as I zigzagged my way down the hill.

And I never used the cane again. When we went back up the hill that night, I walked briskly without going sideways even once. For on that day, I discovered an unusual new fact. After a few drinks, I walked perfectly straight. Brendan was amazed.

17 – A Quiet Convalescence

The summer of 1967 was the summer of love. OK, so I didn't have the love part but Brendan and I were definitely into the spirit of the times. Brendan told me about this great concert in California that he had heard about. It was held in Monterey in June. The Animals and the Byrds and the Who were there, as was the Jimi Hendrix Experience and other exciting new groups that we had only heard about but not yet actually heard any of their songs – like Big Brother and the Holding Company, the Grateful Dead, Canned Heat, just to name a few. And we started to dress the part too. My hair was still short but I had it covered with my paisley cap. I wore brightly coloured shirts and even colourful bell-bottomed pants. And neither Brendan nor I ever tucked our shirts in. To us it was an exciting time. It seemed like we would hear another group that impressed us every few days. The latest was the Doors. And my most recent Rolling Stones' purchase was the album 'Flowers'. As for Brendan's favourite group, that was the year that 'Sgt. Pepper's Lonely Hearts Club Band' was released. Enough said.

One day, Brendan and I got a ride into Napanee. I am not sure what we were doing there but to get home we had to resort to our thumbs. We were only standing at the usual spot by the railroad trestle for a few minutes when a pickup truck stopped to pick us up. "All right," said Brendan, "This is our lucky day." When we got into the truck, we soon realized that our fortune was not as good as we first perceived. The driver of the truck – a big, burly man in his late twenties – talked with a slur and the cab stunk of alcohol. But it was too late to get out. The truck had picked up speed and was roaring down the Newburgh Road barely before Brendan had time to shut the passenger door.

"Where ya goin', boys?"

"Newburgh," answered Brendan.

"Yup," was the reply.

I wasn't sure what that meant but at this point, I didn't care. I was concentrating on the fact that we had accelerated to over eighty miles per hour. And there was a ninety-degree curve straight ahead. I looked at Brendan and saw that he was as concerned as me. The pickup continued its acceleration. "Great," I thought, "I survived 27,000 volts of electricity only to be killed in a truck accident a few months later. If I die, Ma would kill me. She'll never forgive me. And I don't have my cane with me." I gritted my teeth as the truck proceeded straight on without turning the corner. Luckily, there was a small dirt road at the junction which I had never really noticed before. And also luckily, no one was coming around the corner from the other direction. The driver then braked to a stop.

"I guess I missed that corner, eh boys?"

We never said a word. I hadn't recovered from the shock yet. Before we could react and do something smart like get out of the truck, the driver had executed a sharp U-turn, turned left around the corner, and headed on towards Newburgh on the proper road. Before I knew it, we were going over a hundred miles per hour. I looked at Brendan hoping that he had an idea how to get out of this predicament alive. Then Brendan spoke.

"Don't you think that you should slow down a bit?"

The driver then slammed on his brakes causing the truck

to come to a screeching halt, almost propelling Brendan and me through the windshield.

"That's a fucking good idea. Why didn't you say so before? Fuck! That's a great idea. Was I going too fast for ya?"

"Yes," said Brendan. "I thought we were going to crash."

"Then I'll take it real slow the rest of the way. Just for you boys."

And we drove forty miles per hour until we got to Newburgh where we disembarked at the top of the hill. After the truck had continued on its way towards Camden East, Brendan knelt down and kissed the pavement.

"Holy shit, Benny. I thought we were goners for sure."

"And when you told him to slow down, I thought he was mad. I didn't know what to expect. I thought he was going to throw us out of the truck. Didn't you, Brendan? That would have been OK though."

"Or kill us and throw our bodies in the back. That's what I thought."

"I'm glad that that didn't cross my mind," I commented.

"From now on we check out the condition of the driver before we accept a ride. Right?"

"You'll get no argument from me. That's for sure."

After that ordeal, it was time for rest and relaxation again. It was time for Brendan, Dork, and me to travel to Beaver Lake and Dorchestershire. This trip we took our own record player so that we could continue to enjoy our favourite music without having to send Brendan out on a scouting mission. We listened to Brendan's new Country Joe and the Fish album. I thought it was fantastic. We also listened to the Doors. I remember that we were invited to this party with some American girls. When we played the Doors first album, one of them commented, "What's this? It sounds like circus music." It was a very good-looking blonde who said it. Brendan then took it upon himself to educate her. He spent the evening sitting on a bed with the blonde discussing the merits of the Doors. And having a few beers. Dork and I just sat around with the rest of the group discussing I don't know what. And had a few beers. Afterwards, Dork and I ribbed Brendan constantly.

"I can't believe that you sat on a bed with that gorgeous girl and the only thing that came to your mind was the Doors," expressed Dork. "You really are carried away with this music thing, Dickman."

"You're unbelievable, Dickman," I added. But who was I to talk? I never made it away from the kitchen table.

We met another girl at Beaver Lake that summer that I kind of fell for. Her name was Barbra Wood. And she was from Toronto. She spent a lot of time with us at the cottage and went water skiing with us. I should say with Dork and Brendan. My water skiing days were over. That was the sad part about going back to Beaver Lake. I so much wished that I could don the skis once more and jump the waves. But my ankles were too weak for that kind of activity. And I wasn't sure if I fell and landed on my head, that it would be the best thing for me. Anyway, I began telling you about Barbra (who looked good in her bathing suit, by the way). She just remained a good friend of us and that's as far as it went. And I never did see her in Toronto.

When we went back to the village of Newburgh, I was surprised to run into Lily. She had ventured down from Toronto to visit her friend Kelly Weston for a few days and then planned to return home with me. Whenever I was with Sneezy, he suggested that I should spend more time with my sister. It was obvious that he had a bit of a crush on Lily. I always agreed with Sneezy's advice but not just to see Lily. As I mentioned earlier, it had come to my attention that Kelly was not exactly hard on the eyes. Flip, Brendan, and I also went to a barn dance again. And like the previous year, I danced with Jill Washington and Beverly Coleman (who had come down from Sudbury again that summer). I have to admit that I spent more time with Jill though. Of course, part of the time we spent in the parking lot drinking a mickey of

Gold Stripe rye which was in my jacket pocket. When we arrived back in Newburgh, Brendan and I said good night to Flip and headed up the hill intending to head back to Brendan's. However we ran into Sneezy driving his father's new car. After one look at Sneezy, both Brendan and I deduced that Sneezy shouldn't have been driving. Nevertheless, Sneezy invited us to go to Napanee with him to get something to eat.

"Not if you're driving," said Brendan. "We've had enough of riding with someone who's drunk. Haven't we, Benny?"

"Sure enough," I confirmed.

"I'm not drunk," argued Sneezy. "I'm quite all right."

"Yeah, and I'm the Pope," answered Brendan.

"You drive then," said Sneezy to Brendan, "or I'll just go myself if you two don't wanna come."

"OK," agreed Brendan. "Slide over, Sneezy."

"I didn't know you had your licence yet, Brendan," I remarked.

"Shhh," whispered Brendan. "Do you want Sneezy to drive off by himself? I've driven a few times, don't worry."

Flip and I had drunk most of the rye so I knew that Brendan was still sober. So I agreed and off we went on our way to Napanee. I sat in the back seat and the first thing that I saw was an open case of 24 Labatt 50 on the floor.

"Pass me a beer, Dum Dum," requested Sneezy. "I'm thirsty as a camel. And have one yourself."

I was still sipping on the beer as we turned on the Palace Road on the way towards Napanee. Brendan and Sneezy were deep in some discussion. I looked down for a minute and then looked up and out the windshield to see a yellow curve sign directly in front of us.

"Look out," I yelled.

Brendan then directed both eyes forward and turned the steering wheel to try and avoid the road sign. I heard a clang and a thump as we went over the sign and then skidded across the road and into the ditch on the opposite side of the

180

road. We hit the ditch with a thud as I went up in the air and hit my head on the roof of the car. The beer flew out of the bottle in my hand soaking both me and the backseat. We then came to a stop with the car at a forty-five degree angle. There was a limestone wall only a foot or so from the driver's side of the car.

"Fuck!" exclaimed Brendan. "Shit, shit, shit! I'm sorry Sneezy. I tried to miss that damn sign and I guess I yanked the wheel too much."

"That's all right. How are you, Dum Dum?"

"I'm fine," I said, "but I got beer all over your dad's car."

"Fuck, I'm sorry," apologized Brendan. "I forgot about you, Benny. Are you sure you're OK?"

"Yeah," I said. "I hit my head I think. But I feel fine."

"You hit your head! Fuck! Shit! Your mom's going to kill me. Fuck!"

"No, I'm fine, Brendan. Really. And Ma will never know. I'm not going to tell her."

"Let's get out of the car and figure out how we're going to get out of here," said Sneezy who suddenly sounded completely sober.

When we got out of the car, it was evident that we weren't going anywhere too fast. The bottom of the car was resting on rock and the back wheels weren't even touching the ground.

"Shit! What are we going to do now?" asked Brendan.

"Let's get the beer out of the car and hide it somewhere," answered Sneezy. "Brendan, you and I will walk back to the gas station and call a tow truck. Dum Dum, you stay here. You shouldn't be walking too far. Are you sure your head's OK?"

"Yeah, I'm sure."

"And listen everybody," continued Sneezy. "Let's get our story straight in case the cops show up. I was driving. Don't argue, Brendan. I'm in shit anyway. So, I'll just say I was driving. There's no use you getting into trouble too. My

Dad would kill me if he found out that I let you drive. So it's better this way. I'm feeling sober already. By the time we get back with the tow truck, I should be fine. Whatever, I was driving. And a car came at us and I had to hit the side of the road to miss it. And then I lost control in the gravel. That's our story. OK, everybody?"

"I'm not a very good liar," I warned.

"You'll be fine," said Sneezy. "It's almost the truth. Another car did pass us just before. And we did lose control."

"All right, let's hurry and go," said Brendan. "If we're lucky we'll be back on the road before anyone knows the wiser."

Brendan then hid the beer in the ditch across the other side of the road, before he and Sneezy started off in the direction from which we had just driven minutes before. I decided to just sit on a rock by the car and wait for their return. I kept feeling the top of my head to see if there was any damage. My head did feel a bit sore. My head hurt when I touched the point where my bald spot and the former hole joined. I looked at my hand in the dark and saw what appeared to be blood on the tips of my fingers. "Oh, oh," I thought. But I didn't have time to get too worried for something else caught my attention. The headlights of an oncoming car were approaching and it was slowing down. And I thought I could see a bump on the roof of the vehicle. When it came to a full stop about twenty feet away, I was then able to distinguish the unmistakable shape of the red cherry on top of the car. It was the police. Two policemen got out of the car and one walked towards me while the other went to inspect the tilted and suspended car. I probably looked like someone in shock, because I was.

"What happened here?"

"We went in the ditch. I wasn't driving."

"No? Where's the driver then?"

"He went to get a tow truck. My friend was with him."

"Is that right? And they left you here by yourself?"

"Yeah, I can't walk that well."

"Have you been drinking?"

"No, that's not what I mean. I have a bad ankle. I can't walk that well."

"The inside of the car smells like a tavern," advised the other policeman.

"Yeah, it sure smells like beer around here. You reek of alcohol. Are you sure you're not alone?"

"No, I mean yes. I'm sure. They went to get help. I had one beer. I mean just a sip on a beer. But it spilt on me. When we went into the ditch."

"Get up and let me see you walk."

"I can't walk straight. I always walk sideways. That's normal." I almost added that I hadn't had enough beers yet to walk straight, but I thought better of it.

"Come on, get up and let's see you walk the line."

"I wasn't driving," I argued as I got up and stumbled over a rock. "I do have a bad ankle. I was zapped. I mean I was electrocuted. I don't walk very well."

I zigged and zagged all over the road before they finally invited me to get in the back seat of the cruiser. One of the policemen then saw the top of my head as I bent over to get into the back seat.

"Are you cut?"

"I just hit my head. I'm fine."

"Let me see. My God. Your head is a mess."

"That's from my accident. When I got electrocuted. I just bumped it. There's a little blood. Nothing much."

"We better take you to the hospital. But first, let's talk. And wait for these friends of yours to show up. If they ever do. All right, tell us what happened."

"We were driving along. Then a car came at us and we had to go onto the side of the road to miss him. Then Sneezy, I mean Kenny – Kenny Shaker – saw the sign. He swung the wheel to miss the sign and he lost control because of the gravel. And then we were in the ditch."

"How soon did the car come onto your side of the road? When did you know that you had to drive off the road?"

"I don't know. I didn't really see. I was in the backseat. I wasn't really watching. Kenny and Brendan were in the front."

"You didn't see the car then?"

"No, I was sitting back. I wasn't looking." I felt myself digging a deeper hole trying to avoid a direct lie.

"How do you know that it was on your side of the road, then?"

"Because we went off the road. And Kenny and Brendan told me. I saw it go by."

The investigative questioning was then interrupted as a tow truck drove up and parked in front of the cruiser. Brendan and Sneezy climbed slowly out of the truck.

"All right, Mr. Cooper. You stay here while we question your friends."

I sat silently and watched another police car appear on the scene. I first saw Sneezy and then Brendan get into the other car to be cross-examined. I wondered what was going on. After about twenty minutes, my two interrogators got back into the front of the cruiser.

"Well, Mr. Cooper," said one of the police. "We have a little problem here. Your pals tell a little different story." I said nothing and he continued. "They say you saw the car first and yelled, 'Look out'. What do you say to that? Do you still say you didn't see the car coming?"

"I yelled 'Look out' when I saw the sign. I didn't see the car first."

"They were very clear. They said you saw the car first. There was no car, was there?"

"I never saw a car," I admitted. "But I wasn't watching."

"Well, that's what I thought. I think we've got the story straight now. I never thought there was another car. Mr. Shaker just lost control of the car. That's what happened. There never was another car."

"Yes," said the other policeman. "That's obviously what happened. Let's go talk to Shaker and Casey again. I knew we would get to the truth. Wait here again, Cooper. Then we'll

184

take you to the hospital."

"Ah ha," I thought. "You guys aren't as smart as you think. You don't know who the driver really was. We fooled you."

Shortly after, I was driven to Napanee Hospital. I think the look of my head scared the wits out of the young doctor in the emergency, so he gave me two stitches just in case. I never felt a thing. That part of my head didn't have much feeling to it. He then wrapped my head in a large gauze bandage. I looked like I did a month before. When I went out into the waiting room, I saw Brendan and Sneezy sitting there.

"Shit," said Brendan. "I knew you were hurt bad."

"I'm fine. It was only two stitches. The doctor just likes bandages. Don't worry about me. I'm sorry about the story. I screwed it all up."

"That's OK," said Sneezy. "The sneaky buggers interviewed us all separate so they could trip us up. We didn't have enough time to work on our story. Anyway, I'm not being charged with drinking and driving. Just drinking underage. And maybe careless driving. I'm not sure yet."

"And they're charging me with drinking underage as well," said Brendan. "What about you, Benny?"

"I don't know. They never told me. I said that I just had one sip of a beer. I never mentioned the mickey of rye earlier though."

Sneezy's parents then arrived in their other car to drive us home. Mr. Shaker seemed remarkably calm. I wondered what The Old Man would act like in the same situation. I wasn't really sure. He should have been sympathetic considering his own experiences. But I doubted that. Mr. Shaker had talked to the police before and now questioned us to get our side of the story. He also informed us that we would all be charged with drinking underage and that Sneezy would also be charged with careless driving. He said that the cops advised that Sneezy was lucky that he wasn't being charged with trying to mislead the police in an investigation, possessing open beer in a car, leaving the scene of an accident, dangerous driving, and drunk driving. And then he added one more comment.

"I don't feel sorry for you, Kenny. You got off easy. It's Benny here that I feel sorry for. He got himself injured, had only one sip of beer and still got charged. Now, that's a shame. I don't know why they came down so hard on you, Benny."

I looked at Brendan and Sneezy and smiled.

"Poor little innocent Dum Dum," whispered Brendan.

"Shut up, Dickman," I said.

The next day when Brendan and I went down the hill, I still had the large bandage wrapped around my head. We kept bumping into people who wondered what had happened to me and expressed concern. We were then intercepted by Lily.

"Benny, what happened?" she asked.

"We were in a little car accident last night, nothing serious. I just bumped my head."

"Oh no. You know what Mom says. One bump and you could be a goner. You didn't get that plastic plate in your head, remember?"

"I'm fine, Lily. Don't worry."

"Mom's going to kill you."

"She'll never know, will she?"

"I won't tell her. But what about that bandage?"

"It can come off today. In fact, I'm going to take it off now. It looks stupid."

So I then took off the bandage and my head looked fine. No different than usual unless you inspected closely.

"See Lily, I'm fine." I then changed the subject. "Have you been having a good time in Newburgh, Lily?"

"Yeah, great. I hear that Brendan is coming to Toronto with us to visit for a week or two?"

"Yeah, how did you know? I just asked him yesterday."

"This is Newburgh. Things get around fast. Like your car accident. I heard about it before I saw you."

"Oh."

On the last night before our return to Toronto, Brendan, Sneezy, Flip, and I got together for a few beers. For some reason, I wasn't drinking near as fast as the other three. I think I was still feeling guilty about reinjuring my head in the accident. I decided to be a little more responsible. At least for a few days anyway. It wasn't really a conscious decision; it was more just the mood that I was in. We were by the small apartment building (if you could actually call it that) in downtown Newburgh, when Brendan passed out by one of the walls. Flip then decided it was time to relieve himself and went to stand against the wall. We then heard the flow of water.

"Look out Flip, you idiot," yelled Sneezy. "Dickman is sleeping there."

"Oh shit!" exclaimed Flip. "Sorry Dickman. I didn't see you there. Did I get you? I don't think I did. Did I?"

"What?" asked Brendan. "What are you talking about? What am I doing – oh fuck! Why is the ground wet? Oh shit! You bastard, Flip. Get the hell out of here."

Brendan then jumped up while Flip ran down the road about fifty yards. Sneezy and I were too busy laughing to say anything.

"I wanna see that Hemi," said Brendan.

"What?" I laughed. "What do you want to see, Brendan?"

"The Hemi. You know that car with the super fucking engine. I want to see the Hemi."

"The Hemi?" I questioned. I knew exactly what Brendan had said. But it didn't make any sense to me. The Hemi was a powerful engine (as Brendan had so succinctly put it) in a certain car those days. Someone in Newburgh had just recently purchased one. What I didn't understand was why Brendan had wanted to see it. He had never shown any interest in cars before. It was like I had just asked to see the new church. Not what you would expect. I then deduced that it was time for Brendan to hit the sack.

"Come on, Brendan. Let's go home," I said as I grabbed

him around the waist and started to lead him up the hill.

"But I wanna see the Hemi," he argued.

"Yeah, OK. I think it's at the top of the hill."

"Let's go then. I gotta see the Hemi."

I then said goodnight to Flip and Sneezy and assisted Brendan up the hill. I then started to laugh.

"What are you laughing about, Dum Dum?" asked Brendan.

"I was just thinking, Brendan. This is a first. Usually you have to help me up the hill. Now I'm helping you up. And I'm supposed to be the helpless one."

"You're a great friend, Dum Dum," mumbled Brendan. "A really great friend."

"Thanks, I'm just glad to be of service."

"Where's the Hemi? I gotta go see the Hemi?"

Brendan then tried to escape back down the hill but I soon got him moving back in the correct direction. I eventually managed to get Brendan home and in his bed, where he immediately passed out cold. We never did see the Hemi. When I told Brendan the story in the morning, he denied all knowledge of the entire proceedings.

When Lily and I arrived in Toronto (accompanied by Brendan), Ma was ecstatic to see us. She said that there had been no trouble with The Old Man while we were gone but that she still really missed us. I'm not sure that I believed the part about The Old Man. We then learned that Bill would be visiting us for about a week and he would be arriving in a few days. Sitting on the kitchen counter was a letter addressed to me which I assumed contained my final Grade 13 marks. I opened it to read the following: Math A 83, Math B 88, Physics 87, Chemistry 71, English 64. Obviously I was happy with the first three marks on the exams that I wrote. And I had to be content with what I was assigned in English considering how much I had participated in class the first semester. The mark that ticked me off was Chemistry. I know; it's not a bad mark but I thought that I had done better than that in tests prior to being zapped. And that left me just under the 80 percent average required to be an Ontario Scholar. Anyway, I still didn't know what I was going to do come September.

After checking out the marks, I called Diana to let her know that I had returned to the city. Again I was told that she wasn't home and I left a message for her to call me. Two days later, I did the same again. And then I gave up. Obviously, our relationship was over for a reason that was beyond my comprehension. Oh well, that left me more time to spend with Brendan.

While Brendan was there, we took over Lily's room while she was assigned to my bed in our parents' room. And when Bill arrived he got to share the living room with the birds (Corey and Candy) as he slept on the pullout couch. Bill was only able to stay for a few days before he was to get a plane to fly out to Edmonton. He had joined the Airborne Regiment (a paratroopers unit) and would be trained in parachuting from airplanes. I guess I was jealous about the jumping part. I would have been happy just to jump off the couch. However, the idea of being in the army had no appeal to me at all anymore. I was a child of the sixties now. A pacifist. A hippie. I just needed my hair to grow. I was even attempting to grow a moustache. Bill had brought this large reel-to-reel tape recorder with him. And the best part was that you could set it up like a P.A. system and project your voice through the speakers. One day, I was screaming out 'Light My Fire' when Bill arrived home. He said that he could hear me as soon as he stepped off the Bathurst bus. He was not impressed. That's about all that I recall from that visit. Bill was gone before we hardly knew that he was there.

While in a variety store at the local shopping mall, Brendan and I saw the new album by the Jimi Hendrix Experience. It was called 'Axis: Bold As Love'. I decided to buy it as we had both been interested in hearing more of Jimi Hendrix ever since we had first heard Foxy Lady on the radio earlier that year. I remember that Brendan had originally commented that Jimi Hendrix was the first black man that he had seen playing a guitar. And I agreed with him. We were used to the Motown acts like the Temptations, the Four Tops, and Smokey Robinson & the Miracles. Where the singers just twirled around and the band was nowhere in sight. We were ignorant of a whole generation or two of great bluesmen. People like Robert Johnson, B.B. King, Albert King, John Lee Hooker, and Muddy Waters - just to name a few. Of course, we had heard of Chuck Berry and Bo Diddley. I am not sure if we just forgot them or thought that they were white. Brendan and I had a good laugh when I bought the album that day and we recalled how stupid we had been. When we got back to the apartment, we went to Lily's room to listen to Jimi Hendrix on her record player. We didn't think that Ma would appreciate the subtleties of Hendrix. I put the record on the spindle and awaited with anticipation. Brendan and I just looked at each other, when the violins started. That was followed by quiet piano and a few horns. And then the singing started.

"This is weird," I said. "It doesn't sound like anything else that he did off his first album."

"Just wait," advised Brendan. "It's probably just something strange that Jimi's thrown in before the guitar starts." We then listened for about thirty more seconds before Brendan finally broke in. "That sounds like Dean Martin singing."

"Yeah, you're right. That is Dean Martin."

Brendan then lifted the arm off the record album, and picked it up to inspect the label.

"Dean Martin. It says so right here on the label. We're getting worse," remarked Brendan. "Now we can't even recognize the difference between Dean Martin and Jimi Hendrix."

"Yeah, I can't believe it took us half of a song to catch on that something was wrong. They are both on Reprise though."

Brendan then burst into uncontrollable laughter.

"What?" I asked as I started to laugh. "What's so

funny?" I then lost it too. "What are we laughing about?" I finally asked once more.

"I was just thinking," said Brendan before breaking down again. After a moment, Brendan restarted his sentence. "I was just thinking about the poor bastards that bought the new Dean Martin album and got Jimi Hendrix instead. Can you imagine it?" Brendan then changed his voice. "What do you think, Martha? This new Dean Martin album is kind of strange. It sounds like ol' Dino's been in the sauce again." He then switched to a falsetto voice. "I don't know, Henry. Maybe we should give it a chance. Maybe it will grow on us."

Both of us then rolled onto the floor into a fit of convulsive laughter. We kept laughing until Ma and Lily entered the room to find out what we were up to. The next day, I exchanged the album for the correct one. After listening to the opening flying saucer sound effects on 'Axis: Bold As Love', we had to laugh again. We both had to wonder how Martha and Henry would have reacted to that.

Some other albums figured prominently in Brendan's visit that August. While I was in the hospital, someone had given me a couple Bill Cosby records for my birthday. I think it was Mr. and Mrs. Field – Rick's parents. The albums were 'I Started Out As A Child' and 'Wonderfulness'. I loved them both and played them for Brendan. I especially liked the story 'Tonsils' about young Bill's experience in the hospital eagerly awaiting the operation so that he could get ice cream. I could relate to that one. Another favourite was called 'The Giant'. The Giant was what Bill and his brother called their father. Bill Cosby relates how when his father would come home drunk, he would go to bed and drop his pants to the floor with a loud 'chink'. "The Giant has money," one of them would whisper. While Brendan was visiting, The Old Man had so far managed to behave himself. He had been drinking but he never flew off the handle and had kept his vulgarities and insults to a minimum. I think The Old Man found Brendan to be quite a joker and whenever it seemed like he was going to lose his temper, Brendan would say something to make him laugh. Well one day, The Old Man had been out of sight for most of the day. We knew that wasn't good news. We were all in bed when I heard The Old Man enter the apartment. It was obvious that he was drunk. I could hear him mumbling under his breath. I didn't know if Brendan was asleep or not.

"The Giant is home," whispered Brendan.

I started to laugh but not too loudly. I was still fearful of what might occur. I listened intently as The Old Man walked down the hall and into the master bedroom. "Oh, oh," I thought. "Now trouble starts." But I was wrong. I heard him just start to get undressed. I then heard a loud clang as The Old Man's extensive key ring crashed to the bedroom floor.

"The Giant has keys," said Brendan.

I then spent half the night trying to stop myself from laughing out loud. I would lie for a few minutes before breaking back out into a fit.

"The Giant has keys," Brendan said again.

When Brendan left to return to Newburgh, things quickly reverted back to reality. I became an uncle once more; as Ernie and Ruth were proud parents of a little girl named Lizzie. And I received notice that I had been accepted at both Queen's University and the University of Toronto. I also was asked to arrange an interview at the School of Architecture (at U of T) in order to show them my drawings. The only drawings that I had were of Eric Burdon, Bill Wyman, and others. I didn't think that was quite what they had in mind. So I never followed up on that opportunity. In fact, I hadn't followed up on anything. I wasn't sure about finances or my health, so I did nothing. But luckily Mr. Connors wasn't such a procrastinator. He arranged everything for me. And I found myself registered in a four-year General Science course at U of T. I even received a small scholarship to help with the tuition. In early September, I had my picture and story in the paper again. There was an article on both Rick and me, outlining how we were about to head back to school. This was a triumph over adversity. At least that was the story. Lily especially liked the ending of the story. It said that I had spent my 'summer in the hospital and convalescing quietly at home'. She got a good laugh over that one.

18 – Blind Date

In September of 1967 our family grew in size. A little girl was added to the household. No, Ma didn't have another baby. Rather she started to look after a little girl who was the daughter of a young couple who were tenants in our building. Her name was Penny Langdon and she was just over a year old. She was there five days a week from the early morning until about dinner time. Penny was a cute, sweet and lovable girl who added a lot of warmth to the apartment. Lily and I soon saw Penny as a little sister. And needless to say, Ma developed a lot of love and affection for Penny. She was such a delight, I think even The Old Man found her charm irresistible. Here I go again, trying to move the story along too fast. I need to tell you about other things before I get too carried away telling you more about Penny.

Lily started Grade 9 at the same school as the year before. It was a Junior High School, which meant that she wouldn't yet be attending Northern Hills Secondary School. As for me, I started my university days and I loved it. It made me feel like I was finally a mature adult. Well, maybe the mature part was a bit of a stretch. Mr. Connors drove me to the campus the first morning. I had decided to attend St. Michael's College at U of T. You may be wondering why I chose that college when I wasn't Roman Catholic. To tell you the truth, I thought that I was following in the footsteps of my hockey hero (Dave Keon) when I made that decision. Soon after, I learned that Keon had played hockey for St. Michael's School, not the same thing. But it didn't really matter what college I attended since I was unaffiliated anyway. Also your college was only a place where you took a few of your classes and where you went for lunch and breaks. I actually only took English at St. Mike's. The rest of my classes were in buildings on the other side of campus. Almost all of the Science courses were in buildings on St. George except for Botany which was taught in an old building by University Avenue – The Mining Building. That was a good location because I took Botany right after lunch. And the grounds of Queen's Park were an excellent spot to take a short nap in the autumn sun. I found the first few weeks of university courses to be a lot simpler than I had imagined. I had heard horror stories about people getting so stressed over university that they became suicidal. So far though I found most of my classes to be a rerun of what I had been taught in Grade 13. I had to say that I was glad that I had kept up my Math and Physics studies in the hospital and at home. It would have been a far different story if that hadn't been the case. I didn't even mind English. I finally caught on that as long as you stated your own opinion, you couldn't really go wrong. I wasn't even afraid to tackle Paradise Lost.

For the first week or two, I was given a ride to and from the campus by either Mr. Connors or The Old Man. I don't think I mentioned that The Old Man had a new car then. It was a Rambler station wagon. I can't recall what year it was but it was definitely the newest car that The Old Man had ever purchased. Perhaps, it was two to three years old at that time. The one thing that I didn't like about that car was that it had a standard transmission. I had wanted to learn how to drive but I didn't trust that my weak left ankle would yet be able to manage the clutch. So I decided to put off driving until a later date. And then there was also the small problem with my deteriorating eyesight. I hadn't mentioned it to anyone else yet but I was beginning to notice a bit of a cloud developing over my right eye too. I had no wish to alarm Ma so I kept this fact to myself and just decided to see how it went before confessing. So far it wasn't proving to be too much of a handicap.

At the end of September, I had to go back to Newburgh (or Napanee to be precise) for a few days in order to face the court over my drinking underage charge. I told Ma that I was going down for a party that Brendan had planned for Sneezy. That was not a complete fabrication as we did plan to get together after the proceedings and celebrate the closure of the entire incident. But Lily knew the real reason for the sudden trip. On the day of judgement, Mr. Shaker drove us to the courthouse to face our music. Really, there was nothing to it. We stood in front of a judge, said "Guilty" at the right time, and paid our fine. I think my fine was around forty-five dollars. When I paid my fine, the clerk looked at me and commented how it must have been quite a bad car accident. I didn't bother to correct her assumptions. And then we had our little party (nothing too wild) and I returned to Toronto the next day. I felt relief that the episode was now behind me.

That was the year that the N.H.L. expanded to include six new teams. I had mixed feelings over that but mostly I thought it would be kind of interesting to watch the Leafs play new teams. I figured that all the new teams would be pushovers and the Leafs would be guaranteed to win the Cup for many years. With the new Eastern and Western Division format, it meant that the Leafs would be unable to face the Montreal Canadiens in the Stanley Cup final again. All of the expansion teams were in the West which meant that one of them would be assured a spot in the final. That's the part that I didn't like. It didn't sound quite right.

So far I hadn't developed any new friendships at U of T. I mean I spoke to different people who were friendly and all that, but I never met anyone that I would see outside of the university grounds. There was one girl that I would certainly have liked to have seen more. Her name was Susan Wynn. She was a very attractive blonde who I shared a laboratory desk with during Botany class. We would talk a lot to each other and I thought that she was very nice as well as extremely good looking. However I just couldn't get up enough nerve to ask her out for a date. What if she already had a boyfriend? For some reason, I suspected that she did but I wasn't sure. I felt like Charlie Brown and Susan was like 'the little red-headed girl'. I told Lily about The Little Blonde-Headed Girl and afterwards she would constantly quiz me to see if I had yet made any advances.

"Not yet," I would answer, "maybe tomorrow."

"Benny, you are just like Charlie Brown," commented Lily. "You need to be more outgoing."

"Good grief!" I remarked.

"That will be five cents please," countered Lily.

I did run into a few people that I already knew. One day in Chemistry, I bumped into Noah Wayman from Markham Avenue Collegiate. And on other days, I saw two different former classmates from Northern Hills. But we didn't share any classes, so our meetings were infrequent and short. Thus most of the time when I went to the St. Mike's cafeteria (referred to as the Coop), I was alone. One time when I was sitting at a table by myself, I looked over at another table to see two girls and two boys looking towards me. I thought that I heard one of the boys say, "He looks like Spock." And then they laughed. My hair was still slowly growing back and I had these short bangs. So I guess in a way, I did resemble the Vulcan. However there were two main differences between me and Mr. Spock. His ears and my moustache (which was starting to grow in quite well, I thought). At first I was upset that these thoughtless people were laughing at me. But then I thought, "What's wrong with looking like Spock? Better him than a Klingon." That reminds me that it was around that time that I developed a whole new theory about why I had survived the 27,000 volts. What if I hadn't? Maybe in another alternate universe, I had died. And all my family were mourning over me. And Sneezy and Brendan came to my funeral. But the incident had started a new chain of events – one where I had survived. And I was living that timeline. It sounds completely feasible; don't you think? Lily didn't think so. She told me that I was watching too much Star Trek.

There was one guy in some of my classes that I started to converse with on a regular basis. I actually thought that we could become friends. I don't remember his name at all now. For good reason. One day after English, he commented how he found it ridiculous how people would study every single word and punctuation of literature.

"Yeah, I know what you mean," I agreed. "In high school it used to drive me crazy how we would spend a half-hour discussing the meaning of a punctuation mark. I never thought the author put that much thought into it."

"Yeah, they analyze everything to death. It's like the Beatles. Some people go on and on about their lyrics."

"That's right. Some people hear references to drugs that aren't even there. They're often just singing about a poster or drawing or something."

"Right, their lyrics and music are garbage. It means nothing. Just a lot of left-wing, communist sloganeering. That's all it is."

"That's not exactly what I meant."

"They're no better than that communist government that we have in Ottawa. That Pearson is so red it's unbelievable. He's not doing a thing for us WASP's. He's letting all kinds of trash into the country."

"I like Pearson. I think he's doing a good job for Canada. Besides, I'm not a WASP."

"What? What do you mean you're not a WASP? You're white, aren't you?"

"Yeah, I think so."

"You're Anglo-Saxon, aren't you?"

"My ancestors were English if that's what you mean."

"And you're a Protestant, right?"

"No, I'm not any religion. I'm an atheist."

"Bullshit. There's no such thing as an atheist. What religion are your parents?"

"They're lax United."

"Ah ha. You are a WASP then."

"Nope, I'm not. I'm a HEN."

"A hen? What are you talking about, Ben? Don't be stupid."

"I'm not. I'm serious. Just as serious as you calling me a WASP. I'm a HEN – a Human, Earthling, Nondenominational."

The bigot didn't know what to say in answer to that. He just shook his head and walked away.

"A HEN, that's a good one," I thought. I was amazed that I came up with something so brilliant. "I'll have to remember to tell Gordie that one. He'll like it."

I later found out that my former acquaintance was a member of the Western Guard – a small but extreme right-wing group of racist bigots that were cultivating at U of T. We didn't speak to each other too much after that. If we did, we kept our conversations on things like the weather. We certainly didn't have much in common. I could have told him, that to me, one of the highlights of attending university was participating in the anti-war demonstrations on campus. I proudly marched down University Avenue in an attempt to end the war in Vietnam. And I could have told him what my favourite new television show was – The Smothers Brothers Comedy Hour. But I didn't. There was no use arguing with someone like that. You weren't going to change his mind. And he wasn't about to change mine.

On an October Saturday, The Old Man sat at the dining room table drinking beer all day. Ma, Lily, and I went out for the day to keep away from him but at dinnertime we returned back to our apartment. We had our dinner on TV trays in front of the television as The Old Man still occupied the table. The Old Man directed a steady harangue of obscenities and insults towards Ma as we finished our dinner. We were trying our best to pretend that The Old Man wasn't there.

But that was an impossible task. Eventually, the threats began.

"I could kill you, you fucking old bag. No one could stop me. And no one would give a shit. Who the hell would miss you? Do you want me to kill the whore?"

The last comment was directed towards Lily and me. I felt that the question didn't deserve an answer so I ignored it. And so did Lily.

"See," said The Old Man, "your own fucking kids don't care about you? You're a no good gray-haired old bag that's good for nothing. You're a useless fucking whore that lies around the house all day fucking every…"

"Shut the fuck up!" I screamed. "I'm so sick of listening to you. Shut up, please."

The Old Man jumped to his feet. "Who the hell are you telling me what to do in my own house? You think you're a fucking big man now since you started university. With your stupid little moustache and that silly hat, you look like one of those goddamn lazy hippies. I'm the one that works his ass off to keep a roof over our head. I don't need to listen to you. You're no better than your mother."

"If it wasn't for Mom you wouldn't even have a job," Lily snapped back. "All you do is sit around and get drunk all day. It's Mom that cleans the building and does ninety percent of the chores around here. If it wasn't for Mom nothing would get done."

"You goddamn slut! Don't you dare talk to me like that!" The Old Man then stepped towards Lily at the same time that she rose to her feet. He attempted to push Lily but she moved quickly away and hurried down the hall towards the bedroom. The Old Man then followed her down the hall. "That smart-ass, little whore. I'll teach her a lesson."

Mom jumped up and yelled, "Garf, leave Lily alone. What are you doing?"

I too stood up and headed after The Old Man. "Leave Lily alone, you lousy excuse for a father!"

Lily went into her bedroom and tried to shut her door as

The Old Man stuck his foot in the doorway. "You fucking bitch," he shouted as he pushed against the door.

Somehow I beat Ma to where The Old Man was. "Leave Lily alone, you bastard!" I cried. I then tried to shove The Old Man away from the door but his balance was better than I thought. And he pushed back. I stumbled backwards, hit the back of my head against the wall, and slid down the wall to end up sitting on the floor. I tried to cushion my fall by placing my hand on top of a small lamp table. But all I managed to do was tip over the table and bring the lamp crashing to the floor. And this caused Corey and Candy to start squawking with fright.

"Benny!" Ma cried. "Are you all right? How could you, Garf? How could you knock Benny down?"

"I'm fine, Ma. I'm fine."

Lily then rushed back into the hall and came towards me. "You bastard," she screamed at The Old Man. "You bastard."

"What? I didn't do any fucking thing. He just stumbled. You know that Benny can't walk straight. For fuck's sake, I wouldn't hurt Benny. He knows that. Don't you, Benny? It's the old fucking bag. She just drives me crazy sometimes. That gray-haired son of a bitch. She…"

I had heard enough. I wanted The Old Man to stop. I just wanted to rest in peace and quiet. Instead I burst into tears. I was shaking all over and I couldn't stop sobbing. Lily put her arms around me. "Are you OK, Benny?" she asked. But I couldn't answer. I just kept crying. Ma was now hugging me as well.

"Come on, Benny. Let Lily and I help you up. Are you OK? Are you hurt?"

"No," I sobbed. "I'll be OK. I'm all right." But that was all I could say. The sobs just got louder and my shaking got worse.

"I'm sorry, Benny," said The Old Man. "I didn't mean it. You know I do stupid things when I drink. I'm sorry. Let me help you."

When The Old Man got closer, my tears increased in intensity. I thought why am I doing this? I could stop if I wanted to. But I didn't stop. I couldn't stop.

"Get away," said Ma to The Old Man. "You've done enough damage. Now, just go away."

"Yes dear," he said as he went back to the living room. Ma, Lily and I were all still sitting on the floor in the hallway.

"Do you want me to call Ernie to come and get you, Benny? I'll call Ernie and you can go there for the weekend. How does that sound? Would you like that?"

I nodded in the affirmative. And that's what happened. I listened as Ma spoke on the phone to Ernie. I heard her tell him that I couldn't stop crying. That my nerves weren't the same and I needed to get away for a while. I didn't think I was that bad. But if I wasn't, why wouldn't the tears cease? And the shakes. That's the part that I didn't like. It took me quite a while to even get to my feet. I rested on my bed while Lily and Ma talked to me until Ernie arrived. The Old Man stayed in the living room and remained quiet. Corey and Candy had quieted down as well. When I left with Ernie, I never felt so happy to leave. Although I did feel guilty about leaving Ma and Lily in the apartment. But Ma thought it best that I just go by myself. That way I would be better able to forget The Old Man and just try to relax. And she was right. The visit to Ernie and Ruth's Brampton apartment was just what I needed. I played with their baby Lizzie on their living room rug and no one talked about The Old Man. I once more appreciated how lucky I was to have a big brother who could make everything right again.

It must have been somewhere around the middle of November that I discovered I was having trouble reading Moby Dick. I don't mean trouble with comprehension. I mean reading. I was riding the Bathurst bus to the day's lectures, when I noticed that I had been trying to read the same page for the last ten minutes. Whenever the sun shone through the window of the bus, I could pick out a few words; when I was in shade, I couldn't focus on a single word. I then realized that it was time to stop pretending and face up to the truth – I was going blind. The frost on both of my eyes was getting thicker rapidly. I then decided that I had to tell Ma. It was time to call Dr. Curzon. I couldn't wait until my next appointment in January. And it was time to end my university days.

When I arrived downtown, I went straight to St. Mike's administrative offices. I bravely went into the office and told them that I had to quit school because of my health. I filled in all the appropriate forms (with assistance) and headed back home. I never even got a chance to say farewell to The Little Blonde-Headed Girl. When I got home, I confessed everything to Ma. To my surprise, Ma was not shocked. She said that she could tell that I was having trouble seeing just by the way that I sat when I watched TV. She also said that she would call Dr. Curzon's office for me. Then I called Mr. Connors to let him know that I was unable to complete the studies that he had been so instrumental in arranging. "You can try again next year," said Mr. Connors, but I wasn't so sure.

Dr. Curzon was surprised that the growth of the cataracts was so rapid, especially in my right eye. It was his earlier prognosis that I would have been OK until the next summer. He said that the behaviour of the type of cataracts which I was suffering from was relatively unknown. Not many people had developed cataracts through electric shock, because they usually died.

"But don't worry, Ben," added Dr. Curzon. "We'll have your sight back in a few months. You'll need some operations but you'll be seeing again before long."

He advised that it would be best if I waited until the New Year for the operations. I can't explain that reasoning now but it made sense at the time. However, I was greatly relieved. I put all my faith in Dr. Curzon's abilities and I never doubted that he would fix me up. No big deal. Now I could just relax at home, have more time to enjoy Penny, and listen to lots of music. At least it wasn't my hearing that was damaged. Now, that would have been disastrous. I could live without seeing things for a while.

After I left university it seemed that my sight diminished even quicker. It was almost like my body stopped fighting and gave up to the cataracts. About a week later, I went to my Secondary School graduation at Northern Hills. I stood at the back waiting for my name to be called. When it was announced and I walked on the stage, I heard a long, loud ovation. I walked forward and accepted my diploma from Mr. Connors. I looked towards the audience to see if I could pick out Ma, Lily, and The Old Man but all I saw was a large blur. Later Ma told me that everyone had stood when I came on stage. She was so proud of me.

Another day, I went for a walk with Ma and Penny to the corner store. As we passed these two ladies, I overheard one of them say, "That boy's blind. I wonder what happened to him. Poor boy." Ma later told me that I should think about getting a white cane. I didn't like that idea. I had no use for a cane regardless of the colour. Besides, white canes were for blind people. I wasn't blind. I just lived in a fog, that's all. I could make out the outline of things. I just couldn't focus on any features. But I could see well enough to avoid bumping into someone or getting run over by a bus. At least that was my opinion. But Ma wasn't about to let me test my street crossing abilities alone.

"I help you, Benny," volunteered Penny as she took my hand. "Poor Benny can't see, right Grammy?"

"That's right, dear," answered Ma.

When we got home, Penny told the Old Man about our short walk.

"I help poor Benny on the road, Grumpy. He don't see very good."

"Good for you, Penny," The Old Man responded. "You help Benny from now on. Will you do that for Grumpy?"

"Yes, Grumpy. I help Benny."

"Thanks Penny," I said. "I feel a lot safer already."

19 – Exhibit, Eh

As I had deduced, I really enjoyed the extra time that I got to spend at home during the day. Penny and I would keep each other company all day. We made a great pair. I introduced her to rock music and she made sure that I didn't bump into things. She soon became a huge fan of the Beatles, the Rolling Stones, Eric Burdon & the Animals, Donovan, and lots of other performers that I listened to. When one of their songs came on the radio she would usually recognize it before I did. Her favourite song at the time was Penny Lane. She would identify that one after only one chord. And she would sing along to the whole thing. And she would sing it all day just by herself. I wondered what Mr. and Mrs. Langdon would think about their daughter's musical education. But I don't think they minded too much. After all they were a young couple and probably had similar musical tastes.

The Old Man was usually not too bad to be around during the day either. A few times he would be drunk during weekdays but more often it would be the evening or a weekend before he got really plastered. So that was another good thing. I actually got to see The Old Man be human once in a while. Sometimes he would invite one of the tenants into our apartment. Then he would point to the picture gallery on our living room wall where all seven of us Cooper offspring were proudly displayed. He would introduce each of us in the following manner.

"This is Claudia. She is married to an MP in the Air Force. And here's Brad. He's also in the Air Force. He flies the big jets. This one's Ernie. He's in the militia. He shoots the big guns. This boy here is Billy. He's in the Army and he jumps from airplanes. This is the youngest boy, Benny. That's him over there. Say hello Benny. He got electrocuted with 27,000 volts and now he's blind. Oh yeah, this is Gordie. He lives in Napanee."

"Who's the young girl in this picture?" the visitors would invariably ask.

"Oh, that's Lily."

If you were wondering if The Old Man was wrong when he said that Brad was in the Air Force, no actually he wasn't. By that time Brad, Catherine, and the family had returned from Florida and Brad had resumed his military career. He was now stationed at Uplands Base (Ottawa) and they lived in a small town south of the capital city. I heard The Old Man repeat that same family introduction numerous times. It pretty well summed up what he thought about each of our life achievements. And poor Lily wasn't even worth a mention; at least Gordie had accomplished the enviable deed of living in Napanee.

Mr. Connors hadn't forgotten the promise of hockey tickets that Ron Ellis had made to Rick Field and me in the hospital earlier that year. So he called up the Leaf winger and arranged that we would get tickets to a game in December. Mr. Connors probably thought that I was depressed over having to quit university and envisioned that attending a Leaf game would cheer me up. It was a good idea but there was one major problem. By the time we went to the game, my eyesight was not very good. We felt rather privileged when we went into the Special Ticket Office at Maple Leaf Gardens and said that Ron Ellis was holding tickets for us. We got four seats – Rick went with his brother while I was accompanied by Ma. We were sitting in the corner of the end blues which was one of the steepest sections in the building. Ma held on tight to me as we went to our seats. She could probably imagine me losing my balance and tumbling over the railing to the ice surface below. The Leafs were playing one of the new teams – the Minnesota North Stars, I think. From our seats, I could just make out that there were players on the ice. I certainly couldn't tell who was who although I could distinguish to which team each player belonged. As for following the puck, not a chance. For some reason it appeared that every player was wearing a white helmet. If I recall correctly, Minnesota did have more players than most teams that wore helmets that year, but not all of them. And most Leafs went bareheaded. Luckily, Rick provided the play-by-play for me or else I would have had no idea what was going on. All that said, I was thrilled to finally be the witness to a live Maple Leaf game. And they won. And guess who scored two goals. Yes, Ron Ellis. Ma said that he scored them for me and Rick. I couldn't argue with that assumption. Later The Old Man commented, "See I told you that he would score for you. Just like when he saw you in the hospital except this time he got two for you. He should invite you to all their games. Maybe then the Leafs would win more often." He had a good point. So far the Leafs hadn't exactly lived up to my lofty pre-season predictions.

Christmas that year seemed like a dream to me. It was a good Christmas in the fact that Gord and Paula arrived on Christmas Eve and Ernie, Ruth, and Lizzie were there on Christmas Day. And best of all, The Old Man never lost his head. And the tree (decorated with new ornaments) remained standing until the Twelfth Day of Christmas. What made it seem like a dream was the white haze that I viewed it all through. I received some great gifts. From Gord, I got the new Rolling Stones album – 'Their Satanic Majesties Request' – which was viewed as their response to the Beatles' Sgt. Pepper's record. It wasn't well received but I thought it was a classic. Even the liner sleeve had some kind of strange smell to it. The best part was the 3-D picture on the front jacket cover. What was weird about that was the fact that I could make out more from the picture than anyone else. I'm not sure how that worked. I also received two sweatshirts that year. Lily gave me a plain white sweatshirt that had big, bold, black letters printed on the front. They spelled out 'MAKE LOVE NOT WAR'. I loved it. After I put it on, Ruth informed me that she was afraid to sit near me. The other sweatshirt (which was from Ernie and Ruth) was light blue with a large picture of Charlie Brown on the front. On the back it said, 'I Need All The Friends I Can Get'. Considering our earlier discussions about The Little Blonde-Headed Girl, Lily felt that the shirt was very appropriate. And so did Ma. Whenever I wore the shirt, Ma would make the following comment.

"Poor Benny. That saying on his back is too true to be funny."

"Yeah, Poor Benny," Lily would add, "he has no friends."

"That's not true, Fool Barkley Woman," I would respond to Lily. "Well maybe it's true here in Toronto but in Newburgh I have more friends than you can shake a stick at. I'm not sure why you would want to shake a stick at my friends. But in second thought knowing Brendan, Sneezy, and Flip, maybe you would."

"Poor Benny, he needs all the friends he can get," Lily would continue to tease.

"Hush your mouth," I would say, "you Fool Barkley Woman."

That had recently become my favourite pet name for Lily whenever we were teasing each other. I'll let you figure out where that name came from. Her high school friends had taken to calling her 'Coop'. But I didn't like that one. Funny that none of us Coopers had ever been referred to as Coop until Lily was tagged with the name that year. I still think Fool Barkley Woman has a much better ring to it.

I was due to have my first eye operation at the end of

January 1968. But before that, Dr. Curzon asked if I would mind if I attended an eye surgeon conference with him. My job was to be an exhibit – sort of Dr. Curzon's science project. As I described earlier, there weren't many people who had developed my form of cataracts so I made a perfect specimen. I agreed without any hesitation. I didn't mind at all; it sounded kind of cool to me. So I went to a downtown doctors' convention with Dr. Curzon and just sat there while numerous eye doctors examined me and discussed my case with Dr. Curzon. By now, my sight had deteriorated to the point where I couldn't even tell who was looking at me. But I enjoyed the experience as I kind of felt like a celebrity.

My first eye operation was at Toronto Central Hospital which is located downtown near the University of Toronto campus. That made it more difficult for the family to visit me but there was an upside to not being at Camden Hospital again – the food. The meals were much better at Toronto Central although that was not too difficult of a feat to accomplish. Dr. Curzon informed me that I would be awake for the operation as I was only to receive a local anaesthetic in my left eye. That eye was first up on the schedule. When I asked Dr. Curzon about the procedure, he explained how I could watch as they removed my eye and placed it on my chest in order to get at it better. That frightened me until I realized that Dr. Curzon was just pulling my leg. Before the operation I was injected with a drug to relax me. And then when it came time to freeze my eye, they inserted a large needle through my left temple and on into my eye. And boy did that hurt! I thought that I had never felt such pain. But thankfully it only lasted for a moment. During the operation, the relaxant did its job only too well. I talked Dr. Curzon's ears off. I never shut up. I was a talking machine. I wondered where The Little Blonde-Headed Girl was. I wouldn't have been afraid to ask her out on a date at that point. Afterwards, when I had returned back to earth in the recovery room, I apologized to Dr. Curzon and asked if I had talked too much.

"Well, you were kind of talkative," he laughed. "But it

didn't bother me. Everything went really well. You're going to be seeing before you know it."

"When do you take this bandage off my eye?"

"In a couple days to check it. But we'll keep it covered for about a week. How are you feeling?"

"Fine," I said.

I was embarrassed over my conduct during the operation. The worst part was that I could recall talking non-stop but I couldn't remember a single thing that I had said. The way that Dr. Curzon laughed I figured it had to have been an interesting conversation.

A few weeks later, I was back in Toronto Central Hospital for surgery on my right eye. The white fog had been removed from my left eye and I could see everything much clearer. The only problem was that nothing was in focus. In order to remove the cataract, it was necessary to remove my lens. I would be getting glasses to correct that problem after this second operation. The one major difference this time was the fact that I was put right under with a general anaesthetic. To me that was great because I had been dreading a second occurrence of the pain from the needle being injected into the side of my head. But I had to wonder if Dr. Curzon just didn't want to listen to my babblings again.

There's not much more to tell you about the second eye operation, so I'll skip right ahead to late February when I was home and I had my new spectacles. The lenses in the eyeglasses were over a quarter of an inch thick. Dr. Curzon referred to them as cataract glasses; I called them coke-bottom glasses. And they felt like a brick on my nose and ears. Regardless I was ecstatic. I could see again – clearer than I could even remember. Ma looked fantastic, Lily looked wonderful, Penny was beautiful, and The Old Man was – sorry I'm getting carried away now, aren't I? But you can probably imagine how I felt even though I never once doubted that the outcome would be otherwise. The glasses now took some getting used to. Everything seemed too close. I was bumping into things more than usual because my whole depth perception didn't seem right. At first I dared not pour my own glass of milk. And the eyeglasses were bifocals. Whenever I looked down I thought that I was going to trip over something. The floor just looked too close. When I took off my glasses, I could still make out things. It's just that everything was blurry. Look through a camera that's not in focus and you'll get an idea what it was like. Another thing that I looked at right away was the 3-D cover on my new Stones record. I was surprised that I couldn't decipher any more of the picture than I could before my eye operations.

Even though it was still winter, I also had to go for a walk with Penny and Ma to try out my new viewing capabilities. But we didn't go too far. I found that the sun on the snow was blinding. I realized that it was going to take some time to readapt to this new experience of sight.

One of my other senses – hearing – was also enhanced around then. The Old Man heightened my listening pleasure by buying a small tape recorder from one of our tenants who sold them for a living. I thought that was great. Now not only could I tape some of my favourite songs from the radio, but I could tape myself, Lily, and Penny as well. I don't mean singing. At least not me. That would have been scary. I just mean talking or trying to pretend that I was a stand-up comic. Also pretty frightening, now that I think about it.

One night in early March, The Old Man came home late and drunk. But he wasn't the least bit abusive upon his entrance. He was acting more like he does on the morning after a long drinking binge. The reason for this sudden change in attitude was the fact that he had crashed his new car. He had rammed into a couple of parked cars on Bathurst Street and completely demolished his Rambler wagon. And to complicate the matter, he had picked up a hitchhiker a few minutes before. So not only had he lost his car (which was still not paid for) and damaged two other vehicles, but he also feared a lawsuit from his young male passenger who had been slightly injured. But Lady Luck was on The Old Man's side once more. When The Old Man appeared in court to face his drunken and dangerous driving charges he was accompanied by his lawyer friend that lived in our apartment. The lawyer argued that Garfield Cooper had been suffering a lot of stress and depression lately because of the terrible circumstances surrounding an accident to his youngest son Benny. Not only had his son spent months in the hospital near death, but then his son had turned blind and it was feared that he would never see again. Now he was going through a series of complicated operations to try and recover his sight. No man could be expected to live through such trials and tribulations without feelings of despair. This state of depression invariably led Garfield Cooper to the bottle. Mr. Cooper promised that he had now seen that this was wrong and he would never fall to the evils of drinking again. He was now attending AA to seek help for his illness. It was a very touching and moving story, don't you think? The result was The Old Man got off with nothing but a small fine and the insurance company paid for the damage to the other two cars. Even the injured rider felt sorry for The Old Man and decided not to proceed with the lawsuit. The whole thing was enough to make the rest of us sick. How many of his nine lives did The Old Man have left? We figured that he had to have been getting close to the end of them.

Actually the lawyer wasn't that far off the mark when he described that I had to endure a series of eye operations. Dr. Curzon wasn't completely satisfied about the outcome of my first operation and advised that he would have to perform one more surgical procedure on my left eye. This time the operation was carried out at Camden Hospital. That made it much less of a hassle for Ma and Lily to visit me and it also gave me a chance to catch up with some of my old friends – the nurses, the student nurses, and the candy stripers. Not to mention The Vampire. And it also meant that I once more celebrated my birthday in the hospital. I was now nineteen.

The surgery went off without a hitch and soon I was home seeing even better with the aid of my coke-bottom glasses. When people asked me about my eye surgery, I used to kid that I had three operations – one for each eye.

At the end of March, The Old Man quit the AA and to no one's surprise reverted back to his drinking ways. And he did it with a bang. Ma, Lily and I were trying to watch something on TV as The Old Man sat at the table and progressively got drunker. He had started on one of his usual rants. The one that included the following diatribe.

"I've been around the world. I wasn't born yesterday. I know the score. Do you think I was born yesterday, you gray-haired old bag? You can't fool me. I know what the hell is going on. You're nothing but a whore. I wasn't born yesterday."

"You weren't born," I answered back. I then used a line that I was waiting for the opportunity to say. "Your father jerked off on a rock and you were hatched in the sun!"

"What did you say?" asked The Old Man who was obviously shocked by my outburst. "How can you talk to your father like that? That's a sweet thing to say. Where did you learn that? At university? Is that what we're paying for your education for? So you can be a smartass and badmouth your father. You hurt me, Benny. My father was a wonderful man. And there's never been a harder worker. He'd have given you the shirt off your back. What do you know about my father? He was far better than anyone in this room. I loved my father." The Old Man was starting to cry adding to the notion that he had been badly hurt by my insensitive remark. "Benny, I love you too. I love all my family. How can you talk to me like that?"

I was almost beginning to regret what I said. But it did manage to distract The Old Man away from directing his vindictiveness towards Ma. He then left the apartment to go off and drink somewhere else. The next morning, Ma told me that The Old Man still remembered what I had said. He said it had hurt him so much. He couldn't believe that 'dear little Benny' would say such a thing. He realized that he had said far worse things to us. But that was different. He would only say them when he was drinking. He didn't really mean them.

But Benny had never spoken like that before. It wasn't something that he would soon forget. However, I didn't feel any pity for the old bugger. And I never apologized. I just couldn't look him straight in the eye for a few days.

20 – Ten-Eyes

On April 4th we were watching TV when a news flash announced that Martin Luther King Jr. had been shot. I spent the next few days glued to the television watching the events surrounding his death unfold. I watched as they ran and reran the highlights of his life. The rest of the family (including The Old Man) watched most of the coverage with me. But I stayed up late at night alone to watch more. I couldn't get enough. It reminded me of the days surrounding John F. Kennedy's assassination. But Martin Luther King's death had a much bigger impact on me. When Kennedy was shot it was a surreal time but to be honest I hadn't really been following politics that much then. I couldn't say that I felt a lot of emotion over the event. However as I watched the stories on Martin Luther King, I more than once felt a lump in my throat and a tear in my eye.

When I went back to Newburgh later that month, Brendan and I discussed the effectiveness of passive resistance. He expressed the opinion that a more aggressive approach was required if we were ever to change the world. I had to disagree. I stuck to my pacifist philosophy and never agreed that the ends would justify the means. We had some pretty heated discussions. One thing that we did agree on though was our support for Pierre Elliot Trudeau as the next leader for Canada. Brendan even had a big poster of Trudeau on his bedroom wall. We were looking forward to a new society under Trudeau's direction. As I have mentioned earlier, I was a supporter of Lester B. Pearson's policies and felt that Trudeau was the best choice to continue forward along the same path. Brendan thought that Trudeau would prove to be a far better Prime Minister than Pearson ever was. And I was starting to feel the same. I commented that if Trudeau became Prime Minister and Bobby Kennedy became President, the world would experience a major shift away from the politics of war. "There's no need for a revolution," I argued.

Political discussions were not the only focus during my spring trip to Newburgh. There was still time for our usual sources of entertainment. And some new ones. Brendan, Sneezy, Dork, Birdbrain, Pooh, Sean Becker, and other Newburghers were all playing a game of pickup hockey at Tamworth arena. So I went along to watch. I found it kind of painful to watch as I wished I could have laced up the skates and joined them. I borrowed someone's skates to try it out but I kept falling over on my left ankle. I couldn't even stand up straight with the blades on. Before the game was over, I decided that I had seen enough and went to wait in the dressing room for the game to end. I knew that some cold beverages had been brought along for an after-game treat. Shortly after I went into the dressing room two girls entered and started talking to me. One was Valerie Burnside who lived in Strathcona. Her brother Matt was one of the competitors in the game. Matt Burnside had started to hang around with Brendan, Sneezy, and Flip on a fairly regular basis so I knew him quite well. I had never really noticed Valerie before but I did now. She had certainly grown up and developed since I had seen her last. I wasn't familiar with the other girl who was a friend of Valerie. Somehow the conversation turned to the art of kissing. You can probably guess that I wasn't the one that brought that subject up.

"Are you a good kisser, Benny?" asked Valerie.

"I don't know," I said truthfully. "I've never been tested. I mean I've kissed girls but I've never been compared to others. Well, at one time I was told by a girl that I couldn't kiss right and then she showed me how. She said that I was a quick learner."

"Is that right? How are you supposed to kiss then?" inquired Valerie.

"I don't know," I answered slightly embarrassed. "I can't describe it."

"Show me," Valerie replied. "Show me how you kiss. Come over here." She patted the bench right beside her.

"OK," I answered. I then went and sat beside Valerie and put my arms around her. And we kissed. And then we kissed some more. And some more.

"You are a good kisser," commented Valerie. "I liked that."

"So did I," I said. And I did.

"It's my turn now," said Valerie's friend. "Let me see if Benny is a good kisser for myself."

"OK," I agreed. So then we embraced and locked lips.

"Mmmm," commented the girl. "Not bad at all. You Toronto boys are far better kissers then the farmers around here."

I blushed in embarrassment and said nothing in response. I certainly didn't mention that I had found it more exciting when I was kissing Valerie.

"OK, my turn again," demanded Valerie. Being the gentleman that I was I had to oblige her. We were in a deep embrace when Pooh walked into the dressing room.

"What is going on in here? You're an animal, Dum Dum. Can't we leave you alone for a moment?"

"Nothing's happening," said Valerie. "We're just doing some testing. Isn't that right, Benny?"

"Yes, that's right," I said with a big grin. "I think I passed."

And then more and more of the players returned to the

dressing room including Valerie's brother.

"What are you doing in here?" asked Matt to his sister. "Come on, get out. People have to change."

"OK, OK, big brother. I'm going. See you later, Benny." Valerie stated. "That was fun," she added as she and her friend exited from the room.

Matt looked at me and smiled, "What the hell was that about, Dum Dum? Were you making out with my baby sister?"

"Who me?" I said innocently. "Would I do that?"

"Probably," he answered.

"I might have," I confessed.

When Brendan came into the room he apologized that the rest of them had left me alone. "You must have been bored stiff," he surmised.

"Something like that," I said.

I saw Valerie one more time in downtown Newburgh before I went back to Toronto. I was with Brendan, Flip, and her brother Matt. We were pleasant and polite to each other but we never had the opportunity to repeat our previous encounter. But we exchanged a lot of smiles. I don't think Brendan even realized that there was anything going on between Valerie and me. He couldn't understand why I was willing to miss the Stanley Cup playoff game on TV. Anyways, the Leafs weren't involved. They failed to even make the post-season that year.

After I returned home, I watched the remainder of the playoffs. The Montreal Canadiens won the Cup again by defeating the St. Louis Blues in the final. Somehow it didn't quite seem like a final to me. Forget the fact that the Leafs weren't there; it didn't even involve the two best teams. I mean the Leafs missed the playoffs for the first time in something like ten years and yet they had a better winning record than any of the Western Division teams. I'm not saying that the Leafs deserved to have participated in the post-season. They didn't. But the final was certainly anti-climactic to me.

Four days later, I became an uncle one more time. Brad and Catherine became the proud parents of a new baby girl. Brad called us the next day to give us the news. They named their new daughter Jennifer. And we were told in no uncertain terms that she would remain Jennifer. She was never to be called Jenny. And a long time Cooper tradition bit the dust.

May 1968 was also the month that I contracted a serious infection. It was called Trudeaumania and I had it bad. The federal election was in full swing and I was caught up in all the hoopla. So what if I was still too young to vote (the voting age was twenty-one), I could still feel like part of the process. I went to see Trudeau speak at Centennial Arena which was only a short walk away. I was part of the cheering and adoring crowd that welcomed his arrival in a limousine. I listened intently and cheered and applauded his entire speech. It didn't matter that I had to stand outside and listen to the entire proceedings over a loudspeaker. I again cheered when Trudeau made his exit back onto Finch Avenue. I even caught a glimpse of him waving to the crowd. I was mesmerized by the experience and went home on a high. I felt like the Leafs had just won the Cup.

Not many days later on June 4th, I experienced the other end of the spectrum of emotions. I stayed up late in order to catch the results of the California primary in the U.S. election race. I was elated when it was announced that Bobby Kennedy had captured the state. I could now see that my prophecy of a Trudeau-Kennedy era was close to fruition. The Old Man was the only other one in the family that stayed up. He was more interested in drinking than the primary, but so far he had been well-behaved and hadn't caused any trouble. So when the results were known, I went to bed happy about the outcome.

"Aren't you going to watch Bobby's speech," asked The Old Man.

"No, Dad. I'm too tired. I'll watch the highlights on the news tomorrow. Good night."

"Good night, Benny."

I was in a deep sleep when I heard The Old Man come into the bedroom. At first I thought he was probably drunk and was going to wake Ma up so that he could insult her. But it was me that he was calling.

"Benny," he whispered. "Benny, I thought you might want to get up. Bobby Kennedy's been shot."

"What?" I questioned. I felt a lump in my throat as I jumped from my bed and rushed into the living room. I stayed up the rest of the night as my worst fears became real. Bobby Kennedy had been killed. His death hit me harder than anyone else's. I was devastated. My dream for the future had quickly vanished in thin air. The U.S. was killing off anyone that could offer hope. I hardly moved for days. The Old Man watched most of the coverage with me. And he didn't even act up in spite of the fact that he was drinking. Lily and Ma also spent a considerable time in front of the television set during those few days. I just hoped that the other part of my prophecy wasn't about to fall apart.

We all watched later that month when Trudeau faced the angry crowd at the Ste. Jean Baptiste Day parade in Montreal. During the elections the next day, The Old Man and Ma both cast their votes for Pierre Elliot Trudeau. I figured that Ma would vote for Trudeau but The Old Man surprised me when he said, "I decided to vote for your guy, Benny." When the ballot results indicated a Trudeau victory, I called Brendan and we cheered together over the phone.

Towards the end of June after school had completed, Aunt Becky came to visit for a few weeks. When she arrived, Aunt Becky looked over at the couch and viewed me just rising to greet her.

"Hello, Aunt Becky," I said. "How are you doing?"

"Oh my Blessed Father, is that you Benny? I didn't recognize you. Is that you behind all that hair and those thick glasses? Look at your son, Mary. I would have walked right by him on the street. You look like a, a, I don't know what. Like some singer in one of those awful groups that appear on

The Ed Sullivan Show."

"Yes, it's me. I guess I've changed a bit since you've seen me last."

I almost thanked Aunt Becky for her complimentary comparison but I thought it better to just ignore it. I guess I've failed to describe my evolution into a hippie. My hair had grown back in and then it kept right on growing. It was well past my collar now. I had recently started to part my hair in the middle, and with my dark hair and drooping moustache, I was definitely going for the George Harrison look. He was my hero now. I hadn't changed my allegiance from the Stones to the Beatles but George was another matter. He was God. I even carried the lyrics of his song 'Within You Without You' in my wallet. I thought that song pretty much described my philosophy on life. And then there was my choice in clothes. I was wearing one of my turtleneck shirts that zipped up the back. This one was bright orange. My pants were dark green checkered bell-bottoms. I had stopped wearing my paisley cap since my hair had grown back in. I thought it was probably a good thing that I wasn't wearing my gold chain (not real gold) necklace with the large medallion on the end. That was a present from Lily for my nineteenth birthday. I figured Aunt Becky wouldn't have approved of that.

"Benny's got to wear his hair long to cover up his bald spot," explained Ma. "He didn't have much hair for quite a while. So I think he looks great now."

"And you've grown," continued Aunt Becky. "I'm sorry Benny. I didn't mean anything. You just surprised me. It's so good to see you doing well after that terrible accident. You're looking good. I just wish I could have come and saw you earlier."

"That's OK, Aunt Becky. There's no need to apologize. You're looking great too."

Lily then entered the apartment and gave Aunt Becky a pleasant greeting and a welcome hug.

"Oh my Blessed Father," exclaimed Aunt Becky, "look how much Lily has grown too. You're all grown up on me.

You've grown like weeds."

"It must be the dirt in the Toronto air," I remarked. "It makes a good fertilizer."

"Oh Benny. I see you haven't lost your sense of humour."

"Yeah, it's still bad," said Lily.

"You're just jealous, Fool Barkley Woman," I retorted.

A few days later, I made a major alteration to my appearance. Dr. Curzon prescribed contact lenses for my eyes. I wore them for only four hours on the first day; I thought that I would never get used to them. But by slowly increasing the wearing time each day, I was wearing them for a full day within a week. I had to readjust my vision all over again. Things looked smaller again. But this time the adjustment was swift. One benefit from wearing contacts as opposed to glasses was that I could see people and things that were beside me now. With the glasses I could only see straight ahead. I certainly preferred to watch what was going on around me. The purpose of the contact lenses were just to see anything at all; I required a new pair of glasses if I wanted to be able to read as well. These new glasses were trifocals. The top part was just plain glass so that I could still look people in the eye when I had my reading glasses on. The middle section was for reading at an arm's length. And the bottom of the glasses was for normal reading of something like a book. Those took some getting used to. I remembered that kids who wore glasses in public school were often kidded and teased with the nickname 'Four-eyes'. So what did that make me? Using my advanced mathematical skills, I calculated that I should be called 'Ten-eyes'. Not that I was going to suggest that name to anyone. Dum Dum would suffice for now.

Aunt Becky was as taken with Penny as the rest of the family. I remember when she was first introduced to Penny.

"What's your name, little girl?" asked Aunt Becky.

"Penny," she promptly replied. "Penny Lane, I mean Penny Langdon."

"And how old are you?"

"Almost two," said Penny proudly. "I can sing. Do you want to hear me sing?"

"Sure," said Aunt Becky.

"Penny Lane, dere's a barber showin' fotie-graffs, of evey head he's had the preasure to have known…."

I was relieved that Penny hadn't chosen the new Eric Burdon & the Animals song that she had recently been singing around the apartment. It had become one of her favourites.

"Ky Pilot, Ky Pilot, how high can you fy? You never, never, never reach the ky."

In mid-July I took the familiar bus ride to Napanee to visit my Newburgh friends for a week or so. And then I planned to invite some of my friends to come back to Toronto with me. Packing for this trip was now a totally different experience. I had purchased a record case that held about sixty to seventy albums. That meant I actually had room for some clothes in my suitcase. Usually when I rode the bus, I would watch as young girls my age would sit in some other part of the bus. Whenever the largest women or man clambered on the bus, I knew that they would sit next to me. And I was almost always right. But that was my lucky day. A hippie looking girl wearing a flowery short dress came up to my seat and said, "Hi, do you mind if I sit here?" That was the shortest bus ride of any that I had taken so far.

It was a fairly short visit to Newburgh that time, so there isn't all that much to tell you about it. But I remember a couple highlights. Brendan and I went to a concert in Kingston with one of his friends. It was my very first rock concert. We saw the Canadian group The Paupers, who were very popular in New York that year. The show was at the arena where the Kingston Frontenacs (a Junior 'A' hockey team) played. After the performance, Brendan and I talked to Skip Prokop – the drummer. I remember he told us that his favourite new album was the latest from The Byrds – 'The Notorious Byrd Brothers'. He advised that we pick up a copy and give it a listen. He thought that album most closely approached the sound that he was trying to create. Another first that I recollect happening was Brendan and me attempting to write poetry. We would sit down late at night and each of us would write a few stanzas and then we would compare notes. One time we tried it when we were drunk. We thought that it might prove to be an inspiration. However it was all pretty bad. Here's an example now. Perhaps if you are weak of stomach, you may wish to bypass this excuse for a poem and turn to the next chapter.

Misguided Youth's Reply

You tell me there will never be peace
As long as there is a Commie alive
Can't you see it's hate-mongers like you
That cause the wars of today
You say that we must kill to stay free
But when I say it's my right
To decide what I want to do
I am called a "dirty rotten Communist"
The time to start loving is now – right now
It'll be too late when we destroy the world
You can never achieve peace by wiping
Out another nation – can't you see that
So we'll keep on demonstrating
And we'll keep on until you listen
So start talking with your hearts – not your guns
Before you forget how to love

21 – Hippie Down!

It was somewhere around the beginning of August when Flip first came to Toronto for a few days before he and Brendan switched places. I can't recall too much about Flip's visit to Toronto other than the fact that he was terrified to go out on the balcony. It was a warm summer so I would often want to stand or sit out on the balcony. I was surprised the first time I walked out on the balcony and called Flip to join me.

"I'm not coming out there, Dum Dum," said Flip.

"Why not, Flip? It's nice out."

"I don't care. I'm not coming out. The balcony could fall."

"Don't be crazy," I laughed. "Come on out, Flip."

"No, I'm not kidding, Dum Dum. There's nothing holding that thing up. It just sticks out from nowhere. I'll stay in here on a solid floor, thank you very much."

"You're weird," I commented before deciding to try another approach. "Oh wow, you should see the four gorgeous girls standing down there in the parking lot. That's quite a bathing suit that one is wearing. You've gotta see this, Flip."

"No, I'm not coming out there. So stop making things up, Dum Dum. Even if you were telling the truth, I'm staying here."

"OK, I'm just going to stand here a minute then I'll come back inside."

"Why is Benny standing out there while you're in here?" asked Lily who had just entered the room.

"I'm not going out there. It's dangerous," replied Flip.

When Brendan replaced Flip, we decided to set some of our great poetic compositions to music. We sat in Lily's bedroom with my tape recorder as we played along to a few of each other's poems. Each of us sang (that's stretching it – it was more like talking) our own lyrics. Brendan performed one long song in which he rambled on ad lib for about ten minutes. There was one major problem with our recording session. We didn't own any musical instruments. But that didn't slow us down. Brendan played the electric can opener while I rubbed a hairbrush against the lid of my tape recorder. We thought we were musical geniuses. We dubbed ourselves 'The Two Extremes'. We recorded an entire album and called it 'Black and White (And Other Colours)'. All we needed was an agent and a contract and we would have been on our way to instant stardom. One day we ventured down to Yorkville, which in 1968 was Toronto's answer to the Haight-Ashbury district of San Francisco. With our clothes, we fit right in with the rest of the scene. But no one even recognized The Two Extremes.

Just before Brendan and I headed back to Newburgh to spend the remaining weeks of August, we received some upsetting news. Ma was reading the obituaries in the Telegram when she saw something that jumped out at her. I am not sure why she was reading the death notices that day. That certainly wasn't part of her normal reading practices.

"Oh my God, Benny and Lily, listen to this."

She then read out loud about a man named Smale who had drowned while fishing in an Ontario lake. As she continued to read it became painfully obvious that it was our neighbour in Hillsburgh, Sammy, Jenny, and Sarah's father who had passed away. I thought about Mrs. Smale who had always been so kind to us during our years as neighbours. How many times had they helped us escape from the house when the situation merited it? I had often gone in the car with Sammy, Jenny, and Mr. and Mrs. Smale to various places. Also Sammy and I had played in Mr. Smale's truck on numerous occasions. Ma then observed that the funeral was that day. There was nothing more we could do other than to phone the Smales and offer our condolences. I wished that I could have been there for my friend Sammy. If Mr. Smale's death had a meaning it sure was beyond my comprehension.

The next day, Brendan and I headed back to his place in Newburgh. I had decided to spend the remainder of the summer with my friends. However, I still didn't know what I was going to do in the fall. Because of doubts over my health earlier in the year, I hadn't done anything about registering for university again. Now I figured it was too late to get back into U of T. So I just decided to forget it all for the moment and have some fun. One of the first people that I ran into was Kelly Weston who inquired why Lily hadn't come with me. She then informed us that she was going to call Lily and invite her to come on down to Newburgh for a visit. Sneezy said that sounded good to him. And I didn't mind an excuse to see Kelly more often.

In the meantime, Dork had invited Brendan, Sneezy, Flip, and me to join him for a week at Dorchestershire Island. That sounded good to us in spite of the fact the Brewers' Retail was on strike and there was no beer to be had anywhere. We figured that we would be able to come up with other options. The day before our departure to Beaver Lake, Brendan and I were standing in front of the barbershop just shooting the breeze. A few minutes previously the barber had been trying to talk me into getting a haircut but I had respectfully declined.

"But Ben," he argued, "I can cut it so your bald spot would still be covered. You don't have to worry about that. I can leave it longer on that side. I would just cut it shorter at the back and around your ears. And I would thin it out all over. Your hair is very thick. It needs to be thinned out. Come on what do you say? You can pay me later if you're short of cash."

"No thanks, I think I'll just leave it for now. I like it long. Maybe another day. Thanks anyway."

"What about you, Mr. Casey?"

"No, I'm OK for another year or two. Thanks."

It was at that point that we ventured outside of the shop. Brendan was wearing an old and long blue shirt (not tucked in as usual) over a pair of ripped jeans. When he left the house earlier that day, Brendan's mother had taken one look at him and commented on his appearance.

"You're not going out like that are you, Brendan Thomas Casey?"

"Thanks mother," rejoined Brendan. "Now I know that I'm dressed perfectly. See you later."

I was wearing my favourite orange turtleneck shirt matched with green and white striped bell-bottoms (that I had often been told looked like pyjamas) and my gold chain pendant. We were just talking and standing on the sidewalk near a parked green '55 Ford when a strange man came up and stood just a foot or so from us. He looked to be about thirty years old, well over six feet tall, and muscular. Behind him stood a short dark-haired woman of about the same age.

"Have you ever seen a hippie down?" sneered the stranger.

"Excuse me," said Brendan. "What did you say?"

"I said, did you ever see a hippie down! You're a couple of damn hippies. I could take you down in a flash."

"We're not doing anything," argued Brendan. "We're just standing here minding our own business."

"You're offending me; that's what you're doing. Why aren't you two working? Too goddamned lazy, eh? Just standing around taking up space. Why don't you damn hippies get out and work for a living? Then you'll know what it's like to be a man in this world. Fucking hippies. Look at this," the stranger said as he grabbed hold of my pendant.

228

"What the hell is this? Does this belong to your sister?" He then let it go. "I'll leave you standing for now. I could take you down but I don't want to waste my time on sissies like you. Just get the hell out of my sight. You sicken me!"

"Come on, Benny. Let's go back inside," advised Brendan.

"All right," I agreed.

But as Brendan turned to go into the barbershop, I had a change of heart. If I just turned and walked away then I would be a hypocrite. It was time to stand up for what I believed in. To practice what I preached. So I waited and watched as the couple got back inside the car. Brendan poked me in the arm but I ignored him. Then the stranger noticed that I hadn't departed and he rolled his window down and once more directed his attention towards me.

"I thought I told you to leave, hippie!"

"Why, why should I? This is a free country. I have a right to stand here as much as anybody." I was surprising myself. I could feel shakes coming on but I ignored them.

"Think you're damn smart, do you? Talking to me about a free country."

"No, I'm not smart. I just don't understand why you're upset by the way we look. We weren't bothering you. It's just the way we like to dress."

"Well, I don't like it!"

"And I don't like your hat. But I don't let it bother me. That's your business. And the way we look is our business."

At this point, Brendan was doing everything to get my attention short of kicking me. "Benny, come on," he whispered. You don't want to get in a fight with this guy."

"You do think you're a smartass, don't you?" shot back the stranger. "You're just a stupid hippie."

"I may be a hippie. I don't know. What is a hippie anyway? And I may be stupid. But that doesn't mean I don't have the right to stand here. Where do you live?"

"What? Where do I live? You're asking me? Where do I live?"

"Yeah, where do you live?"

"Near Centreville, why? What's it to you?"

"Well my friend here lives here in Newburgh. In this town. Don't you, Brendan? That means we have more of a right to be here than you do."

"Shut up, Dum Dum," pleaded Brendan. "You're going to get yourself killed."

"Why am I wasting my time talking to you two?" said the stranger. "Do whatever you want. Just leave me alone." He then rolled up his window.

"OK, Brendan. I'm ready to go inside now. Let's go."

When we went inside, the barber asked if the stranger had been bothering us.

"We just had a little discussion. That's all," I said. "He wasn't so bad once you got to know him." I watched as the '55 Ford pulled away.

"You're nuts, Dum Dum. What were you trying to prove?"

"And you said passive resistance doesn't work. Ha, see it does. I certainly wouldn't have wanted to fight him."

"What would you have done if he had jumped out the car after you?"

"Ran like a deer. What do you think? I'm not that nuts. And I wouldn't have stopped until I was on the other side of Shit Creek."

For the first few days at Beaver Lake, there was only Dork, Brendan and me. Sneezy and Flip were to arrive later in the week. The first day it was so hot that Brendan and Dork decided to go for a swim off the end of the dock. I had not been in the water since I had been zapped so I originally decided just to watch them. But then I thought why don't I go in to cool down. I just needed to take out my contact lenses and I could go right under. So I walked up the short steps to the deck and then on into the cottage. I then put on my bathing suit and removed my contact lenses. I put on my coke-bottom glasses before I had a better idea. I put my clothes back on over my bathing suit before taking my glasses back off. I then walked back outside and carefully down the stairs to the dock. I could make out the outline of Dork and Brendan in the water only enough to know that they were watching me.

"Do you have your contacts out, Benny?" asked Brendan.

"Yeah, I'm thinking about going for a swim but I'm not sure yet." I then started walking towards the end of the dock.

"Be careful, Benny. Or you'll walk right off the end."

"Don't worry, Brendan," I said. "I can see fine. I know right where the dock...."

"Look out!" yelled Brendan and Dork in unison as I stepped off the end of the dock and went under the water. When I came up, Brendan and Dork were right beside me.

"I told you to be careful, Dum Dum," said Brendan. "I knew you couldn't see."

"I could see fine," I laughed. "I did it on purpose just to fool you."

"Sure you did. You never planned that. I saw you looking straight ahead and step right off into the water."

"Yeah, that's what I planned. It was a joke. I have my bathing suit on."

"And your clothes and your shoes. There's no way you did that on purpose."

"Yes, I did. It worked. I scared you shitless."

"You scared me alright. Now we'll have to watch you at all times. You're still not very steady on your feet."

"It was a joke, Brendan. A joke."

"It didn't look like a joke to me," added Dork.

And they never did believe me. For the rest of the stay at the cottage I could drive them crazy by just standing close to the water. They both kept expecting to have to rescue me at any minute. I guess my acting abilities were better than I realized.

That night I sat out on the deck drinking rye and coke and listened to my transistor radio. I was listening to a program on the Kingston station on which they played new albums. They were playing the debut album of a new Canadian group called Steppenwolf. Brendan and Dork were inside the cottage reading. I listened to all of the first side of the record and I loved it. I thought they sounded fantastic. When they started playing the second side and the loud, crunching guitar at the opening of 'Desperation' was in full swing, I cranked up the volume as high as it would go and carried the radio on into the cottage.

"You guys gotta hear this new group, Steppenwolf. They're fucking amazing."

"Hear it!" yelled Brendan. "You've got it so loud it sounds like static! Turn it down!"

"You've got no appreciation of good music, Dickman. I'm going back outside."

"It sounded good while you were outside. But you're waving that thing around so much it just sounds like a wind storm."

"They're fucking great!" I exclaimed. "See you later."

After 'Desperation', the DJ announced that they had to skip the next song because of bad language and drug related content. All he would say was that the song was called 'The Pusher'. And then 'A Girl I Knew' started playing.

"Hey, Brendan," I shouted. "They just skipped one of the songs on the Steppenwolf album. Something to do with bad language and drugs or something. I wonder what that song's about."

"Hey, that sounds interesting," said Brendan as he walked out on the deck. "I'd like to hear that song. We should buy the album. Bad language and drugs, eh. Did they say what the song was called? Hey, this song is good. You're right, they're pretty good."

Brendan then listened to the remaining two songs with me while Dork stayed inside and tried to read over the sounds of the blasting radio.

I knew it was going to be a fun day when I saw Dork and Barbra Wood (the girl from Toronto that we met at Beaver Lake the previous year) together in the shower washing each other. The shower was in the boathouse and I walked in on them by mistake. But before you let your imagination get carried too far away, you should know that they both had their bathing suits on. And there was more giggling going on than anything else. And then I turned and walked away. I'm sorry but if you are looking for a book with cheap, gratuitous sex in it then you picked up the wrong one. Earlier in the day Sneezy, Flip the Sausage, and Sean Becker had arrived. They were yelling and waving their arms across on the mainland while I decided whether to row across and pick them up. But eventually I did. Later Barbra arrived by boat and shortly thereafter a friend of Dork's arrived in another boat. No one except Dork knew him before; his name was Peter. After introductions we discovered that Sneezy, Brendan, and I had a connection with Peter. His father was the judge that we stood in front of and said 'Guilty' last fall. I found it kind of ironic that we were going to sit and drink with the son of the man who had convicted us of drinking underage. If Barbra was feeling uneasy about being the only girl among a group of drinking boys, she never expressed any reluctance. Even though there was no beer there was certainly no shortage of alcohol. Everyone had brought along their favourite liquor. As well as my usual rye whiskey, there was rum, gin, vodka, and who knows what else. I guess we all missed the beer and weren't experts at drinking the hard stuff, because we all seemed to be feeling pretty good before we knew it. Later that night after Barbra had long since departed and our liquor stocks were depleted of everything except vodka, we started a friendly game of poker. Eventually we also ran out of anything to mix with the vodka. Peter started drinking it straight. At first I thought he was nuts but he said to try it. So I did. It went down pretty smooth, I thought.

"There's a car sitting across on the mainland with its headlights on," said Sean suddenly. "They're pointing right at the cottage."

"That's weird," said Dork as he went to the window. "I

wonder who that is."

"Is that a cherry on top of the car?" asked Sean. "I thinks it's a cop car."

"I can't see," said Dork. "Maybe it's the O.P.P. They sometimes parole this lake."

"They wouldn't come in here, would they?" I asked. "So who cares? This is a private residence."

"If someone complained about the noise they would," commented Dork. "And if they suspected illegal activity such as drinking under-age."

"Well, there's none of that around here," said Brendan.

"Nope. None," said Sneezy. "We weren't noisy either."

"I'm not so sure about that," said Dork. "We do get pretty loud when we drink sometimes."

"Who us?" I asked. "Where's Flip by the way."

"Passed out over in the corner," informed Brendan. "On that couch."

"They're getting out of the car," said Sean. "Look."

"So, I won't pick them up if they wave to us," I said.

"We don't have to," said Dork. "The O.P.P. have a boat over there."

"Oh," I replied. "Well, they won't charge us. We have Peter here. His father will get us off."

"Not likely," said Peter. "He'll probably throw the book at me."

"Shhh, quiet," cautioned Sean. "I think I hear a boat starting. Listen."

"Yeah, I hear it," said Dork. "Look there it is. It's coming this way."

"Fuck!" yelled Brendan as he went flying out the back door of the cottage.

"Everyone be quiet," said Dork. "Let's pretend that we're sleeping and maybe they'll go away."

So that's what I did. I jumped on the free couch and closed my eyes. I felt like I did many years ago when I was hiding from the ghost. Except this time I didn't have any covers to pull over my head.

"Wake up, Dum Dum," someone was saying to me. "Look at yourself. Oh god, you're disgusting. Boy, do you stink. You've got puke all over you. Why didn't you go outside?"

"What? Where's the police?"

"That was hours ago. There was no police. It was just some people going to their cottage or something. Get up and clean yourself up."

"What? No police? What time is it?" I finally realized that it was Sneezy who was talking to me. "Oh, Sneezy. I don't feel too well."

"Well, get the hell out of here. You've done enough damage."

"I'll try. Help me up, Sneezy. What time did you say it was?"

"I didn't say. It's around eight o'clock or something. I don't know. God, you reek!"

"Sorry. Where's everyone else?"

"Still sleeping. All except for Brendan. I haven't seen him since he ran out of here last night."

"Oh shit!" I exclaimed before I made it outside just in time to release more of the vodka and part of my stomach from my system.

Suddenly Sean poked his head out the back door and yelled out, "Who wants bacon and eggs?"

"Not me," I attempted to say before continuing my regurgitation.

"Has anybody seen Dickman?" Sean asked.

"No," said Sneezy. "I'll go scour the island. Maybe he's hiding up a tree."

"Good morning," said Flip far too pleasantly as he walked outside. "What's wrong with you, Dum Dum? You look like death warmed over. Boy, I'm hungry. Did I miss any excitement last night? How about some nice greasy bacon and eggs, Dummer? Sean is cooking up a feast."

"Go away, Flip. And let me die in peace."

"Hi there," said Brendan. "What's up? You don't look

good, Dum Dum."

"Brendan," I answered, "where the hell did you come from? We thought the bears got you."

"And what happened to your pants, Dickman?" asked Flip. "You look like you pissed yourself. There's no bears on this island, is there Dummer?"

"First tell me what happened with the police," Brendan requested. "What did they say?"

"The police never showed up," I answered. "It was just someone who lived on the lake. I'm not sure if that was just Sean pulling a fast one again or not."

"Oh," said Brendan. "You mean I sat in the reeds for nothing."

"You did what?" I asked.

"Well, I went to the other cottage. But it was closed up as I thought. Then I saw a good place to hide – among the reeds in the lake. I waited there about ten to fifteen minutes before I waded out and sat on the deck of the other place. I guess I fell asleep there."

"Or passed out," I corrected.

"Hey everybody," yelled Flip as he reentered the cottage, "guess what. Dickman hid in the lake. What an idiot!"

"Well, I think I've finally seen it," commented Brendan as he looked at me with pity.

"Seen what?" I asked somewhat reluctantly.

Brendan looked straight at me and replied, "A hippie down."

"Brendan! Dickman! Brendan Thomas Casey! Brendan!"

"Who the hell is that?" wondered Brendan.

"Oh, that's Sneezy. He went hunting for you a while ago."

"Should I tell him that I'm here?"

"Nah, he's having fun. Let him be."

"Brendan! Hello Brendan. Where are you? Dickman!"

I didn't eat any bacon and eggs. I tried some toast but that wasn't going to stay down either. For the rest of the morning, I told the guys that they could set a clock by my stomach. Every half-hour on the half-hour it was time to be sick again. I swore that it would be a long time, if ever, that my lips tasted vodka again. Around noon, Barbra came back in her boat to see how we had recovered from the previous night.

"You don't look good, Ben," she said to me. "Were you a bad boy last night?"

"I was a very bad boy, Barbra. Were you a bad girl?"

"I'll never tell."

Later in the afternoon we returned to Newburgh. Somehow, I survived the car ride back. And then I finally discovered something that I could eat that my system wouldn't reject – a Popsicle. When Brendan and I walked back into his house we were greeted thusly.

"Hello Dummer, hello Peckerboy," said Brendan's brother Jimmy.

"Hey boys," said Brendan's mother Mary, "I'm glad you've made it home. I'm cooking a big turkey dinner just for you. Won't that be good?"

22 – The Black Plague

By the next night I had fully recovered from my alcoholic transgression and Brendan and I were staying up late listening to some music. Brendan had the same stereo record player that I had. The one that you got for free (or was it only dirt-cheap?) from Columbia Record Club for ordering a bunch of records. It had detachable speakers that you could spread out across the floor. That way Brendan could lie beside one speaker while I was near the other. We were listening to the Donovan album 'Mellow Yellow'.

"This record is what I call psychedelic, man," said Brendan.

"Yeah, you're right. It's really psychedelic. There's no loud guitars or anything. But the music is kind of – I don't know how to describe it."

"Psychedelic."

"Yeah, that's right. It's psychedelic."

"Psychedelic, man."

"Psychedelic."

"If I hear that word psychedelic one more time," yelled Mary Casey from her bedroom, "I'll come out there and clobber the both of you. Then you'll be seeing psychedelic stars. Let me tell you. It's bad enough listening to that music without your commentary. Just listen and shut up. Or else go to bed."

"Yes, mother," said Brendan. "We're going to bed after Donovan finishes." He then turned towards me and whispered, "Psychedelic, man."

Brendan and I were sound asleep in his room when the sound of something banging woke us up. I didn't know what it was until Brendan informed me that someone was knocking on his bedroom window.

"Who would be knocking on your window at this time?" I asked. "Probably Sean being The White Man again."

"Brendan, Benny, wake up," pleaded a distant voice.

"That sounds like Lily," I commented.

"You're right that's who it is. I wonder what she's doing here."

Sean then went and opened the front door and Lily entered.

"Lily," I said, "I didn't even know that you were in Newburgh. When did you get here?"

"This afternoon," replied Lily. "I was at Kelly's place until just a while ago. I've been banging on the window for ten minutes. You guys are hard to wake up."

"What time is it anyway?" I asked.

"About three in the morning," said Lily. "Kelly and I had a little fight. I don't even remember what it was over. She invited me down and then for some reason it didn't seem like she wanted me there. So I left. I hope you don't mind, Brendan."

"No, of course not. You can sleep in my bedroom with me and Benny can go to Kelly's."

"Ha, ha," I said.

"Seriously though, Lily. You take my room. We can sleep out here. It wouldn't be the worst place that we've ever slept. Right, Benny?"

"Thanks Brendan. Will your mom be OK about me staying here for a few days? At least until I can talk to some other of my friends."

"Sure, no problem. It's kind of nice to have a good-looking Cooper stay here for a change."

"See if I invite you to Toronto anymore," I said.

"Lily would invite me anyway, or Ma for sure."

"Yeah, you're probably right. I think Ma likes you for some odd reason."

"It's my good looks and charm. What else?"

It turned out that Lily only stayed at Casey's for one night. The next day she went to stay with another one of her friends. I can't remember who it was now. Perhaps it was Margaret Forrest. As for me, I was still confused about my relationship with a few different girls. One day, Jill Cox came to visit Brendan. And I thought, "Oh yeah, now I remember. I like Jill." But there was never anything between us. And then I ran into Valerie Burnside on the street. We talked and everything seemed very friendly but we didn't resume our kissing lessons. Next, I went to a barn dance with Brendan, Sneezy, and Flip. I danced half the night with Janet Washington and the other half with Beverly Coleman. Remember Beverly? She was the girl from Sudbury. She looked more attractive than I had even remembered. During one of our drinking breaks (while the square dancing was going on), Flip conferred with me.

"Dum Dum, you are nuts. You should go after Beverly. It's obvious that she really likes you. And she's the hottest girl here."

"Do you really think she likes me?"

"For sure. Go after her. What are you? A dumdum."

I wasn't so sure. I could still recollect Beverly making out with Pooh a couple years back.

Later that night, I spent an hour in front of Janet Washington's house talking to her about I don't know what. We seemed to get along great. But all we did was talk. I just couldn't get up enough nerve to make a move with any of these girls. Besides, I liked them all. And lastly, I was starting to notice Flip's younger sister, Karen. Sneezy told me that she had a crush on me. I didn't know what to do so I just cruised along and waited for someone else to make the first move. But there was no first move; I'm not so sure that the game had even started.

One day, Brendan, Sneezy, Flip, and I, and our friend Teddy Lennon were sitting in front of the Newburgh Lunch when we decided to form a rock band. I would play bass, Brendan would be on drums, Sneezy would play rhythm guitar, Teddy would play lead guitar, and Flip would play keyboards as well as be our lead singer.

"What should we call ourselves?" asked Sneezy.

"Flip and the Sausages," suggested Flip.

"How about the Dickmen?" said Teddy.

"I've got it," I said. "We'll call ourselves The Black Plague." That was after one of my favourite Eric Burdon & the Animals' songs. "We'll spread like a plague."

"I like it," said Brendan. "The Black Plague it is."

Now all we needed were two things and we were on our way to a huge success story – talent and musical instruments. At least we had the name. That was the most important thing.

That summer we discovered a new place to hang out. It was a canteen in the middle of nowhere not too far from Yarker. It just seemed to be in a farmer's field. But it served food and had a big jukebox. It was a good place to go to get a late snack and to listen to some music. Brendan and I would search out the loudest songs to play on the jukebox just to drive the other customers crazy. Brendan would often select the flip side of 'Lady Madonna'. It was a George Harrison song called 'Innerlight' which consisted of mainly sitar.

"What's this damn Chinese music that's playing?" one of the farmers would always complain. "It sounds like my cat when it's in heat."

Brendan and I would just laugh and keep playing it. 'Jumping Jack Flash' was my favourite to play. It never quite got the reaction that 'Innerlight' would though. We went to the canteen more than once in the car with Gordon Day. What was great about that was the fact that he had a new eight-track stereo system installed in his car. It sounded fantastic. I remember how good the new Stones album 'Beggar's Banquet' sounded when I first heard it on eight-track. I decided that whenever I got a car, I would definitely need one of those new sound systems.

What else do I remember about Newburgh that summer? Well, Dork, Brendan, and I went in the Skunkmobile to the Napanee Drive-in to see a movie called Barbarella. After the opening credits, I had already fallen madly in love with Jane Fonda. There were two other things that I remember about August 1968 and they were both on television. Brendan wanted to watch the Democratic Convention from Chicago, so we sat down to catch that with Mrs. Casey. We sat in shock as the television reporters focused on what was going on outside as opposed to inside. As we witnessed more and more protesters get beat over the head by the Chicago police, Brendan got angrier and angrier.

"See, Benny. See what passive resistance does for you. You get yourself hit over the head."

"What do you think they should do? Fight back?"

"Yes. And get organized. Not just sit there and take all that shit. This is sickening. It's unbelievable."

"Oh shit," I said, "the cops have gone wild. That girl was just sitting there. The U.S. has gone nuts. I bet everyone will just say that those kids deserved it. They're just hippies. Unbelievable."

A short time later we watched in shock and anger again as the Soviet Union sent the tanks into Prague. So much for my prediction of a changed world. It had changed all right – for the worse.

By the time that I finally made it back to Toronto, Ma informed me that Mr. Connors had called several times. When I returned his call, Mr. Connors couldn't believe that I hadn't done anything about re-enrolling at U of T. "Don't worry," he said, "I'll take care of everything." And he did. I was accepted back into the four-year General Science curriculum and would once more be attending St. Michael's College. It was a good thing that someone was looking after my education. However before my formal tutelage resumed, I discovered a new institution to assist in my continuing musical education. It was called The Rock Pile. It was a new music club located in a Masonic Temple at the corner of Yonge and Davenport and I was a card-carrying member. Over the ensuing months I saw performances by groups such as Country Joe and the Fish, Procol Harum, the Jeff Beck Group, the Chambers Brothers, Iron Butterfly, Deep Purple, Canned Heat, the Mothers of Invention, and Spirit, just to name a few. I also saw some of the blues greats who Brendan and I were totally ignorant of only eighteen months earlier. This included legends like Muddy Waters, Buddy Guy, Albert King, and Howlin' Wolf. The house band was a local group that called themselves Transfusion. Also not quite a house band, but semi-regulars was a Toronto blues band by the name of McKenna Mendelson Mainline. I loved everything about The Rock Pile. I would go every weekend regardless of who was playing. Some of my favourite concerts were those by people I knew nothing about. For example, I knew that Jeff Beck had once been in the Yardbirds and that was all. And he blew me away. His guitar wizardry was amazing and I enjoyed his young lead singer. A fellow called Rod Stewart. The bass player was an unknown by the name of Ron Wood. But what I liked best about The Rock Pile was the atmosphere. I could decide at the last minute to go to the show and I never had any trouble getting in. Everyone would sit on the floor, so that meant that you could see well from everywhere. I would often see some of the same people in the audience each week. There was one young girl with whom I often shared food and conversation prior to the show. I don't think I ever knew her name.

Anyway to get this book back on track, I started back at U of T in September 1968. That meant that Lily was now entering Grade 10 at Northern Hills Secondary School. The only advice that I had for her was to avoid flying balloons. She thanked me for that. Lily had developed quite a few friends that I also would associate with. I guess Lily remembered the words on my Charlie Brown shirt and decided to share some of her friends with me. I certainly didn't complain, after all most of her friends were female. There was Jenny Farr, Melanie (and her boyfriend David), and a girl with the curious name of Wendy English. Combine the name of my first two girlfriends and you'll see why I say 'curious'. In typical fashion, I liked all three of these girls plus other friends of Lily who I can't recall anymore.

As for me and the U of T, I was repeating all the same classes such as Chemistry, Botany, Zoology, Physics, Mathematics, and English. If I found some of them repetitive of Grade 13 the previous year, you can imagine what I thought about the first couple of months of that year. It was definitely a rerun. That wasn't all bad though. It didn't hurt me in subjects like Zoology where I really needed a refresher course. It's amazing how much you can forget in ten months. I still declined when it came time to dissect frogs though. I wanted proof that they couldn't feel anything after jabbing them in the back. At least at university they would let you sit with someone else and watch. I recalled that when I refused to perform the same procedure at school in Napanee, I was just given zero on that portion of the curriculum. As for Botany, I had a new lab mate. Her name was Paula. Guess what. I liked her. Even though it was mostly the same classes, I wasn't running into any of the people that I had met the year before. The campus was that large. Then one day as I was heading to Botany class, I saw Susan Wynn enter the lab across the hall from ours. "The Little Blonde-Headed Girl!" I said to myself, "I've got to show Lily that I'm getting braver." And then I found myself standing beside The Little Blonde-Headed Girl in her lab.

"Hi Susan," I said. "How are you doing?"

"Ben!" she replied in surprise "It's good to see you. How are you doing? I heard you had to quit school last year." She then reached out and touched me on the arm. "Welcome back."

Did you hear that? The Little Blonde-Headed Girl was

glad to see me. And it sounded like she missed me. Wait until I tell Lily. Now's the time. I should ask her for a date. She must like me too. No, I'm not sure. I guess I'll wait until another day.

"I'm fine, Susan. It's good to see you again. I guess I better head back to my lab. I'll see you again later."

"OK, Ben. My lab is the same time every Tuesday and Thursday."

"Oh, that's good. I'll come see you again. Bye for now."

"Bye, Ben."

So that became my routine two days a week. I would leave my lab whenever there was a chance for a break and go visit The Little Blonde-Headed Girl if for only a few minutes. And I promised myself that I would soon ask her for a date. I just had to wait for the right moment.

23 – The Pusher

Sometime that fall, our lawyer had arranged that I meet with the lawyers that were representing the school board. As I mentioned earlier, we had launched a lawsuit against the school board, the school, and one of the teachers. What I didn't tell you was the amount of damages that we were seeking – $250,000. That was an astronomical sum in the sixties. I couldn't imagine what I would do with a quarter of a million dollars. Earlier I had visited a psychiatrist in order to assess the extent of any possible mental damage because of the accident. I even got to participate in the inkblot test. I thought a lot of them looked like the projections on the screen at The Rock Pile but I never admitted that. The outcome of that examination was the prognosis that I hadn't suffered any brain damage. Are you surprised? So now I was going to sit across from the enemy and discuss the effect that the accident had on my lifestyle. I followed my lawyer's suggestion and wore my coke-bottom glasses for the examination. I don't really recall a lot from that meeting. It sort of seems like a dream now. I know that I was asked how the accident had affected me personally. They were more interested in the permanent results of being electrocuted. The months of pain and suffering were glossed over pretty quickly. The effect on my family (especially Ma) was not even an item of discussion. So what was left to tell them then? I had lost my eyesight. But I could see now. It hadn't affected my education other than losing a year. My earning capabilities weren't harmed unless I had planned to climb telephone poles like The Old Man – not likely. If only I could have been dumber. Then I would have had a stronger argument for a loss in future wages. So I told them that I couldn't ice skate anymore. And that I couldn't water ski. I couldn't think of anything else. They asked if the accident had affected my relationship with girls. Was I having a problem getting dates because of my scars and other noticeable injuries? So I told them the truth. Yes. I was having a problem getting a date. And that was about it. Afterwards my lawyer said that I had done well. He said that he would be getting together with the other lawyers and it was possible that an out-of-court settlement could be reached. He would keep Ma apprised of the situation. Since I was still a minor, it was Ma that was officially launching the suit. I was told that the proceedings could go on for years, so I once more just put it all out of my mind.

I decided it was time to make a trip to Newburgh again. Already, you may say. Well, as I had mentioned the first few months of classes were repeats, so I decided to head back down now while I had the chance. So sometime in October I found myself once more on the bus heading towards Napanee. Since I was only going for a few days, I left my record case at home and only brought along a dozen or so albums in my suitcase. Just like old times. One of the records was Steppenwolf which I had purchased as soon as I had returned to Toronto a few weeks back. But this time I had something else in my case – a nickel of hashish. I had never smoked hash before in my life let alone buy it, so this was a first for me. I had smoked marijuana a few times but I had never purchased that either. I guess it was at some of the concerts where one of those cigarettes might have gotten passed my way. I don't really remember now. But by that point I hadn't yet even experienced any kind of high from the drug. So I thought that I would give it a go. You may wonder how someone with no Toronto friends was able to purchase such a thing. Well, keep wondering. On the first night in Newburgh, Brendan, Sneezy and I went to Flip's house. His parents and sister were not home at the time so I brought up the subject of the hash and inquired whether anyone wanted to try it out. They all said, "Why not?" So we put it in the centre of the table and passed out straws. After igniting the hash, we all took turns taking a whiff of the smoke.

"I don't feel anything yet," commented Brendan.

"Neither do I," said Sneezy.

"Or me," added Flip.

"Be patient," I said. "Do you get drunk after one beer? Give it time."

"Sneezy gets drunk after one beer," remarked Brendan.

"Shut up, Dickman," replied Sneezy.

"I still don't feel anything," said Brendan after a few minutes.

"I don't feel anything at all, all, all," laughed Flip.

"Me either," I laughed. "Nothing. I feel nothing. Do you feel anything, Sneezy? Whoa, what was that?" I then started giggling.

"What, I didn't see anything," said Sneezy.

"Whoa, there it goes again," I laughed. "I'm just joking, Sneezy. There's nothing. But I think I feel something. Nope, I feel absolutely normal" I started to laugh uncontrollably. "I don't feel anything. Do you, Flip?" I then burst into laughter.

"I feel nothing," laughed Flip. "I am; therefore I feel nothing. I feel; therefore I am. I am what, Dum Dum?"

"You are higher than a proverbial kite. That is what you are. Just don't go close to the hydro wires. Then you will be zapped."

"I think I feel it now," said Sneezy. "My head is going in circles. Is that what you feel?"

"No, my head is in trapezoids," I replied. "What about you, Flip?"

"I think it is gone. My head is gone."

"So what else is new," said Sneezy.

"I still don't feel anything," complained Brendan. "This stuff is useless. It does absolutely nothing for me."

"Oh, poor little wee Brendan," I chortled. "Do you want a refund? But you didn't pay anything."

This continued on for several minutes as Sneezy, Flip, and I progressively became more and more prone to fits of uncontrollable giggling. Brendan was just getting more and more frustrated.

"This is stupid," he finally expounded. "I'm going to get a beer. Does anyone else want a beer?"

"Not yet," we all said. "Maybe later."

"Mmm," that's good commented Brendan after taking his first sip of beer. "Now this is something real. Not like that other junk. What a joke that stuff is. I can't figure out what all the fuss is about. And the government thinks that stuff is going to ruin a generation. Not likely. We'll all be old or in our grave before we get a high on that stuff."

I just stuck my tongue out at Brendan and then made some of my patented screwed up faces before finally speaking. "You're right again as usual, Mr. Brendan Thomas Casey. Your royal highness. King of the nation. It's all a hoax perpetrated upon us poor unsuspecting masses by the bourgeoisie."

"Let's bow to the king," said Flip.

"Long live Dickman the first," shouted Sneezy.

"Long live the king," the three of us cried out before we lost it all together. We kept looking at the puzzled expression on Brendan's face and laughed even harder each time.

"You three are nuts. I'm having another beer."

The next day, Brendan and I decided to go into Napanee to visit my brother Gord. We also concluded that it would be a good idea to take along some of my records so that we could continue our quest to bring Gord's musical tastes into the sixties. Gord and Paula were now living in a small house situated in downtown Napanee. After locating the house, saying our hellos to the two of them, consuming a few beers, and discussing what was new in the world and with each other, we finally got around to putting some records on the turntable. Country Joe and the Fish were first up on the agenda. After hearing 'The Fish Cheer' and the opening few chords of 'I-Feel-Like-I'm-Fixin'-To-Die Rag', Paula said that she had heard enough of the shit and left the room. Unfortunately, with it being a small house, Paula couldn't really escape from the music (or noise depending on your point of view) altogether. We listened to the entire 'I-Feel-Like-I'm-Fixin'-To-Die' album before progressing along to Steppenwolf. I think it was during 'Born To Be Wild' that Paula yelled down the small open stairs.

"How long do I have to listen to this shit? This is ridiculous."

"This is the last record," said Gord. "We'll turn it off after this one."

"Thank God. I can't stand much more."

"OK, honey."

"Maybe you should turn it down a bit, Gordie," I suggested.

"No, then we won't be able to hear it. It won't hurt Paula to hear some music. I don't play this thing very often. My little brother and little Brendan Casey are here to see me. She should understand. I guess we should not sing along as loud though."

"All right," we agreed.

But we broke our promise. When 'The Pusher' commenced, Brendan and I couldn't help ourselves. We had to sing out. The number of beers that we had consumed by this moment may also have had something to do with our inability to practice vocal restraint.

"Goddamn the pusher," we sang along with John Kay. "Goddamn the pusher man."

I guess that was just about enough for Paula, because she soon hurried down the stairs and stood amongst us.

"Turn that goddamned thing off, right now! This is my

house and I don't have to sit upstairs and take this shit anymore." She then started for the record player.

"OK, OK," said Gord as he lifted the arm off the record and then removed the album from the turntable before Paula could reach it. "It's my house too, you know. And Benny and Brendan are my company."

"Your company! Your company! I can tell them to go whenever I want. Get out of my house right now," Paula shouted at Brendan and me.

"You can't throw out my company," argued Gord. "Stay you guys. Come on, Paula. We've turned off the fucking music for Christ's sake."

"Get out! Get out all of you. You too, you drunken bastard." Paula was directing her words towards Gord. "Out! Out! How dare you swear at me. You're just like your father when you drink."

Brendan and I then scurried out the front door but not before I had collected my records. Gord was right behind us.

"And stay out!" yelled Paula as she slammed the door shut.

"I'm sorry about that," apologized Gord.

"Don't be sorry, Gordie" I said. "It's not your fault. We shouldn't have sang. I guess that record's kind of loud."

"Yeah," Brendan added. "I'm sorry to get you in trouble with Paula. Where will you go?"

"Oh, she'll let me in when she calms down. This is not unusual. We fight all the time. I just wish I could have heard the rest of that Steppenwolf album. It was good. That 'Pusher' song is amazing – what I heard of it. You'll have to play it for me again some other time."

"Not when Paula's around," I suggested. "I think she's had enough of the goddamn pusher man."

That reminds me that a few weeks after I returned to Toronto, Brendan wrote me a short note to tell me about a rumour that was circulating around Newburgh.

Hey, Dummer. You better be careful the next time that you come down. There's a story going around that you have been supplying drugs to all the kids in Newburgh. That you buy them in Toronto and sell them down here for a profit. What a joke, eh? Mother's OK though. I told her that it was all a bunch of lies. She believes me. She thinks she knows where the gossip started. She doesn't care much for the person who started it. I'll tell you about it the next time you're down. I wouldn't bring any funny grass next time if I was you. Not that I would miss it. It's up to you. I don't care. But I thought that I better tell you. How do you think the Leafs will do this year?

And don't bother trying to deduce who could have started that rumour. It wasn't anybody that's even mentioned in this book. And I'll just leave it at that. Anyway, at first I laughed. It seemed funny to me. The way that stories could take on a life of their own in small towns just amazed me. Then I realized that it wasn't that funny. Brendan had a good point. I had better cool it when it came time to pack my bags for Newburgh. Not that I had planned to buy a lot of drugs anyway. So I heeded Brendan's advice. I certainly wasn't going to complain about sticking to beer.

I realize that I haven't spoken much about The Old Man lately. That's just because I couldn't think of any more original stories to narrate. He was getting as drunk as usual. Or to be more truthful, he was getting more drunk more often. It seemed to be almost daily. But what new can I tell you about it. You've heard it all already. His drinking habits were getting to be well known around the building. So much so that the management got wind of it. The Old Man was told to move along. They had only tolerated him as long as they did because Ma was so well regarded. Both for her hard work and her personality. All the tenants loved her. And she kept the building spotless. But it came to a point where the management could no longer ignore The Old Man's drunkenness. Especially after he told one man in the building to, "Go fuck yourself and mind your own fucking business." In spite of all that, he was still told that he would be given a good reference if he wanted to be a superintendent at another building. And before long, The Old Man applied to an ad as a superintendent for two small buildings located in the Yonge-Sheppard area of the city. And he was hired. So on December 1st we would be moving once more. This move wouldn't be near as dramatic for Lily and me as was usual. I would stay at U of T, of course, and Lily would remain a student at Northern Hills. And we didn't have to worry about Corey and Candy not being allowed at our new place. But there was one part about the move that upset us all. We would have to say our good-byes to Penny. Her parents wouldn't be able to take her over to our new location every morning. They had no car and rode the TTC to work each day. So they found another tenant that would look after Penny.

"Why do you have to go, Grammy?" asked Penny. "I'm going to miss you, and Benny, and Lily too. I'll even miss Grumpy."

We had to laugh at that comment. I guess that's one good thing that you could say about The Old Man – he never went into one of his profanity filled tirades while Penny was around. Funny, when we were young kids that had never stopped him.

Before we had to move, I can tell you about three new things that entertained me that fall. The first was The Electric Circus, a new rock club that opened on Queen Street. I also became a card-carrying member of that establishment. Although, I enjoyed the club I thought that it never had the same atmosphere as The Rock Pile. It just wasn't the same relaxing feeling there. For instance, people stood up rather than sitting down for the show. I don't know; The Electric Circus just worked too hard to be cool rather than just being natural. For example, the manually operated dish of water and oil to display patterns on a front screen at The Rock Pile was replaced by an electric light show at The Electric Circus. Regardless, The Electric Circus gave me the opportunity to once more see the Jeff Beck Group and Country Joe and the Fish. I even talked to Bruce Barthol (the bass player in the Fish) between sets. I can't imagine what I would have said to

253

him. I wonder if I told him that I played bass in a group called The Black Plague.

It was at the Electric Circus that I first heard the new album by a group formed from the remains of the Yardbirds – Led Zeppelin. It sounded pretty good blaring out over the sound system.

The next source of entertainment that I wanted to mention was Rowan and Martin's Laugh-In. It was hilarious and "Very interesting." And lastly, I have to tell you that Ma ordered a guitar for me from Eaton's. It was a Stella acoustic guitar. I bought a book of guitar chords but I have to admit that I was an impatient learner. I didn't want to learn chords in order to play 'Home On The Range'. Not me. I wanted to go straight to playing lead. I used to play my Canned Heat album and pick along to all the blues licks. I should say, I attempted to pick along. But it was fun. I even tried playing the bass notes. But I never got by the first chord in the book. I wonder what chord it was.

24 – Where's the Week Gone?

On the first of December we sadly said goodbye to Penny and moved to our new home. Penny's parents and Ma promised each other that we would still get together on a regular basis; but I knew that it would probably not work out that way. Maybe for the first month or two but then we would become distant and we would never see Penny again. And that's exactly what happened. And that's why I had more than a tear in my eye when I kissed and hugged bye-bye to Penny. I wondered who would continue the job as her musical guru. I would certainly miss her smiling, happy face.

Our new home was a two-bedroom apartment in one of the two apartment buildings that The Old Man was now maintaining. They were small two-story buildings situated a block or so apart on different streets. Since it was a two-bedroom, I had the choice of the pullout couch or having my bed set up in my parent's room. I chose the couch. The Old Man informed us that this move was only temporary anyway. Just for two months. Then we would move into the other building and have a three-bedroom apartment. Which meant that I would have my very own bedroom for the first time in my life. That would be a thrill. However I would have gladly shared it with Billy or Gordie if they had wanted to return.

But before then it was the two-bedroom apartment and the couch. I would describe the layout of the place like I usually do but I can't recollect one single feature of the apartment. All I remember was that it was a short walk to the Yonge bus if you cut across an open field that was attached to one of the businesses located south of Sheppard and east of Yonge.

As the year of 1968 was winding down, the classes at U of T became a little harder. I had gone past the point in the lectures where I was forced to resign the year before. But I was still doing well in my courses and I was having a ball. There were the anti-war demonstrations and marches in which I was an enthusiastic participant. I actually felt like I was making a difference. Then there were the anti-war rallies. Twice during a rally at Convocation Hall, we had to evacuate the building after a bomb scare. I wondered if my former friend or one of his Western Guard buddies had something to do with that. We occupied the U of T President's office for a day on another occasion. I can't remember why now. I know that I was one of the few males participating in the sit-in so I think it must have had something to do with women's rights. One of the women (it's probably time that I talk about women and men as opposed to girls and boys since I was getting close to being twenty years old) from my Math class commented that I was a brave and dedicated person to face the threat of bombs and other unknowns to fight for what I believed in. But that was just being part of the times, there was certainly no involvement of bravery on my part. The campus (like that of most North American universities) was full of dissent and protest and I felt that I had to be part of it. If I just went to class and then went home, I would be like the rest of the system. I thought things were going to change and I wanted to be included. Was it exciting and fun? Sure. But is that why I contributed to the protest movement? No, I don't think so. I honestly was looking to influence the direction of society. All right, I'll get off my soapbox now and tell you about what you really want to hear. No, I still hadn't asked The Little Blonde-Headed Girl for a date. And worse, once the New Year of 1969 commenced she was no longer taking botany at the same time as me. I'm afraid that I completely lost track of her.

On the second anniversary of my transformation into Electric Man, we moved to our new apartment. I now had my own bedroom. Which meant that I could hang up posters and place pictures wherever I wanted. I taped on one wall the poster from The Beatles ('The White Album'). The wall above my bed was reserved for the Bob Dylan poster with his silhouette and rainbow coloured hair, which came inside 'Bob Dylan's Greatest Hits'. I framed the pictures of John Lennon and George Harrison (again from 'The White Album') and placed them prominently on my bedroom dresser. The frame at one time had contained a photo of my favourite Marlie – Brian Glennie. Why nothing pertaining to the Rolling Stones? That's easy to explain. None of their albums had free pictures or posters. Unless you count 'Big Hits (High Tide & Green Grass)', but I wasn't about to rip those pictures out of the jacket cover. Afterwards The Old Man commented to Ma that I had gone a bit weird.

"Benny's putting pictures of bloody Beatles on his dresser like they're his family or royalty or something," he said.

"Gods," I corrected to Ma. "Not royalty. I'm not a monarchist."

The first few months of 1969 seemed to fly by. I thought that time was travelling far too fast now that I was older. When I was a young boy, a year seemed to last for an eternity. Now it felt like nothing. I wanted things to slow down a bit. I had enjoyed being a teenager. Why did I have to get older? I could empathize with Peter Pan's viewpoint. I didn't want to grow up. Ma also felt that life was passing by too quickly.

"Is this Tuesday already?" she would ask.

"Yup, Ma. Tuesday it is."

"That means tomorrow is Wednesday, the next day is Thursday, and before you know it, it's Friday. Where's the week gone?"

I loved that interesting perspective on the passage of time.

For the first time since 1966, I was able to celebrate my birthday at home. In spite of my protestations, I got older and turned twenty. I was now a grownup. If it had been possible, I would have gladly returned to the days when I was 'only nine'. But that didn't mean that I couldn't enjoy the present. A few days later, I was sitting alone in the Coop at St. Mike's having my lunch. I was listening to Jimi Hendrix playing 'All Along the Watchtower' on the jukebox (my selection), when I noticed the most gorgeous woman that I had ever seen enter the room. She had long blonde hair and a smiling face. She was wearing a short mini-skirt and long white boots. And then I noticed something else. It appeared that she was walking towards me. And her smile got wider. She was walking to my table. It was The Little Blonde-Headed Girl – Susan Wynn.

"Hi, Ben. How are you? It's great to see you."

"Hi, Susan. I'm fine. How about you?"

"Good. Do you mind if I sit with you?"

"No, that would be great. Have a seat."

"Tell me what you've been up to, Ben. I've missed your sense of humour."

She missed me! She thought that I had a sense of humour! I was in the clouds. The most beautiful woman in the Coop was sitting and talking to me. I had noticed the eyes of other men follow her to my table. I was the envy of every man in the room. At least that's what I thought. We talked for about fifteen to twenty minutes before it was time to head to my next class.

"I hope to see you again soon, Susan," I said.

"Yeah, I'll see you, Ben. Good luck on your exams."

"Yeah, same to you. Bye."

"See you," she said with a smile.

When I got home that evening I had to tell Lily.

"Guess who I saw today, Lily."

"The Little Blonde-Headed Girl?"

"Right on. She looked great. We had a long talk."

"Did you ask her for a date?"

"No," I said shamefully.

"Well, will you see her again?"

"Sure. I mean, I don't know. We just said goodbye."

"Ahhhhhhhh! You're hopeless."

"She missed me. She thinks I'm funny."

"That's for sure. You're a funny guy, Benny."

"But you should have seen what she looked like. And she sat with me. I think next time I'll ask her out. The worse she can say is no, right?"

"Or she could have a boyfriend that's seven feet tall and very jealous," laughed Lily.

"So what? He wouldn't dare hit a blind cripple."

"And brain-damaged. Don't forget that."

"I love you too, Sissy."

"Don't call me Sissy, dear little Benny."

"OK, Fool Barkley Woman."

When it came time to study for the exams, I shut my bedroom door and tried to read the textbooks and my notes. But I could never really study for Math or Science that easily. If you weren't picking it up as you went along then you would be hopelessly lost anyway. So I found that a lot of the time I spent picking notes out on my guitar along to Bob Dylan singing on 'Nashville Skyline'.

The exam writing itself was a strange experience. For some of the exams, I sat on the floor of Varsity Arena along with hundreds of other students in rows upon rows of seats. It didn't seem to be exactly conducive to higher learning to me. I had to walk through the penalty box to get to my seat. I figured that's where they would send you if you were caught talking. "Cooper, two minutes for unsportsmanlike conduct." Nevertheless, I figured that I had done fairly well on most if not all of the examinations.

By the time that my school year was completed (around mid-May), there were a few new developments to tell you about. Not on the dating front though. I had not seen The

Little Blonde-Headed Girl since our chance encounter in the Coop. No, it was a few other things. The Montreal Canadiens had won the Stanley Cup once more. "Just wait until next year," I thought. "The Leafs will be there." Also our lawyer told us that the other side had presented a reasonable settlement offer. And he recommended that we accept it. It was for $70,000. I was kind of looking forward to a quarter million dollars. It had a nice ring to it. But, if the lawyer thought that $70,000 was fair who was I to argue. That was still a lot of money. More than The Old Man would earn in fifteen years. So Ma and I informed the lawyer to go for it. He told us that the settlement would have to go before a judge so it would be a few weeks before it was official. I figured that I could wait.

The other news was the fact that Dr. McCoy wanted me to go back in the hospital to redo the graft on my neck. The tissue there had gotten progressively thicker and redder. Kind of ugly. That's one of the reasons why I wore a lot of turtleneck shirts and dickeys. Besides the fact that I liked them. Almost as soon as I was finished my year, I was readmitted to Camden Hospital. I couldn't wait to sample those delicious veggie-burgers again. It turned out that this was the worst skin graft operation to recover from, worse than all of the previous ones. Maybe that was because I was more alert this time. My leg (where the skin was extracted) was shooting with pain. My neck was in agony. Every time that I awoke from a drugged stupor, I would call for the nurse to bring more drugs. I wondered if I was turning into a baby. I was definitely not saying, "I'm fine," whenever someone asked. And then the worst part. I had to lie with my neck completely still for forty-eight hours. I was on my back and my head was propped up by pillows. Cushions were positioned around my neck in order to discourage me from accidentally turning the direction or tilt of my head. So much for time travelling too fast. That was the longest forty-eight hours of my life. Even with all the drugs. I thought that the time period would never expire. I couldn't even watch TV.

The visits of Ma and Lily certainly helped diminish the sentence.

When the two days were up, I was ecstatic. The pain was no longer such a big deal. And a day or two later it had subsided substantially. And then I had a surprise guest – Bill. He was in Ontario for some training before heading back out West. He brought along a gift to help kill the time. A wood-carved chess set. Bill then taught me to play and continuously whooped me. After I got a little more mobile, I played chess with another patient. When I finally won a game, I felt triumphant. I ignored the fact that the patient had beaten me five times in a row before that. By the time I left the hospital to go home, my neck felt good. And it already was a large improvement over the thick red version.

"I'm glad to see that you're no longer a redneck," teased Bill.

"Not me," I laughed. "I'm what you call a long-haired hippie or a dirty rotten communist. Take your choice."

The hospital stay had lasted only about ten days. A day after my release, Bill had to leave. And on May 29th, I got word that my suit settlement was official. I was rich. I was now part of the class of society that I railed against. I hoped that the money wouldn't change me. I didn't have to worry about that just yet though. Since I was not yet twenty-one, the funds would be held for me by the Official Guardian of Ontario until I reached the legal age of adulthood. I was too young to know what to do with $70,000. That could buy a lot of records. Actually it wasn't $70,000 because $13,000 of that went to pay off various costs like lawyer fees and medical bills. Thus, $57,000 was put in trust for my receipt the following Ides of March. In the meantime, it had been arranged that I would receive a generous monthly stipend. That would certainly assist in my education costs come September.

Informative newspaper stories about me appeared in various papers again. More clippings for Ma's scrapbook. One of the stories mentioned that I had just got out of the hospital after getting a plastic plate inserted in my skull. I think that was based upon some comments from The Old Man. He continually talked about the plastic skull in my head. The one I never had inserted. He insisted that I did. If I did, I certainly don't recall the operation. And someone has stolen the plate since. Anyway, I had just had what I hoped to be my last operation related to the accident and now the case was settled. I felt as if another chapter in my life had just been completed.

25 – And Your Bird Can Sing

Since we had moved to the smaller apartment buildings, The Old Man was drinking even more than usual, if that was possible. I came home late from The Rock Pile one June night and walked into an all-too-familiar scene.

"Fuck you! You goddamned gray-haired old bag. You think you're smart, don't you. You ain't nothing but a fucking old hag, a useless old whore. You're dirt under my feet. I should put you out of your fucking misery."

The Old Man was standing up in the living room and yelling down the hall towards his bedroom. His face was bright red with rage. I walked in and shut the front door.

"Is that you, dear?" Ma's voice asked from down the hall.

"Is that you dear! Is that you dear!" The Old Man repeated sarcastically. "You make me sick. Yeah, it's your hippie son out fucking the dog all night finally coming home. It's about time. Why the hell don't you get out and get a job like everyone else? You think you're a big shot now, do you. You're better than the rest just because you've got money now. You and that gray-haired old bag of a mother of yours.

You're two of a kind. Worthless tits."

"Greetings to you too," I said. "It's sure nice to be home."

"Think you're fucking smart now, do you? Just because you're going to college doesn't make you any better than me. I can take you with one hand tied behind my back. And that whore you call a mother. Shit, I'll take on that bitch of a sister of yours at the same time. You think I'm afraid of you. I'm not afraid of you. Come on, just try it."

"Aren't you a brave bastard," I commented. "You can take on two women and a cripple all at the same time. You must be really brave."

"You fucking asshole!" yelled The Old Man as he lunged towards me.

"Garf, what are you doing?" screamed Ma as she entered the room at the same time as The Old Man made his move. "Benny's just come home. What the hell's the matter with you?"

Luckily The Old Man was so plastered that he missed me and lost his balance. He ended up spread out on the floor behind me.

"Benny," yelled Lily. "Are you all right? Did that bastard hurt...." She stopped when she saw The Old Man on the floor.

"Why don't you all go to bed and leave me alone?" said The Old Man as he regained his feet. "Can't a man get any peace in his own house? I'm just trying to have a quiet drink. Let me be."

"Sure," I said. "I wouldn't want to bother you. Have your drink. I'm going to bed. Come on Ma and Lily let's go to bed and leave this poor gentleman in peace."

"Thanks, Benny," replied The Old Man. "I love you. You're a good boy."

You could almost laugh at him, but it wasn't funny. Not by a long shot. I went to the washroom and removed my contacts. Then I laid down on top of my bed with my coke-bottom glasses on and still fully dressed. I wanted to be prepared. I drifted in and out of sleep as the night abruptly changed from quiet to full of curses and then back to solitude again. I could see light start to crawl through my window before I finally succumbed to my tiredness and fell asleep.

The next day while The Old Man was in bed recovering from his ordeal, Ma, Lily and I discussed the evening.

"I've had enough, Ma. I can't stand it anymore," I argued. "I shook all night. I hate it. I'm afraid to even go to concerts anymore. I don't know what I will find when I get home. I want to leave home but you know I'll never leave while you and Lily are here. I don't know what to do. When I get my money, let's leave the bastard. I can pay the rent and for the food. It will last until I get a job. But I don't know if I can wait another year. I'm scared, Ma. I feel like killing him. And I don't even believe in capital punishment. I hate the feelings I get."

"I know, dear," answered Ma. "I feel like that too sometimes but you know what I always say."

"Yeah, he's not worth it."

"Right. I've been thinking too, Benny and Lily. Let's not wait. Let's leave him now. Not right now but in a few weeks. We can go to Brad's. I'll call him."

"But I don't want to live in Ottawa," said Lily. "Can't we stay in Toronto?"

"Lily's right, Ma. I don't want to change university now."

"No, I mean we'll just go to Brad's for the summer. Then we will find a place in Toronto to come back to in September. I'll get a job too. I can find something. There were people back at our apartment building near Bathurst that said I was a good worker. One tenant said to let him know if I ever needed work. We can leave now. What do you say?"

"It sounds good, Ma," I replied. "But how will we do it? How do we take all our stuff?"

"We won't," explained Ma. "We'll just take a suitcase each. We can get the other stuff later. I'll speak to Ernie when he and Ruth come for dinner tonight. Ernie and maybe you,

Benny, can pick up the other stuff after we've been at Brad's for a while. What do you think?"

"Can I bring Corey and Candy now?" asked Lily.

"Of course, dear. Everyone can bring what they can carry."

"And I'll bring some records in my case," I added.

"Sure. Just leave room for clothes."

"So when?" I asked.

"Let's pack the next time that The Old Man is out. We'll have our suitcases all ready to go. And then the next time he is away for a while or the next time he is drunk, we go. We'll take the train to Ottawa. I'll check out the schedule."

"I'm getting goosebumps just thinking of leaving him," Lily informed. "I can't believe that this is finally going to happen."

"Me either," I said.

"It will," reassured Ma. "I've let you live through hell all these years. It's time that you got to live a normal life for a change. I'm sorry that I got you both in this mess."

"Don't be sorry, Ma," I said. "If we hadn't of had The Old Man for a father then we wouldn't be here, would we? I think we still managed to have a pretty good childhood. All because of you. If it wasn't for you, I don't know where we'd be. I'd hate to think."

"Thanks, Benny. I love you and you too, Lily. You know that it's only you kids that kept me going all these years. All right. It's a deal. When The Old Man goes out, it's packing time."

"We love you, Ma," expressed Lily.

"I love you too, Ma."

"Oh, I feel sick," said The Old Man as he walked in the room. "Can I get some toast, dear?"

That night we discussed the plans with Ernie whenever we had the chance to speak without The Old Man overhearing the conversation. He was all for it. He said it was about time that we left him. Over the following few days, Ma phoned Brad and explained our plans. She called CN and

266

found out the train departure schedule from Union Station. And we packed our cases. We each had one case ready to go. Mine was in my clothes closet. I also picked out my fifty to sixty essential albums and stuffed them in my record case. And then we waited. It was not a long wait.

It was a Sunday night when we had first formulated the plan. And on the following Friday, The Old Man was drinking beer at the kitchen table. He had been drinking all day and as a result, there was only one bottle left in the case of Red Cap by his feet. And of course, he was drunk and nasty.

"You must think I'm stupid. I wasn't born yesterday, you know. I know what the hell's going on around here. You think you have me fooled, don't you? I know what the old gray-haired bitch is up to. All of you, I know what's going on. You can't fool me. I wasn't born yesterday. I've been around the world. I know the score."

The three of us conspirators looked at each other. We wondered if our secret was out. Had The Old Man seen one of the packed suitcases? None of us spoke.

"You've been stealing my beer, haven't you? I don't know which one. Maybe all three of you. You can't fool me. You've been stealing my beer. You fucking thieves. Think you're fucking smart. I'm going to go get more. There better still be that one bottle there when I get back. Or there will be hell to pay." The Old Man then got up and started to head out the door. "Fucking old bag. She's stealing my beer, now. What will be next? Fucking whore." He then shut the door behind him.

"Now!" we all yelled in unison. I went in my bedroom and packed up my few remaining items such as my toothbrush, grabbed my record case and walked out into the living room with both arms full. Lily was standing there holding her case and the birdcage containing Corey and Candy. Ma had her case by her feet and was putting some things into a shopping bag.

"What are you packing, Ma?" I asked.

"Just some of the family pictures. I don't trust what your Old Man will do to them. OK, I'm ready. Is everyone else ready to go?"

"Ready," I said.

"Ready," said Lily. "Oh, just one second." She then went over to the case of beer on the floor, took the one bottle out of the case and into the kitchen, opened it and poured the contents down the sink. "Now, I'm ready. I always wanted to do that."

"Hurry, let's go. The old geezer won't be that long," warned Ma.

"We're off," I said.

We all walked out the door and started up the road each carrying something in both hands. I don't think any of us looked behind to take a second look at what we were leaving behind. We had only gone a few hundred yards when we saw someone approaching.

"Oh shit, it's The Old Man," said Lily. "What are we going to do now?"

"Shit!" I exclaimed.

"Just keep on walking," recommended Ma. "I'm not turning back now. He can just try and stop us."

So we took Ma's advice and just kept walking straight on. The Old Man was only a few yards away from us and yet he still hadn't reacted to our presence. We came up to him and he started to walk by us.

"Good evening, ma'am," The Old Man said politely as he tipped his hat.

"He didn't even recognize us," I whispered.

"Shhh," said Ma.

After we had travelled a few hundred yards more and were crossing the field towards Yonge Street, I finally looked behind me. The Old Man was nowhere in sight.

"The old fool didn't know it was us," I laughed. "I can't believe it. I was shitting my pants wondering what he was going to say and do and he didn't even recognize us."

"And he said, 'Good evening, ma'am' so sweetly," added

Lily.

"And tipped his hat too," said Ma. "Did you see that? I don't believe it. God must be on our side tonight."

"I think it was more likely the alcohol," I argued.

Soon we were standing at the bus stop. Lily was singing and dancing in circles as we waited for the southbound bus.

"I'm not going to feel relaxed until we get on the bus," I said. "The Old Man might come to his senses and come after us."

"I won't be relaxed until we're on the train," Ma said. "Then it will seem real. I can't believe we've left The Old Man yet."

"Here comes the bus," said Lily. "Whoopee, we're free. We're free."

The bus ride seemed longer than usual. But eventually, we arrived at Eglinton Station where we switched to the subway for the remainder of the ride to Union Station. We rode in silence and finally arrived at our destination. The train to Ottawa was scheduled to depart that night as planned. We bought our tickets and waited for the announcement of our train.

"For service to Oshawa, Whitby, Coburg, Belleville, Kingston, Smith Falls, and Ottawa, please proceed to Gate 17."

"Another sign," I thought to myself. "My lucky number."

When we boarded the train, we found three seats together and I stored our bags overhead. I left my records by my feet, Ma left her pictures on her lap, and Lily placed Corey and Candy's cage on the seat beside her.

"Ahh, now I feel relaxed," said Ma. "We did it! We finally left the old fart. I hope I never have to see him again."

"It's great," I said. "I feel so relieved. And excited!"

'We're free, Benny," said Lily. 'The Old Man can't hurt us anymore."

All of a sudden Cory and Candy started chirping. They were singing louder than any of us had ever heard them before.

"Even Corey and Candy are glad to be rid of the old bugger," I commented.

"You better put the cover on them, Lily" suggested Ma. "I think some of the passengers are trying to sleep."

"OK, Ma," replied Lily.

Lily then draped the cover over the cage so that Corey and Candy were in darkness. Within seconds they had settled down and their singing had ceased. However, no amount of covers could have made us three Coopers settle down.

~ The End ~

Acknowledgements

Thanks to John Brooks, Barb Burton, Chris Burton, Gary Burton, Gillian Burton, Marilyn Burton, Meghan Burton, Sam Burton, Scott Burton, Wayne Burton, Jean Delaney, Gord Delaney, Eric Dennis, Sabrina Dennis, Arlene Déry, Christina Evans, Bob Rainone, Annette ter Stege, Anna Webster, and Wayne Webster for encouragement, suggestions, and story ideas. Special appreciation must be added for Meghan and Gillian Burton for reading, re-reading, editing, and proofreading my manuscript while attempting to curtail my excessive use of commas and semi-colons. I wish to thank Jacqueline Moss for proofreading the final version for publication. As well, I would be remiss if I did not mention my thankfulness to Christina Evans, who not only provided constructive criticism, but also inspired me to keep writing whenever I reached a creative impasse. I must also extend extra gratitude to Gary Burton and Scott Burton who continually provided input to much of this book and never seemed to be bored, although I never stopped talking about it. But most of all, I would like to express my indebtedness to Wayne Burton. Without his continuous support, advice, criticism, prodding, narrative contributions, and enthusiastic interest, this book would never have been finished.

www.ingramcontent.com/pod-product-compliance
Lightning Source LLC
Chambersburg PA
CBHW061553170626
46811CB00001B/186